The Unravelling

Also by Thorne Moore and available from Honno Press

A Time for Silence

Motherlove

The Unravelling

by

Thorne Moore

HONNO MODERN FICTION

First published by Honno Press in 2016.
'Ailsa Craig', Heol y Cawl, Dinas Powys,
South Glamorgan, Wales, CF64 4AH

1 2 3 4 5 6 7 8 9 10

© Thorne Moore, 2016

The Author would like to stress that this is a work of fiction and no resemblance to any actual individual or institution is intended or implied.

ISBN 978-1-909983-48-9 (paperback)
ISBN 978-1-909983-49-6 (ebook)

A catalogue record for this book is available from the British Library.

Published with the financial support of the Welsh Books Council.

Cover image: © altanaka/Shutterstock, Inc
Cover design: Graham Preston
Text design: Graham Preston

Printed by Gomer Press

For Janet Thomas
who encouraged me to write this book

Many thanks to my editor, Caroline,
and the Honno team

"When you ask him which he would rather have, a gingerbread-nut to eat or a verse of a Psalm to learn, he says: 'Oh! the verse of a Psalm! angels sing Psalms;' says he, 'I wish to be a little angel here below;' he then gets two nuts in recompense for his infant piety."

Jane Eyre *by Charlotte Brontë*

When thou from hence away art past
Every nighte and alle
To Whinny Muir thou com'st at last
And Christe receive thy saule.

Lykewake Dirge

Late October, 2013

She is here. Somewhere.

Don't look. Not yet. She will be here still, after this.

We approach the chapel through a garden where recent wreaths are on display, a couple of cypress trees strategically positioned to mask the brutal stub of the crematorium chimney. Benches for the bereaved are banked by pale roses, with a few ornamental trees. They may have been planted for their spring blossom, but it's autumn now, and there is no blossom, just hints of anonymous fruit. One drops as I pass, rolls across the grass, over the verge and onto the gravel…

And in an instant, I am back, on an icy January night, watching an apple dropping and beginning to roll. Starting the chapter that demolished my already ruinous world.

An apple rolling into darkness, and the unravelling begins.

— 1 —

Twelve years earlier

Miserable January. The new year was a few days old, but it already felt tired. This was supposed to be a time of ridiculous resolutions, a brand new start, an opening up of the future, but to me, January always seemed an interminable no-man's-land of mud and barbed wire. It wasn't a new anything. Hopeful expectations might begin to reassert themselves with the first glimmers of spring and the lengthening of daylight, but these early days just sank into a post-yuletide quagmire.

The roads and pavements and slate roofs streamed black in a freezing rain, as my windscreen wipers struggled, shrieking and grinding against the deluge. One failed completely as I turned into Hobson Street. The other was juddering on its last legs as I parked up. Switched off.

Silence, apart from the steady hiss of rain. I sat watching it slanting, scalpel-sharp and mesmerising, through the cold glow of the street lights. An occasional glimmer of lamps behind half-drawn curtains intensified the darkness of the night, small defiant declarations of exclusion.

The Slough of Despond – a miserable month, a miserable day, and a miserable, middle-aged woman, sitting in a miserably decrepit car, trying to summon up the energy to do something, anything.

I swivelled the mirror around and looked at myself. Long face. Sheep's face, my sister used to say. Hollow. Pallid. At least in this weather, the freckles faded. That had to be a bonus. I pulled up a strand of my hair to catch the streetlight. I ought to do something with it, but what? Restyle? Colour? It hadn't changed with time, neither lighter nor darker. Not light enough to be fair, and not quite dark enough to be what my mother desperately called light auburn. Not even decent ginger, just sandy. Poor Mother, she always despaired of me.

No good sitting there, contemplating hair dyes. I needed to get on. Unpack the shopping, phone the garage to get the windscreen wiper sorted out, finally face up to the electricity bill. Or maybe just curl up in my flat, under the duvet, with a good book, and disappear into some golden, flickering world of fire and foe and escapist fantasy that didn't have bills and windscreen wipers. *Come on.*

A mighty heave of will and I emerged into the embrace of the rain. Instantly, it found its spiteful way over my collar and down my neck, while I struggled to pull my shopping from the back seat. Something caught, of course. It always did. The bag tipped and apples escaped. Before I could grab it, one bounced into the gutter and started to roll down the street, hustled by swirling rainwater. I followed, lunging for it, but too late. It slipped from my grasp over the jagged lip of a broken gully cover and plummeted into the gurgling, foetid drain. As I watched, a surge of water enfolded it and pushed it out of my sight into the blackness of the sewers.

Serena Whinn turned, and smiled at me.

My hand was halfway into the gully, groping for the lost

3

apple. How ridiculous. It was lost, destroyed. There was no point trying to get it back. I pulled back, wiping my fingers in disgust on my wet coat, and concentrated on the other apples – one on the pavement, two in the well of the car – squeezing them back into the carrier. They were bruised, already pulping and inedible, but I had to pick them up. I couldn't just walk away and leave them to rot...

Serena Whinn turned, and smiled at me.

Odd that, remembering a ten-year-old girl I'd known briefly, decades earlier.

I picked up my carriers, locked the car – as if anyone could possibly want to steal it – and headed, hunched against the sharp, icing rain, into the passage that led to the rear of No. 114.

A narrow alley. For the first time, since moving in, I saw its sinister potential, a darkening lane, full of shadows, where anything might be lurking. I brushed away the cold fingers that were beginning to stroke the back of my neck.

Serena Whinn turned, and smiled at me.

Serena. A lovely girl. Everyone had wanted to be her friend. I used to be her friend once.

I fumbled with my keys, couldn't find the keyhole, it was so dark. Everything was dark. The fingers were back on my neck. Found it! I threw the door open and lurched inside, stepping by instinct round the piles of books, dark ramparts in the gloom. I dumped my bags in the cramped kitchenette and wriggled out of my coat. My hair was dripping rats' tails, soaking my already damp blouse.

One shoe squelched. I pulled it off – the sole was split. My cold foot prickled with pain – a stone must have worked

4

through. I turned my foot up and in the dimmest of light saw the darkness of saturation, the pink bloom of blood spreading around a hole in my sock.

My stomach lurched.

Serena Whinn turned and smiled at me.

That was the moment, looking at a hole in my sock, when I stopped the instinctive fight to keep her out and let Serena in. I knew it was going to be one of those bad times, everything splitting, a double helix coming apart, and I knew what I was meant to do, how I was supposed to cope, but I didn't care. Serena was smiling at me and suddenly, nothing else mattered in the whole world.

*

Serena has seen me. Me! She's coming. She doesn't just wave, she comes to join me, smiling, skipping down the road.

'Are you going home?' asks Serena. 'Can I come with you?'

My heart swells, with nerves and joy. She wants to come with me! 'Oh yes!'

*

I abandoned my shopping, curled up on the sofa and pulled the paisley throw over me, so all the lingering light of today's world – the crimson pinpoint on the phone, the green digital numbers on the clock radio, the glimmer from houses beyond the fence – all were expunged in the darkness of a world that had vanished thirty-five years before. It was too late to turn away, to blink Serena out of existence. I wanted to look at her, nothing but her. I wanted to let her possess me.

*

I am trying not to shuffle. We've been told not to shuffle, because we might push Colin onto the stage too soon. But it's difficult not to shuffle if you're wrapped in a sheet, with cardboard wings slipping down your back and a tinsel halo that makes your scalp itch. Me and Jacqueline Winstanley. We're attendant angels. We get to chant 'Glory to God in the highest' when Colin's finished, and that's it.

Colin Chivers is Gabriel, who is sort of angel house captain. He does all the talking. He's really loud. That's why Miss Hargreaves picked him, only now she keeps having to say 'Don't shout, Colin. You're not broadcasting the good news to Scotland.'

I'm an angel, which is loads better than having to wear socks on my hands and a woolly hat and pretending to be a sheep, but I'd really, really wanted to play one of the big parts where they have real lines to learn. Kings or shepherds or Gabriel. It's not like you have to be a boy. Angela Bryant's a king, with an orange wool beard that keeps tickling her nose and making her giggle. I could have done that. The innkeeper would have been great, but Michael Wiley got that because he's good at making people laugh, and the innkeeper's supposed to be funny. Michael's really small and Barbara Fulbright, who plays his wife, is really big and that's supposed to be funny too.

Trouble is there were too many of us squabbling over the good parts, so I didn't have a chance. I never do. Others got chosen and I got to be in the crowd, snivelling over the unfairness of the world and being handed tinsel and white socks.

We never squabbled and snivelled over Mary, though. It

6

went without saying, there's only one girl in the whole world who could play her. Serena Whinn. None of us even sighed with disappointment when Miss Hargreaves beckoned her forward and said 'We'll have you as Mary, shall we, Serena? I'm sure you'll play her beautifully.' Of course she will. Serena was, is, and ever shall be, Mary, Mother of God.

Now I'm standing in the wings, trying not to scratch, with Colin blocking my view and roaring his lines.

'Fear not! Behold! I bring you great tidings of good joy!'

Miss Hargreaves is hissing, 'Good tidings, great joy!' but Colin is roaring on. If I peer round him, I can see one of the shepherds, Shirley Wright, finger in her nose, kneeling up to peer into the audience. She's not interested in what the angel has to say, or in Miss, who's flapping her hand to make her sit down. She just wants to see if her parents are watching.

My parents are out there too, but I don't want to look for them. I just want to rest my eyes on the pool of light at the far side of the stage – at the kneeling vision in blue, Serena Whinn, still and quiet at the heart of a world that spins around her, hands pressed together in prayer as she gazes down with angelic blessing on the plastic doll, wrapped in a nappy, that is our Lord and Saviour. My heart is bursting with love.

*

I was awash with that remembered love. This was how it had been. All-consuming. Of all the world, when I was ten, before all thoughts of sex and hormonal turmoil, I had eyes only for Serena Whinn, a girl I worshipped with a love so pure I knew I had to find it again. If I could only recover that, surely I could get the world back into balance once more. Until then it would split and keep splitting and splitting, till nothing was left.

I pushed back the throw, before I suffocated under it, and drew a deep breath. What was weird was not that I had suddenly remembered Serena Whinn, but that I had ever forgotten her.

Thirty-five years. That was what had passed since I'd last seen her. At the age of ten I'd been living in Lyford, attending Marsh Green Junior School and Serena had been my idol, my lodestar, my all. Then, on the whim of an adult world, my life had turned a page. I was in a new town, new school, new home, in a life that didn't contain Serena Whinn, and it was as if she'd ceased to be. Until this moment, thirty-five years later, I hadn't given her another thought.

I was appalled at my own disloyalty. How could I have wiped her out?

Serena turned and smiled at me, a smile of disappointment – oh the pain – but her dark eyes melting with forgiveness.

I scrabbled for the table lamp, for the paper and pencils under the sofa, and began to pour out my memories, scribbling, furiously scribbling. Serena's face, Serena's smile, Serena's hands. I was going to bring her back. That way, I would deserve her forgiveness.

Scribble, scribble. Another sheet. Scribble. I only had to shut my eyes to see her there in front of me, beckoning me into her circle of light.

How do you draw a circle of light? There was one around her, I'd swear, and everyone had longed to be in it. The teachers and the sour-faced caretaker, the school swots, the giggling girls, the sporty bouncers. Even the hard bully boys. We'd all worshipped from afar and hopelessly dreamed of edging closer, of being chosen as one of Serena's bosom friends. I knew the exquisite pain of that dream, because I'd shared in its hopelessness. But I had also known the numbing bliss of its fulfilment.

*

The playing field is chill, the wind is brisk. The rest of the class are stamping, or jumping up and down, eager to be on with the game and running around to get warm.

I don't stamp or jump, because I know nothing will warm me. Life is cold and miserable and full of despair, as the crowd of fellow pupils around me dwindles, summoned one by one into the growing teams. Their names are shouted and off they bound. The loud and athletic went first. Now it's the earnest and eager, and I'm left standing there, me and… well, everyone else. The ragbag useless ones that never get called. The tightness and the little misery grows within me.

Then Serena's voice, clear as a bell, comes to me on the chill wind. 'Karen Rothwell!'

She's looking at me. At me! In my joy I rush forward, stumble, trip and fall flat on my face. I feel the fire in my ankle, my knee, my nose, but any physical pain is swamped by the excruciating humiliation. All ten thousand of my cruel schoolmates hoot and roar with laughter as I struggle up and my tears begins to flow. But there is Serena, smiling down on me, her hand reaching out to pull me to my feet, and suddenly nothing else matters.

*

It was as if she were pulling me up out of reverie into wakefulness.

Loud, rude wakefulness. A crash of bins. The distant grind

9

of a refuse lorry. Where was I? All through the evening, I had dimly heard the sound of children, TVs, clicking heels, dogs barking, a cat prowling, until the night noises had petered out into silence. Now, out of that silence, the clatter of the bin men burst like a shrieking klaxon into my consciousness and I flung off the throw, the cushions and the papers that had wrapped themselves round me like swaddling clothes.

An avalanche of sketches and a forest of blunted pencils slid chaotically to the floor. I peered down at them. That was all the movement I could manage for the moment. Every joint had stiffened, every inch of me was aching. I had to roll off the sofa onto my knees before struggling to my feet, my clothes still damp, clinging to me like mermaid hands, dragging me down.

Still pitch dark outside but it was morning, the world was waking, and I had been scribbling and thinking all night, giving form to shards of memory that kept emerging like shattered pots from an archaeological dig. Shards that I couldn't quite fit together, but I knew that at the centre of all of them was Serena Whinn. The meaning of it all.

I dragged myself to the window, supporting myself on the books piled high on the sill, and stared out into muffled darkness. Icy rain had given way to icy fog, seeping into the joints of the world. At the end of the yard, on the narrow alley separating the houses of Hobson Road from those of Leopold Street, luminous jackets were yellow blurs, dragging wheelie bins.

I rubbed my eyes, thinking of the bin men back in Marsh Green. The way they used to hoist the bins on their shoulders, crashing the metal lids, loping along at the double like strange bowed beasts. Like the coal men, bowling along with their sacks on their backs. Sacks of coal and coke. Their memory overlapped with an image – some medieval depiction of the Last Judgement – of humped devils dragging souls down into the jaws of hell. Demons come to drag us down. Too many of them...

Clatter. Grind.

I tugged at my tangled hair, till it hurt, and forced demons out of my mind. They weren't demons in the alley. They were poor sods, out there in the freezing fog, breaking their backs to empty our garbage. Except, not mine. I'd forgotten to take it out again. Too late, now.

High up through the greying blanket, where I knew a bathroom at the rear of a house on Leopold Road to be, a halo of light appeared. The sound of a distant radio came at me through cotton wool. There was a fog inside my head, mirroring the frozen grey outside, swirling confusion as present reality tried to force itself back into focus. Why did it have to? Who needed reality? Who wanted the tedium of another day? Just like the last, and the one before and the one before. Block it out.

I drew in the condensation on the clammy window pane.

A sun. Around it, encompassing it, a five-pointed star. Five sharp points.

Very sharp. The golden girls. Barbara Fulbright, Denise Griggs, Angela Bryant, Ruth Jefferson and Teresa Scott.

There. A surge of satisfaction. I even remembered their names. They were the seraphim surrounding Serena, armed to the teeth and ready to turn their spears on any trespasser who came too close. Not on her command, let it be understood.

11

Serena smiled on everyone. She would have poured her sunshine out on the whole world. It was her court favourites who were determined to keep the rest of us out. They were jealous, terrified of being usurped. Barbara, Denise, Angela, Ruth and Teresa.

I dropped on my knees and searched through the night's scribbling. Yes, I'd captured each of them in the night, burly Barbara, petite Ruth with her purse on a strap, gangly Angela and her tartan hair ribbons, rotund Denise, serious Teresa with the glasses. I couldn't draw Serena and not draw them. They were welded into one. Except that in my last year at Marsh Green Junior, Teresa Scott had left and the ring was snapped. It needed emergency repair and I, Karen Rothwell, the unworthy and yet the most blessed, had been chosen to take her place.

I could remember the joy.

Karen, come and play with us.

Yes!

And? Nothing more. Just that moment of joy.

The bin men were finished. More lights were on, and louder radios. Doors slammed. Engines started. Daylight was beginning to seep into the fog. How could they do this? How could people just get on with life as if the second coming of Serena Whinn hadn't happened?

I couldn't. There was a riddle here. It had arrived on my doorstep and eaten me whole. At ten years old, I had achieved my dream. I had stepped into Serena's circle of light, and then – what? Something incredible must have followed. Did I acquire mystical enlightenment? Or superhuman powers? Did I conquer the world? Did I achieve greatness or have it thrust upon me? If I did, I couldn't recall any of it.

All I could remember was that first glorious joy of acceptance. Nothing else, except a lurking sense that wasn't akin to joy at all. I could feel it, fingers on my neck, thudding in my heart, thundering in my ears, threading its way into my veins to reclaim me.

Fear.

There was my riddle. How was it that this episode, which had begun with a blazing memory of bliss, left me haunted by a sensation of overwhelming dread? Serena Whinn would have the answer. No one else. Just her. I had to have the answer, had to find her.

The problem was, I didn't have the first idea how.

— 2 —

The council car park was jammed with cars. My windscreen wiper had failed to mend itself miraculously overnight, and the fog was still thick, smothering the deluded headlights as they attempted to pierce it. At least, that would do as an excuse for my misjudgement, as I clouted the White Witch's Corsa with my wing mirror. I reversed, found another place, at the far end, then got out, pulled my hood up and walked back to the revolving doors, studiously not looking at the scattered shards of orange plastic from the Corsa's tail light.

The White Witch was standing at the photocopier as I entered, in prime position to note my arrival and the clock above me. Gail Creighton, red lips pursed, pencilled eyebrows raised.

'11:04, Karen. 11:04! You do realise that, do you?'

In reply, I fixed my eyes on my desk on the far side of the office, and concentrated on unbuttoning my damp coat. It was the best way to avoid punching her.

She followed. I could hear her high heels clacking behind me. 'Karen. Karen Rothwell! 11:04. You are supposed to be at your desk by 8:45. What, precisely, makes you think it's all right to stroll in here more than two hours late?'

I shook my mac and she flinched as the fine spray caught

her. 'Thank you! I'd like an explanation, please. Why are you late?'

'I had an appointment.'

'What sort—' she began, then changed her mind. She knew about my appointments and made it a point of not pursuing the details. 'There was nothing in the diary. You've been told, Karen, repeatedly, appointments, doctors, dentists, that sort of thing, must be arranged beforehand and approved by Mr Parry.'

I sat down and switched on my screen. I was forty-five, she was not much more than thirty, at least ten years my junior, but she spoke to me as if I were a naughty child. I could remember her as a giggling young junior in a crowd of giggling juniors, squealing over clothes and movie stars and office gossip, no more offensive than any of them, but this is what promotion and office power does to some people. It can turn a friendly Mrs Beaver into the White Witch overnight. I never caught Gail Creighton handing out Turkish Delight, though.

'Are you listening to me?'

I looked up at her. Her fingers were twitching, itching to slap me, but, of course, she didn't quite dare.

'Oh for God's sake.' Nostrils pinched, she turned on her stilettos and marched off, like an irate stork, to the far end of the office, to confer with Uriah Heep.

Stewart Parry to everyone else. It was easier dealing with people I found, if I could fit them into a book. Gail Creighton was obviously the White Witch. I had been torn, with Stewart Parry, between Uriah Heep and Wormtongue, but Uriah Heep won. He was, after all, just a jumped-up clerk whose 'umble' abode was the cluttered end desk, behind a pile of files, half-empty coffee mugs and trainers. In the pecking order of line managers, the White Witch was mine and Uriah Heep was hers. I wasn't sure who his was – one of the men in suits.

Gail was making her report in what was supposed to pass for a confidential tone, but just loud enough for me and everyone else to catch the necessary emphasis above the clicking of keyboards, the ebb and flow of gossip and the perpetual white noise of Caz Philpot's Radio 1. 'I mean, how long…pointless… bloody waste of space…' Every few words, she would glare back in my direction and his smirking gaze would follow.

This was a regular occurrence, even if it didn't usually go on for quite so long, so I paid no attention. Okay, I was two hours late. Shoot me.

I didn't care. I really didn't care. I had a job, a daily grind, not a career. This office was my place of punishment. I came in, I typed, I went home, I got paid, minimally, and at this moment I didn't care about any of it. I didn't care if they shouted at me, mocked me, picked on me or sacked me.

Serena Whinn had kept me standing rigid at my window for hours, long after I should have set off into the rush hour traffic. The only reason I had finally broken free and made the effort to come in at all had been the dreary realisation that the yard, the bins, the one dead buddleia and the steamed-up bathrooms beyond were not going to provide me with answers. I could stand there staring forever and Serena was not going to appear, magically, like Mary Poppins, on the chimney pots of Leopold Road. I needed to snap into action, do something positive.

The only positive move I could think of was to come into work. At work, there was the internet.

I waited until the bustle of the office was back in full swing, everyone playing their regular musical chairs, then I slipped into the corner where an unattended computer terminal was connected to the World Wide Web. There were office rules about accessing the internet, and number one was: 'Don't let Karen Rothwell mess around on it.' No one was supposed to mess around on it, which is why it was restricted to one terminal, supposedly under the White Witch's control. But the White Witch couldn't be watching it all the time.

She wasn't watching now.

Computers were far too expensive to be a part of my home life, but I'd learned my way around them at work. I tried Yahoo. 'Serena Whinn.' Nothing.

Altavista. 'Serena + Whinn.' Nothing.

What was I expecting? The internet was useless. It promised caviar and delivered candy floss. I was better off with books. Books were my portal to everything. I was at home with them. I could always find my way around with books.

The office was short on books, but it did have a full run of telephone directories, lined up below four shelves of box files. I worked through them. Every one of them. Nothing. Serena could be anywhere in the country – but she wasn't.

If she'd been an actual book, there would be no problem. I could always find books. Ask me to track down any volume, in bookshops, at market stalls and rubbish dumps, even on the internet, and I would find it. Might take me time, but I'd do it. People were another matter. How exactly do you find people? I had no idea where to start, unless I tried the adverts for private detective services, thrown up by Yahoo. Services I'd have to pay for, and I didn't have the money.

'Karen, what are you doing with that?' The White Witch

was standing over me as I wrestled directories back into place.

'I was checking an address.'

She took the last volume from me. 'Fife. And who do we deal with in Fife?'

'Wrong one. I was putting it back.'

She tutted hard enough to rip off the roof of her mouth. 'I take it you are going to complete that report before lunch.' She followed me back to my desk. I could see how much she longed to settle the Karen Rothwell problem – to sweep my work to the floor, hurl my coat at me and stab an outstretched arm at the door, crying 'Go, and never darken my doorstep again!'

Unfortunately for the White Witch, sacking was far above her pay grade and all she could do was ferry a constant stream of complaints up the chain. She pushed round to see my screen, which was displaying the report I'd been asked to type up two days before. I had added two words since coming in that morning, but what could anyone expect? How was I supposed to concentrate on stock lists when I had Serena Whinn living in my head? The White Witch continued to hiss and fizz over me but I could barely see her. It was so easy to block her out.

All I saw, in her place, was Serena, dark eyes smiling down on me, chestnut hair flowing like a curtain to encompass me, hand extended to—

'You've done virtually nothing, Karen! Have you been on the internet? You have, haven't you? I knew it! How many times do I have to tell you the rules? You know them perfectly well, and don't pretend you don't! No private work, no personal stuff, no internet except in your lunch break. In fact, even that privilege is discretionary, isn't that right, Mr Parry? If that report isn't finished and printed and on my desk in the next two hours, you'll be banned altogether. I'll change the password and lock you out!' She was sounding more and more like a little girl stamping her foot, and she must have realised it, because she lowered her voice. 'Do you understand? Karen! Are you listening to me?'

'I'm working,' I said. 'Got a lot to do.' I was too busy typing. No idea what I was typing, but my fingers were moving.

She stiffened, the tendons on her neck vibrating like over-tightened harp strings. If she'd spoken, she would have spluttered, so she worked her lips furiously, until she could manage, without foaming at the mouth, to say, 'Just get it done, Karen.'

As she stalked away, I glanced back at the computer in the corner. But why bother? It wouldn't tell me anything because I didn't know where to look. I felt as if I were ramming myself at full speed into a brick wall. Over and over again. I had to break through. I had to, I had to.

'Karen! Here!' Anne Elliot beckoned me across the crowded department store café. She wasn't really Anne Elliot, she was Charlie Freeman, but to me she was Anne in *Persuasion* because she was always worried about people, sorting out their problems without seeming to have a life of her own. She probably did have one, but I never shared in it.

There'd been a time when I thought she really was Anne Elliot. How daft is that? The mind plays tricks.

She was already at a table, which was lucky, because it meant I didn't have to queue at the counter, pretending to select something. I could predict, without looking, the unappetising array of pre-wrapped sandwiches and trays of lukewarm brown sludge with a thick skin.

Thick, brown skin.

*

It's meat pie. Minced beef under bouncy suet pastry. A round of mash. A dollop of cabbage. I don't like cabbage much, but I'll eat it, just as long as... No! The gravy jug hovers over my plate and I watch with horror as the slimy skin on the thick brown gunge tips over the lip and lands on my plate.

'Go on,' says the dinner lady, poking my shoulder and smirking at my distress. 'There's plenty of starving black children in Africa would love that. Won't kill you, you know.'

It will though. It makes me choke just thinking about it. I'm not eating it. I'm not! I don't care if I miss dinner. I'm not eating that slimy skin. Doesn't matter. I'll have fish fingers and beans when I get home. I pass the disgusting thing on, to someone else. Someone who'll happily scoff it down because they'll probably be lucky if they find so much as a bit of bread and marge when they get home.

I am snorting, folding my arms, ready to sulk for the rest of the day. Then, at the next table, Serena turns and smiles at me in sympathy.

And suddenly, I feel silly and petulant, and embarrassed that she's been watching me having a paddy. All right! I'll stop snorting. I'll eat my pudding, even if it is sultana sponge and I get the thick skin off the pink custard...

*

It's a universal thing in places like this – brown sludge with thick skin, just like school meals. Maybe it's because they know

20

shoppers are nostalgic for school days, when their mummies did the shopping for them.

It wasn't all shoppers crowding the tables, though. Most of those council workers who didn't head for a two-hour break at the pub (women, I mean) came here, because it was convenient. They were the ones who went for the pre-wrapped sandwiches.

I scrambled my way through, between protruding legs, shopping bags and pushchairs, to the corner table and Charlie rose to greet me. She was my oldest friend in this city. We often spent my afternoons off in the park or the shopping centre, just nattering, or we'd come here to grab lunch. She was a great one for lunch, was Charlie.

She took my hands and looked me over. 'Thought you were going to get your hair done.'

'Couldn't be bothered.'

She shook her head. 'Karen Rothwell, what are we going to do with you?'

'As little as possible, please.'

She laughed and sat down, pulling me onto a chair beside her. 'I bought you lunch.' She pushed it across the table – a child's bubble-gum pink milkshake and a sandwich. Chicken and salad by the look of it.

'There was no need, honestly.' I hated being treated, even by the best of friends. It heaped the weight of obligation on my shoulders.

Charlie waved away my objection. 'I know you, Karen. You'd rather talk than eat and I'm starving and I hate eating alone, so keep me company.' She sliced a huge ham baguette in half. 'Go on, get yourself comfortable, and then we'll talk and eat.'

I sighed in defeat and wriggled my coat off. I tried a sip of the milkshake. It tasted horribly sweet, sickly and artificial. God knows what it was supposed to be. Raspberry or strawberry, probably, but it didn't taste like either. I pulled a face and pushed it away.

Charlie nudged it back.

'Go on. It's not that bad. Try the sandwich.'

I picked up the carton and tried to break through the rigid plastic. Impossible. It was built like Fort Knox. I put it down.

Charlie reached for it and ripped it open. 'I went for something simple. I know you don't like spicy things.'

'Thanks.' I took a nibble.

She watched me swallow, then smiled. 'Okay, so tell me. How are things at work? Not so good, I've been hearing.'

'You've been receiving smoke signals from the White Witch, I suppose.'

Charlie pretended disapproval. 'Now, now. But yes, Ms Creighton was chewing my ear, having a good old grumble about you.'

'She loathes me.'

'Oh come on. She must care a tiny bit or she wouldn't have called me, she's worried… Yes, all right, she loathes most people, does our Gail. Certainly doesn't like me very much. But then she's not my line manager, she's yours. I know how difficult it can be when there's a personality clash. She likes to complain. Makes her feel in charge. Has she got a lot to complain about at the moment? She claims you've been coming in late for two or three weeks now. Missing whole days sometimes, with no explanation.'

I couldn't deny it.

'What's up, Karen? I can see something's eating you.' She looked at my lunch. 'Which is more than can be said for that poor sandwich.'

'It's stale.'

'No it's not. It's freshly made today.'

'Doesn't mean they didn't freshly make it with stale bread.'

'Right. Just eat the filling then. It's only chicken and lettuce and tomato.'

'And mayonnaise. Way too much of it. Why do they have to put so much gunge in everything?'

Charlie looked hard at the sandwich, as if she wanted to challenge it to a fight. Then she looked back at me, smiling broadly. 'All right, forget lunch for a moment. Just tell me what's wrong. Something's upset you.'

She wasn't the first to ask. There were well-meaning sorts in the office, who'd noted my distraction over the last couple of weeks and enquired if I were all right, in a faintly patronising way. They hadn't really been seeking a detailed reply, so I hadn't given any. But Charlie and I went back a long way and I owed her more of an explanation.

'Sort of.' It was so difficult to explain. 'I feel – frustrated. I can't… There are things… I can't quite… and then I get these feelings. Of panic. Fear. Like I'm… like there's something… I'm not explaining this very well, am I?'

'No, you're not explaining anything at all. But don't worry. Go on. Keep talking. Tell me what it is that's frustrating you. What's making you panic?'

'It was the apple, you see, rolling into the drain.' I started to shred the lettuce from my sandwich.

'No, I don't see. An apple rolled into a drain.'

'And it made me think of this girl I'd known at school.'

'Ah!' Charlie put her baguette down. She wiped her lips with a serviette, her eyes urging me to continue. 'Go on. A girl you knew.'

'In Marsh Green Junior School. Way back. In Lyford, I mean, before we moved up north. This girl. I worshipped her. Honestly. I know it sounds ridiculous, but I really did. And then we moved away and I never thought about her again. Isn't that odd? You don't do that, do you? Completely forget someone who meant everything to you?'

'Well, children, you know. They live in the moment and moments change and they just move on. It's us oldies who carry the past around with us, and sometimes it can surprise us. We remember things we didn't know we'd forgotten. Is that what you're doing, Karen? Beginning to remember something?'

'I don't know. I just remember her.'

'But that's good. Tell me all about her. What do you remember?'

'She was lovely. It's like thirty-five years have vanished and I can remember her so vividly, she's all I can think about. I know I have to find her, but I can't. I don't know how. I feel so...' I started shredding the bread.

'Well. You've found her in your memory, Karen. That's a start.' Charlie thoughtfully rescued the chicken and tomato, manoeuvring them to the side of my plate. 'Tell me more.'

'She was an angel.'

'I see. An angel. Meaning what? Do you think she's in heaven?'

'No, no!' My turn to laugh. Charlie was being ridiculous. 'Just lovely.'

'Tell me all about her, Karen.'

'She was just, I don't know. She was Serena.'

'What?'

'Serena Whinn. That's her name.'

'Hm.' Charlie sat back, her face puckered up into a frown of deep thought. 'Serena Whinn.'

'Do you know her?'

'No, sorry. Are you sure? Serena Whinn. It does sound a bit like a character in one of your fantasies. Is that what you're doing? Thinking of someone in a book?'

'She's not someone from a fantasy novel. Or a historical romance, or a wartime thriller or science fiction. She was a girl at school. Though she was so beautiful, she should have been a heroine in a novel. She was in my class. She had long dark hair and dark eyes and the most beautiful smile.'

Charlie smiled fondly. 'You had a crush on her. That's all right. We all did it. I remember a girl, when I'd just started High School…'

'It wasn't a crush. It was – it was…' Whatever it was, it was far more significant than a crush. The memory of a crush would make me laugh. It wouldn't produce this weird reawakening of joy and fear. 'Why did I forget her? Why did I suddenly remember her now? I can remember, so vividly. All about her. I can even remember where she lived. Just off the estate, on Rowlands Avenue. I checked in the phone book and there's no one called Whinn living in Rowlands Avenue now.'

'No, well, that's hardly surprising, is it?' Charlie shrugged. 'It was thirty-five years ago, didn't you say? Her parents will have retired to Eastbourne, or died, and anyway, she's probably married, so she won't be called Whinn any more.'

'Oh. Hell. Of course. I hadn't thought of that.'

'She's not going to be there, where you left her, Karen. Not geographically. But she is still there where you left her in your head, and that's very important. It's so interesting that you've started to think about her now. Because of an apple, you say. I wonder why. Did she ever give you an apple?'

Mirror, mirror on the wall... I could see Snow White's Wicked Queen holding out a lovely apple. A hand reaching out, holding... I jerked my head to shake the image away. Serena would have been Snow White, not the Queen.

'It wasn't the apple. It was the drain.' My fingers clenched as I realised. It *was* the drain.

'All right.' Charlie patted my hand. 'Don't get fraught. Do you feel it's time to dig a bit deeper into all this? It's up to you, Karen. I don't want to push you.'

'But I want to push. Of course I do. It's like I'll never be able to sleep or breathe or do anything again until I find her. I don't know why, but now she's there in my head, she won't go away. So how am I supposed to sit there in the office all day, typing accounts and all that crap, when all I can think about is Serena?'

'All right.' Charlie smiled broadly. Too broadly. The very broad smile of a woman telling other people to stop looking at us. Was I getting a bit loud? 'Why don't we go and see Miles? You know he's always there to help.'

'Miles? Why? He's not a private detective. That's what I need. Someone who can track people down. Except I can't afford one.'

'No, but you know, Miles is a sort of detective. I think he could help you with this.'

'No.'

'You're in pieces, Karen. You're not turning up for work, and when you do, you don't do anything. And you're not eating again.'

'I am!' To prove it, I picked up lumps of chicken and tomato and swallowed them whole.

'Don't choke yourself to death.' Charlie firmly placed the milkshake in front of me. 'Drink this. It's nourishing.'

I sucked up a disgusting mouthful.

'I really do think we should go and see Miles,' she said. 'It's been a while.'

She phoned me later, at work. The White Witch put the call through to my desk with a sharp bark. 'Karen Rothwell. Charlotte Freeman for you. Pick it up. Quickly please.'

I couldn't quite drag my eyes from the paper on which I'd been scribbling a picture of the gates of Marsh Green Junior School. Wire mesh fencing. Greening bronze plaques of busy bees set into the gate posts. Mr Jefferson, rising on his toes, hands behind his back, moustache bristling...

'Karen! Now!'

I picked up my phone.

'Karen?' Charlie sounded breathless. 'All right, good news, Miles is going to be here, end of next week. I'll pick you up at lunchtime on Friday. I told him all about what you'd remembered and he's very keen to see you. So we'll go, shall we, and see him and tell him all about Serena? I'm sure he'll be able to help.'

'Do you really think so?'

'Yes, of course. I've arranged for you to have the afternoon off, so don't forget. All right? And keep eating!'

'Of course,' I said. I had to do as Charlie said. Because she was more than just my friend. She was the one who'd been given the job of sorting me out.

— 3 —

Friday. I woke in one of those moods. A mood of resistance. Which sounds great. I'd have liked to see myself as one of the French Maquis, rifle over my shoulder, diving behind rocks as I took on the Nazis. Or a flame-lit revolutionary, one of Les Misérables shouting defiance as I manned the barricades. But my version of resistance wasn't quite so picturesque. It was usually termed 'being difficult,' by Charlie and other well-meaning souls. Or 'bloody-minded pig-headed stupidity' by the less generous. Call it what you will, there were times when immovable stubbornness set in, and this was one of them.

It had set in even before I'd grasped what it was I was determined to resist. I woke with my fists clenched, my toes curled and 'No!' screaming in my head. Then I remembered. I didn't want to go and see Miles.

Nothing wrong with Miles Pearce, in his way. I pictured him these days as Beorn. Quite helpful if you need to find your way through a dark forest but with a tendency to turn into a real bear if you didn't obey orders. A thoroughly growly bear with big teeth. When he was being nice, offering me bread and honey, I liked him well enough, but I knew that on this occasion I wouldn't be able to behave. No way could I sit there and rabbit on and on for his entertainment because I knew that, for all his detective skills, his being a professional listener, he wasn't really going to be able to help me find Serena Whinn. And that was all I cared about, so what was the point of wasting an afternoon talking about it?

He wouldn't know anything about Lyford unless I told him. I did. Sort of. I was born there. I went to school there.

*

It's my own world, Marsh Green Estate. Like a country all on its own, like the way countries are shown in different colours on the map on Mr Gregory's wall. Marsh Green Estate is purple. I don't know why I think that. It's not really, only it makes me think purple, so that's how I'm doing it. Maybe it's because there's all that tarmac and concrete and when shadows fall across the empty streets, they look purple.

Marsh Green is a purple square, very neat. I'm drawing it for Geography. There's Pirton High Street on the west side, with an old pub and a thatched cottage in among all the new houses because Pirton used to be a village before it became part of Lyford. There's Merecroft Road on the south side, with smelly little factories and yards where lorries are parked up. There's Foxton Road on the east side, very busy, with traffic roaring along, and beyond it the allotments and the railway. There's fields and Thornton Farm on the north side, beyond a line of elm trees, and in the middle of the square is Marsh Green estate, with lots of rows of brick council houses.

There are lots of empty roads too, that haven't got anyone living on them at all, because they've knocked down all the prefabs. They're going to build more houses, but there's nothing there for now except concrete foundations and wire fences and tall weeds.

Where the prefabs used to be, I draw a mouse.

There's the Parade in the middle, with shops and a place for buses to turn, and there's the school and there's the Rough, where we play and scream and roll, and boys chase us with creepy crawlies, and we swing across the brook on ropes…

*

I could remember it. Not just Serena and her friends, but the whole estate, just as I'd drawn it in class. I never told Mr Gregory why I drew a mouse, and now I no longer knew why. One of my resistance spells, probably, doing something I wasn't supposed to do.

Could I draw the map again? Maybe but it was still a broken and deceptive image, in my mind. Like a cracked mirror, but it was coming together, the little world I inhabited until I was ten. A month ago I probably wouldn't even have remembered the name of the estate, but I'd had three weeks to conjure it up and reconstruct it in my mind like a Lego model, piece by piece. Some bits still missing, but you could see what it was going to be.

I'd figured out, by now, why I had wiped it out for more than three decades. The answer was obvious. I should have sussed it at once, but when Serena suddenly materialised, I'd been taken by such huge surprise that my prolonged lapse of memory had seemed utterly mystifying. The truth, as I realised now, was that my early years had faded into invisibility because they'd been blotted out by The Thing.

That thing. My accident.

31

When I was eleven we'd moved up north, away from Lyford, and I'd had an accident. A major accident. It had refocused my entire life. Hospital, operations, rehabilitation, relapse, more hospital… The world takes on new and frightening shapes when you see it through an oxygen mask or a medicated haze. Old memories are tidied away into a sealed trunk, where your troubled soul can't trip over them. You wipe them out because the present is so overwhelming, it takes all your resources to cope with it.

But thirty-five years had passed since the accident and even though its consequences still dragged around with me, like a ball and chain, I could open that trunk again without trauma, and look on a world that used to be. An apple had rolled and Serena had shot back into my thoughts, as if she'd been waiting to push the lid wide. It was wide. My early years were marching through and I could swear I was more confident of my childhood address than of my current one.

12 Linden Crescent. No postcode. We didn't have postcodes then.

Marsh Green was a council estate on the edge of Lyford. All my memories were contained within its borders. I still had no joined-up recollections of Lyford itself, but then Lyford was just 'Town'. It was somewhere with a library full of polished wood and people who said 'Sh!' It was a town hall, with long chilly corridors, for paying rent, and it was a Sainsbury shop, with cold white tiles and women in hairnets cutting huge chunks of Cheddar and Red Leicester with wires. It was somewhere I went occasionally with Mummy and Hilary on the bus, to eat doughnuts at a Lyons Corner House, but I had no idea what route the bus took.

I wasn't even entirely sure that I could place Lyford accurately on a map of Britain. It was south, near London but not London.

How could I possibly go to work, or think about a meeting with Miles, if I couldn't even be sure where exactly Lyford was? I stopped any pretence of getting ready and pulled out a decent-sized atlas of Britain.

What I mean is, I set to work pulling out an atlas of Britain. It wasn't as easy as it sounds. My flat had a lot of books. And when I say a lot… My trouble – not that I saw it as a trouble – was that I'd buy anything and everything if I passed a second-hand stall, regardless of content. It was why I was living in Hobson Road, in what the agents called a garden flat. Garden, meaning a square of tarmac and a tub of dandelions. I'd been more than happy with my old place, despite the leaking dormer windows and the arctic winter temperatures, but Charlie said the floor of the garret apartment wouldn't take the weight for much longer. I think she'd hoped I'd weed out my collection when I moved, but I couldn't. She regularly warned me my home was a fire hazard.

'There'll be a disaster one day and you'll be trapped in here, unable to escape.'

Which was ironic, because my books were my escape.

There was a rhyme and reason to their distribution, which other people didn't always realise. The easy-access books, piled on the floor, on the table and chests, like fortress walls around me, were the ones that constituted my reading of choice. Fantasy, science fiction, romances, historical novels, anything that would whisk me away from the real world. I could cope with dragons, aliens, evil villains armed with swords or

Regency sneers. Just not with the grey, blood-sucking monsters outside my door.

Contemporary realism was out. But I still bought it. It was piled up on the window sills and along the passage. Reference books, which were all coldly and relentlessly about the real world, were shunted to the high shelves of the corner bookcase, above and behind everything else, where they could be ignored. They included atlases.

I had to move a mountain of stacks and boxes to get near the bookcase, and it took time. Time that was easily diverted towards other goals. With my arms full, a copy of *The Silmarillion* slid loose, tumbling to the floor, and as I struggled to retrieve it, it occurred to me that I might not be too sure of the whereabouts of Lyford or the general layout of the United Kingdom, but I could confidently draw a map of Middle Earth. And Earthsea and Narnia and the Drenai lands and the world of the Belgariad.

Could I? Before I knew it, I'd put the books down and was rummaging for paper. There was always some around. It floated like confetti through my library, mostly already scribbled on.

I was at work, positioning the mouth of the Greyflood on the coast of Minhiriath, when Serena Whinn turned in her seat and smiled at me.

She kept doing that.

Instantly, I remembered what it was I was supposed to be doing. After more tectonic shifts, I managed to clamber up to the corner shelf and found my road atlas.

Slightly damaged. Not by me. It had come to me with the hard cover already buckled, which is why I had it. It was a discard from Gem's Books. Dear Mr Tumnus – Malcolm

Garnet – had let me take it, rather than adding it to the recycling pile. It's always good to have a pet bookshop owner.

I found Lyford. Oh. How uninteresting. I was able to place it precisely among the amorphous satellites of London, but that didn't really give it an identity. It was a grey blob. An amoeba threaded with a spider's web of roads, merging with neighbouring Stapledon and surrounded by its own satellite villages. Some of them triggered faint memories of bus rides and ponds and clambering on chalk downs. Others meant nothing. Foxton, Thorpeshall, Cambingley, Tillsworth and Pye Green. The villages didn't matter. I'd lived in Lyford. But where? North, south, east, west? No idea. The map wasn't detailed enough to name the different suburbs. What I needed…of course, what I needed was an Ordnance Survey map.

I had quite a few. Years before, the library I'd belonged to had thrown out its old ones, the ones with red covers, when the pink ones had come in, and I'd fought with another deranged collector, to grab what I could. I'd managed to squeeze about three dozen into a shopping bag and pockets. My rival was intent on searching for specific areas. I wasn't so choosy. Any would do. My compulsion to rescue and rehome any orphaned books extended even to maps.

My Ordnance Surveys hadn't been banished onto far shelves like the road atlas, because they didn't count as reference. They were much closer to fantasy. You can disappear into an OS map, construct everything, craggy hills, waterfalls, woods and railway cuttings and church steeples, all in places you will never really visit.

It was just possible that in among my three dozen fantasy

worlds, there was one that overlapped with the reality I was seeking. They were in a box, under my bed. Not that one. That held Beatrix Potter, the Flower Fairies and Little Grey Rabbit. This one. I emptied them out on the only vacant bit of bedroom floor.

I shuffled through them. Taunton and Lyme Regis. Buckingham. Market Weighton, Selkirk. Montgomery and Llandrindod Wells. And Lyford! Or at least part of it. The countryside that constituted Lyvale, a couple of small market towns and down in the bottom right corner, most of Stapledon and the northern part of Lyford itself.

If it turned out I'd lived in the southern part, I was stuck. I didn't have the adjoining map.

I opened it out, pushing the others aside, and poured over it. Now... There was a main road leading northeast, out through Cambingley and off the map. Another leading northwest, through Foxton – and Foxton Road had bordered the eastern side of our estate, so... The road coming down from Foxton village disappeared into the built-up mass of Lyford.

Marsh Green wasn't named, but I found it. I found the railway line and Thornton Farm and what must be Pirton High Street. I found the Parade, and the school.

My school, Serena's school, infants and juniors. My stomach lurched. It was weird, more than weird, seeing it there, jiggled into a precise place in the real world and not just a figment of my imagination. If it were marked on this map, it stood to reason it must be there still.

I had to go and see, didn't I? Whatever it was I was looking for, Marsh Green was far more likely to give me answers than an afternoon with Miles Pearce.

I consulted the road atlas again. Lyford. It must be getting on for two hundred miles from my Yorkshire home, but most of it would be on a motorway. I'd never driven on a motorway. I'd never driven much further than the city centre where I worked. Before today, nothing would have persuaded me to attempt it. I was too old for new experiences, I'd have said. Silly little lady, can't cope with all that rush and traffic.

But today. Today the traffic could go hang itself.

Today, I'd drive to Lyford.

It wasn't that hard, motorway driving. At least not when it involved just driving. It was the complications along the route that got me. Complications like actually getting on to the motorway in the first place. I know you're just supposed to feed on, but everything was going so fast. I stopped to wait for a big gap and ignored the hooting behind me. And then there was the changing and merging. How do people cope with this on a daily basis? I knew which roads I wanted – I'd written them on a Post-it note and stuck it to the windscreen, but I still found myself going three times round a massive roundabout before I managed to get to where I wanted to be. Once I was in the flow, on the right motorway, safely heading south, everything was fine. Not particularly fast because I refused to move out of the inside lane, so I spent most of it stuck behind crawling lorries, but I didn't care. It brought me, eventually, to the exit for Lyford North.

Once I turned off, I pulled over, opened up the atlas, and tried to equate its roads with the urban sprawl that spread, like a grey fungus, beyond the next couple of ploughed fields to the distant curl of downs. The atlas map didn't really compare with the Ordnance Survey. Might have something to do with the thirty years that separated them. Lyford seemed to have doubled in size. I found the motorway junction marked. If I turned right, to a roundabout, and then right again, I should be able to turn left onto Foxton Road, and then trust to luck. The atlas would be no use once I'd entered the maze of the council estate, but I was convinced I'd remember it, when I was there.

In a way, I did. A house here, a shop there, a corner. Little details that had the skin on my neck crawling with an imminent recognition that refused to explode into life. Everything had changed so much since 1966. It had been changing, even while I was there. I could remember the prefabs smashing down. I could remember bulldozers and diggers and cranes trundling in, to get to work on the rubble and weed. They'd been busy since I'd left. It wasn't just the prefabs that had vanished. Thornton farm too, along with its fields and elm trees, and the pig farm at the end of the allotments. Anything suggesting countryside had been rubbed out. Marsh Green had been on the outer edge of the town, but Lyford had swallowed, belched, and now the estate was halfway down its gullet.

I crawled along Foxton Road, missed what I was looking for, turned in the car park of Pirton station and drove back.

There it was. The first entrance to Linden Crescent. My street. Not a crescent, really. It was three sides of a square, abutting Foxton Road at both ends. I parked and walked its length, but I had to look at the house numbers to identify number twelve. My old home. New door, new windows, new roof tiles, the front garden paved over. I didn't recognise a thing about it. Except... the fire hydrant marker, by its gate.

That was still there. Yes!

A prickle ran up my arms. What was I seeing? The past superimposing itself on the present, or the present, fat and loud, sitting on the echoing caverns of the past?

I locked the car and left it in the street. Day after day, for five years, I'd walked from this house, across the estate, to school. Not many of our families had cars, even though our fathers nearly all worked at the car factory. We didn't need them. We had buses. We walked.

It was as a pedestrian that I'd had known Marsh Green, so that was how I needed to rediscover it. But everything was so hopelessly changed, I doubted my instincts would be enough to guide me. My old Linden Crescent had been marooned, detached from the rest of the estate because the road supposed to link it in hadn't been completed. A concrete stub ran out from the crescent and stopped abruptly at a hawthorn bush and a wilderness of boggy ground. We children had marked it out for hopscotch… More and more little details were coming back to me.

Hopscotch markings had long gone. The connecting road was completed now – Meadow Way, apparently. I wasn't sure where it would take me so I followed the Crescent round and set off up Foxton Road, as I'd done every morning, with my sister Hilary. I counted off the streets that led into the estate. Capstone Way. That was the street I turned up to go to school. Beech Road, leading to the Green, the knot of streets where Angela and Denise had lived. Lucy Road, leading to the Rough. And then, Rowlands Avenue.

Rowlands Avenue had really been part of a different world. The last street off Foxton Road, before the road ran out into

39

farmland. It must have been the work of some 1930s developer. Someone with ambitions that never materialised beyond one short cul-de-sac in the middle of nowhere. Even though it found itself rubbing shoulders with the later council estate, it contrived to stand apart, quietly gathering its skirts in bourgeois disdain for its hustling cheap-rent neighbours. A dozen or so houses primly perched along it, not huge or overtly grand but privately owned and deeply conscious of it. They had blue posters in their windows when there was an election. Everyone on the estate had red ones. When I was ten I'd been unaware of the cultural significance of its detachment, but I'd known it was magically apart. Like Linden Crescent, it didn't quite connect, but unlike Linden Crescent, it didn't want to. You could reach Rowlands Avenue from the estate, but only by a footpath.

Not any more.

It had doubled in length, disappearing into a tight web of eighties housing. But I found the house where Serena had lived. The house where we, her tribe, had gathered in a garden among roses to drink orange squash and eat chocolate fingers. It had changed less than my old home, maybe because it was posher. Really posh - it had a garage. Still had a garage. The windows were new, double-glazed, but they'd kept to the old design. There were still roses in the garden. They couldn't be the same ones, surely. Not after thirty-five years.

I ventured in through the gateway, my pulse racing, and realised there was a woman in the garden, bent over one of the shrubs, her back to me. My heart stopped.

The scrunch of gravel under my foot raised her up, turning towards me.

'Serena!' I said it, because she was Serena, but even before I'd got to the end of the word, she'd transformed into a completely different woman. Short, dumpy, twenty years older than me, her neatly styled hair dyed ash blonde. Her look was imperious, eyebrows raised in a question.

'Yes? Can I help you?'

'I…' My tongue felt twice its normal size. I was tripping over my words. 'Serena Whinn. Sorry. I – sorry, I was looking for Serena Whinn.'

'Yes?' Well, I don't know a Serena Whinn, I'm afraid, so you'll have to look elsewhere.'

'She used to live here.'

'Not for the last twenty years, she hasn't.'

'Oh. No, of course. Before that, then.'

'I wouldn't know. We bought this house from a couple called Jackson, in '82.'

'Yes. I'm sorry. To have bothered you.' I was retreating, then I stopped. 'You don't know anyone, do you, who was here before then?'

She laughed, with a hint of indignation, as if the notion of anyone having lived in the area longer than twenty years was too preposterous for words. 'I can't say I really know my neighbours, but as far as I'm aware, we've been in Rowlands Avenue the longest.'

'I see. Thank you. Sorry to have bothered you.' I stepped back out of the rose garden and turned along the avenue, blindly walking, while the disappointment sank in. Seriously, had I genuinely expected that this stupid, impulsive trip would bring me face-to-face with Serena? Or with anyone at all from that era? I walked down the original stretch of Rowlands Avenue

41

and on to the end of the later addition, facing a road that led right into a new estate and left, between blocks of flats, into Marsh Green proper.

I turned left, without at first appreciating that it was Marsh Green. So much had been built up, I couldn't work out where I was. Then, in a broad gap between two blocks of maisonettes, I looked down a paved footpath, over a bridge, to Marsh Green Junior School.

My numbing despondency was drowned in a new flood of prickles and stirring memory. My old school was the same and yet changed utterly, like everything here. The past and present swimming in and out.

I walked down the path, across the bridge and stared through metal fencing. The brick-built halls, for gym and dinner and assembly, the long wings of classrooms with French windows and paved patios were still there, rather shabby, smeared with graffiti, damaged glass boarded up, but the wide tarmac playgrounds were cluttered with Portakabins and the huge, daisy-studded playing fields had been reduced to a patch just big enough for five-a-side football. New housing occupied the rest.

I stood there, fingers entwined in the wire netting of the tall fence – taller than in my day – and as I peered through, listening to the shrieks and laughter of children in the playground, I could hear the echo of us, thirty-five years earlier, calling, jabbering... Serena's silvery laugh.

*

There are clouds piling up, looking dark. The wind is getting colder. I wish I had my cardigan as I stand watching. Soon, in another week perhaps, we'll be in our woollen kilts and

42

jumpers and our gaberdines, but for now we're still in cotton frocks. All the same, our cotton frocks – different prints but the same pattern, with sashes and gathered skirts. Except Angela's. She has straight dresses without waists, made of Crimplene because her mother works in a clothing factory. Our mothers don't go out to work. They sit at home sewing our cotton frocks on their Singer sewing machines, and knitting our winter jumpers.

I think maybe Serena's mother buys her frocks too, even though she doesn't go out to work, because they always have smart little lace collars, and puffed sleeves with cuffs and ours are just plain.

I watch her powder-blue skirt whirling as she skips. It's like she floats, like a fairy. She's so lovely.

Then she turns and waves at me, gathering her skipping rope in one hand. 'Come and play with us, Karen! You can be with Ruth.'

Dare I step forward? Serena has smiled at me, but I'm still too bashful to do more that stand on their periphery, admiring.

Serena holds out her hand, drawing me in, and I run up obediently to Ruth's side.

Angela's unknotted one end of her rope, and Denise's, and taken the wooden handles off and now she's tying them together to make one long rope.

She hands me one handle and Ruth the other. We're to turn the rope for the others.

I'm not very good. I knew I wouldn't be.

'No, no!' Barbara stamps. 'You've got to do it together. You're making it go all wiggly.'

Serena smiles encouragement and with her sunshine all around me, I manage to get the rhythm right. When she smiles, I always get everything right. At the far end of the rope, Ruth begins to look less pained.

Serena is first in, skipping lightly over each flick, graceful as a fawn. The others are chanting the rhyme. 'Teddy Bear, Teddy Bear, turn around. Teddy Bear, Teddy Bear, touch the ground.'

She can do anything. I'm glad I'm not skipping, because I'd keep tripping on the rope, but Serena never does.

'...Teddy Bear, Teddy Bear, say goodnight!'

'Barbara!' says Serena, as she floats free of the rope, barely losing breath.

Barbara charges in, like a bull. Her feet land heavily with each jump. Angela is standing ready for her turn, straining like a greyhound. Denise is bouncing behind her, looking anxious. They – we – are one. The golden girls, the skipping rope uniting us in an endless circle. Beyond us, nothing matters. Through the whirling rope, across the playground, all alone, I see...

I see other children watching, mournful, unchosen, longing to be where I am. Just as I used to stand, watching and longing.

*

What was so hugely significant about a skipping game? It was just normal play. Maybe that was it. Its very normality had a golden allure that was swallowed up by what came next. After my accident, normality ceased to exist. Things can't be normal if you have a fractured skull, broken this and that, internal damage. I'd been in hospital for months, and I was in and out – more in than out – for the rest of my childhood. A few days, or maybe a few weeks at school and then I'd be back, to my new normality of bright lights, needles, pills and the smell of sick and disinfectant. When I did make it to school, teachers couldn't remember who I was. They gave up. I didn't bother taking O levels or CSEs, because there was no point. My education came from the books I read, lying in hospital wards.

That was where I learned to escape into books. To shut out the pain and tedium of real life and hide in exotic worlds, peopled with impossible heroes and villains.

But there'd been none of that, when I'd lived here, in Lyford. Nothing to predict that I wouldn't have sailed through school normally, like all my friends. Never brilliant, never Oxbridge material – haha, that would have been a joke, coming from Marsh Green council estate – but I could hope to do well enough if I worked hard. Maybe that was why the image of Serena Whinn was haunting me. The ghost of what might have been, if only I'd stayed on here, with Serena's charm to protect me. The dread that accompanied her memory was simply my subconscious dread of the accident still to come.

Someone blew a whistle. The playground noise subsided. Not instantly, but it settled. An adult voice barked. Quiet.

*

Dead silence. It's like the sky has fallen in. We all stop. Even the teachers on playground duty stop talking, and look in shocked disbelief.

And Kenneth is shocked too. That's what's so impressive about it all. Nothing shocks or worries Kenneth. Nothing ever cows him. But now he stands silent and aghast.

45

Kenneth's the boy nobody messes with. He's the boy they step into the gutter to avoid, the boy they hand their sweets and marbles and cigarette cards to, in order to escape a kicking. He'll give them a real kicking if they don't, not just a bit of a shove.

He's the boy Mr Cutler chased round the dining hall, roaring, 'Come here, boy! I'll see you hung, drawn and quartered for this, you little wretch!' Which was a bit disturbing, seeing a teacher get so angry and Kenneth not caring, just running out laughing.

He's the boy who shouted a bad word in assembly, who lets off in class, who smells, whose skin is scurfy and whose hair is nitty. Kenneth is afraid of no one and nothing, but now, there he stands, frozen, horrified.

He's been in a barney with other boys, throwing punches, kicking, snarling as usual. I watched, keeping well clear, but others were cheering on him or his opponents. Barneys are part of playground sports. I hadn't been watching him exactly. I've been watching Serena Whinn and her friends, playing a game that has them running from one end of the playground to the other. I want to join in so much, but I know I never will.

And then it happened. Kenneth stepped backwards, arms windmilling, and a flailing blow caught Serena as she'd run past.

Serena Whinn had tumbled.

That's why the silence has fallen. We freeze and watch in silent horror as she pulls herself up from the gritty tarmac, teetering, tears of unexpected shock welling in her big dark eyes. There's a collective intake of breath. Serena Whinn is in tears! Someone has made her cry!

The universe rocks in horror, but it's Kenneth's horror that impresses itself on my mind. He has done what no mortal can do without facing the fires of hell. He has hurt Serena. For the only time in his wicked life, Kenneth looks appalled at what he's done.

*

He was caned, of course. Mr Cutler had a cane, but I think Kenneth was the only one it was ever used on. Kenneth…the rest of his name wouldn't come to me. What had happened to him? Hung, drawn and quartered, probably, just as Mr Cutler had predicted. Kenneth was an argument for predestination, if ever there was one.

Who cared? I didn't want to know about Kenneth whatever his name was. It was Serena I wanted, and she was gone. Everything was gone.

I pulled back from the school fence, onto the bridge over the brook.

It was a new bridge, one of those characterless slabs of concrete with grey metal railings, tightly spaced for fear of compensation claims by tumbling children or pensioners. It seemed ridiculously large to span that tiny brook.

My brook.

Did it have a name? It was always just The Brook to us. I looked down into its sluggish waters, and ice crystals began to form in my stomach.

Dark water, and I was drowning in it. It was closing over my head. I couldn't breathe.

Stop it! I couldn't drown here. The water was barely a foot deep. Look. This was just the brook that wound among our houses, sometimes in meadows of buttercups, sometimes in deep gullies between backyards, sometimes disappearing entirely underground. Even less of it was left above ground now, as the estate had filled in. No more buttercups or grassy banks. Just a short stretch of deep ditch.

My mesmerised eyes followed the flow of empty paint cans, shopping trolleys, black plastic as the ditch skirted the fences of back gardens before slithering into a culvert. A black mouth, half-blocked by a rusting grid that dammed up scum and foul debris.

I couldn't take my eyes from it. My head began to swim. The sense of dread began to coalesce into...

A monster standing right behind me, its fangs brushing my neck, its claws biting into my shoulders.

It wasn't a sense of mere dread any more. It was sheer, writhing, all-consuming terror. Why? Why did the brook bring a scream bubbling up inside me? Why did the sight of a drainage culvert leave me suffocating, unable to breathe?

I was back on that chill, wet January evening, watching my apple being swept along the gutter into the dark, gurgling drain and...

Again, I was drowning, sinking. Sweat was breaking out all over me, but it was cold, not hot. Ice cold. I was shaking, dizzy. That driving ache to find Serena Whinn, that surge of obsession and desire, gave way to an overwhelming need for flight. I had to get out. Get away, find somewhere to hide. Some corner where no one would ever find me.

Bile rose. I would have been sick, but I had nothing to bring up. Just burning acid.

I forced my head down, forced my lungs to work, desperate

for oxygen.

The trembling calmed. But the terror was still there, at my shoulder, waiting to fold me in its black, suffocating wings. I had to get away.

I forced my legs to work, one step, then two, then I was running.

I ran, driven more by instinct than by memory, back to Foxton Road, back to Linden Crescent, to my car. It took me minutes to unlock it, my fingers were numb, the key wouldn't go in. Someone or something was chasing me.

Kenneth Dexter.

That was his name. Dexter. Coming for me.

Dexter.

I started the engine. Was it left or right? I didn't care. Just as long as I drove far away from Marsh Green.

And whatever had happened there.

— 4 —

I made it home. Must have done, though I have no memory of the drive. I just remember running through the passage in pitch darkness, into my flat and slamming the door.

I drew. Scribbled and scribbled and scribbled. Faces. Brooks, culverts, wells, more faces. Snarling faces, sinister faces, scary faces, faces of dragons, faces of beasts. Anything to give faces to the monsters lurking out there – except that they weren't out there, any more. They were in here, with me, behind the sofa, under the bed. They were my memories, and they were black and terrible, but no matter how I scribbled, they wouldn't come clear. They were always just beyond my sight.

Even daylight couldn't make them clearer. It seeped grey into the room like a smothering mist, sucking the life out of the yellow glow of my lamp.

I looked at the heap of scribbles around me. Black, black, black. And the face of Kenneth Dexter.

I stared at it, watching it change, fluctuate, like Frankenstein's monster, coming to life. It had a pulse!

And then, for the first time, I noticed the thing that was giving it a pulse. Not evil life, but the message light on my phone. It must have been flashing all night. I wanted to ignore it. How could I deal with phone messages, with present day inanity at a time like this? But I had this little cattle prod, deep inside me. I don't know if I was born with it, or if it had been implanted with all the rods and staples that had reconstructed me, but it was there, and now it began to prick and prick, telling me I needed to listen. I needed to hear a real human voice before I drifted into completely detached insanity.

'You have four new messages.'

Karen, where on earth are you? Charlie. She was the one who'd had the phone installed. Said I needed to be able to keep in touch. Meaning she could keep in touch with me. *Why didn't you come into work? Miles is waiting. Don't tell me you've forgotten. He's giving you another half hour, so jump to it.*

'End of message.'

It's Hilary. What time is it there? Thought you'd be home from work by now. Anyway, ringing to say happy birthday for tomorrow. We'll be away. Shaun has a match. So… hope the card arrives. Bye. My sister, who lived in Australia and kept in touch on birthdays and Christmas when she couldn't very gracefully get out of it. Yes, if it was Saturday, it must be my birthday. I'd forgotten.

Karen, it's Charlie again. Where on earth are you? I came round to look for you when Miles gave up waiting. What are you up to? Please contact me.

Next message.

Karen. I'm seriously worried about you now. It's late and no one's had sight nor sound of you. I've asked your neighbours. Maybe you're tucked up in bed and fast asleep. I hope so. Phone me in the morning. You must. If I don't hear from you, I'll have to go to the police.

I couldn't cope with Charlie and her worrying and nagging.

Not today. I had to get out. Always, I had to get away. I took a long swig of cold water, splashed some on my face and staggered back out to the car.

Just as well it was early and a Saturday. I'd left it skewed halfway across road and pavement. I jiggled it back and forth, clear of bikes and parked cars, and drove. Just drove. Quarter of a mile, and then the car began to splutter and hop. Then it stopped. In a side street, fortunately.

I hadn't been paying any attention to the petrol gauge. Empty. Drained dry. Hardly surprising. I didn't know what to do about it, so I got out and left it. There was a park down the road. By the river. I walked round it, down the riverbank, staring into the waters.

Water.

Dark water. Water to drown in and suck me down.

Dark as dark glass. Through a glass, darkly.

For now I know in part, but then shall I know, even as I am also known.

I was crouching on damp grass. I kept trying to recapture Serena's face, turning to smile at me, but every time she turned, instead I saw Kenneth Dexter. Blue eyes wide with horror. Blue eyes screwed with anger.

Go away, go away! I want Serena, not you! She's turning to me, she's…

I was sick, shivering again. The sky was grey above me, spitting on me. I couldn't stay here. The cattle prod was pricking. Straightening, feeling all my joints grinding, my head throbbing, I walked out of the park.

I walked the two miles to Gem's Books. I don't know why. Because it had always been a refuge in the past, a place of escape and there had to be somewhere.

'Karen! Long time no…' Malcolm Garnet's remorselessly cheerful greeting petered out. He was beside me. I didn't see him coming towards me. One moment he'd been down the shop, behind the counter, and the next he was by my side, taking my arm, leading me to a chair.

'Oh dear, you are in a state, aren't you, Karen? Has something happened?'

I shook my head violently, and then, perversely, said 'Yes!'

'What?' His voice was very soft. He was my Mr Tumnus. 'What happened?'

'I can't remember! But something happened.'

'All right. It's all right. When did it happen?'

'1966.'

'Ah.' That floored him, but he had other things to think about. I keeled over.

'Oh, oops, there we go. Come on now. Look at me, Karen. Focus. You're shaking. When did you last eat?'

'Breakfast.' I'd had cereal. I think. I'd held the packet. Maybe I'd poured some and eaten it.

'Today?'

'Yesterday.'

'Right. Come on through.' He was leading me into the back office, sweeping books off the spare chair to make room for me. It was cluttered, more cluttered even than the shop, which was chaotic enough. I liked the clutter. It was like my flat. Just books…everywhere.

Malcolm was messing with a kettle and a toaster. 'I was just about to have breakfast, so you can have some with me. Will you do that? Karen? Can you hear me?' He was holding a mug to my mouth. Tea, too hot, burned my lips, but he made me sip. Then he was feeding me a piece of toast. The oiliness of the butter turned my stomach. I was heaving.

'All right. All right. Just wait there.'

He left me in the office, but I didn't want to be sitting there, on the chair in the centre of the room, like I was on display. In the centre where monsters could creep up on me. I retreated behind his desk, among the boxes and crates, my back to the wall, and crouched, wanting to disappear. To be swallowed up.

Malcolm was hunkering in front of me, holding my hands. He started to say something, then sighed, then started again.

'Oh dear, Karen. Will you come out? No? Don't worry. Stay there. Listen. I've called Charlotte. She's coming, with Dr Pearce.'

'No!' He really is Mr Tumnus, offering me toast and then betraying me. He has horns.

'You've got to have help, Karen. They'll help you sort yourself out. It's for the best. You know it is.'

You see, what I did is, I'd go about my daily business, or I'd pretend to, and I got by from week to week, month to month, occasionally even year to year. And then something would happen and I'd unravel. That's how I think of it. My mind was shattered into a million pieces, just like my body, and someone, the doctors, I suppose, put it all back together again, like they did with my body, with needle and thread, and bandages and sticky tape, all back into one lump. But every so often, I'd brush against something sharp that snagged on a thread and the whole thing came undone. Then the doctors had to move in again with new thread and they'd start to sew and it hurt.

It always hurt.

I hate doctors.

'So, Karen. How are you, today?'

'Very well, thank you. How are you?'

'I'm fine.' Miles sat back and surveyed me, over the tips of his fingers. He was tapping them slowly together. He was very thin. All his joints were sharp. He was like a spider. 'Who am I?'

'You're Dr Miles Pearce and you're a pain in the arse.'

He allowed himself a thin smile. 'And am I anyone else today?'

Shelob, actually. 'Well, I'd say you exhibit certain tendencies which might lead me to equate you with Uncle Andrew, in *The Magician's Nephew*. Or maybe Steerpike.'

'I see. You equate me with these characters.'

'I could.'

'But you don't think I'm either one of them?'

He had to ask. Because sometimes I wasn't Karen Rothwell. Sometimes I was someone completely different. I'd been Jane Eyre for a while. And he had been St John Rivers, trying to bend me to his will. That had been all right, because I'd just argued with him. I'd refused point blank to go to India. But then there'd also been a time when I discovered I was Éowyn, warrior princess of the Rohirrim. And he had been the Witch-king of Angmar. Our session got a little heated. A little physical. I can't remember what I did, but I know he finished up with a black eye.

That was then.

'No, I'm not identifying you as anyone other than a very

55

tedious psychiatrist who's holding me prisoner.'

'You're not a prisoner, Karen. You know that. This is a hospital.'

'Oh good. Can I go?'

'When I'm convinced you're ready. Are we happy to talk today?'

'Well you are, obviously. What do you want to talk about?'

'What do we always talk about?'

'My accident.'

'Yes, let's start there.'

Start and finish. Always the same. I don't know where our talks ever left us. I suspect their purpose was not so much to explore the trauma of my fall and its aftermath, but to assess how close to functioning sanity I was. And after three months, this time, he was beginning to conclude that I was close enough. Talk, therapy and medication. Mostly medication. They made me eat. Made me smile and walk and read. Made me sit up and beg.

Malcolm Garnet came to visit me. Not for the first time, though I don't remember his earlier visits. He felt responsible, I suppose, since I'd chosen his shop for my meltdown. Besides, he didn't have much else to do. Since his wife had died about eight years before, he had made himself comfortable in his own world of books and had about as much of a social life as I had. I was his best customer, and often his unofficial shop assistant, too, so he visited.

'Karen, you're looking so much better.'

'Thanks. I am. Better enough to be embarrassed at the exhibition I put on in your shop. Did I frighten off all your customers?'

'Customers? What customers? No you didn't. Here, what do you think of this?' He produced an ancient and very chewed copy of *The Hunting of the Snark*. 'I rescued it from a house clearance. Thought of you, clambering into that skip, that time. So. Do you think it's saleable?'

We pored over it and considered the market, a little oasis of normality. The oases were spreading, linking up, mastering the desert. The medication was working.

Finally, Charlie was in my room, helping me to pack up my toiletries.

'You're looking fine, Karen. Almost roses in your cheeks. We'll have you back home and leading a normal life in no time at all. And you know I'm always there for you.'

Of course she was. She was my social worker. I was being released back into the world on condition that she monitored me. I'd have to demonstrate to her that I was eating, regularly. Eating and digesting, not just throwing up. We'd been playing this game for years. She insisted on weighing me.

'I think I've found you a new job. Much better. You never liked it in accounts, did you?'

'Would anyone? I bet the White Witch did a jig at the thought of being rid of me.'

She laughed. 'Way too undignified for Ms Creighton. You're the one doing the jig. You're free of her at last. But you want to keep working, don't you? There's a vacancy in Learning. Office work, like before, but much nicer people.'

'Local gov again, Guv?'

'Well, why not? They're always keen to help.'

What Charlie meant was that the council had to earn its

Brownie points by employing a quota of problem people like me. So she'd found me another job where I could sit and type all day and it wouldn't matter too much if I messed it up. Or if I didn't turn up some days.

So I went back to my flat and my books and I started a new job, which was very much like the old one, but it was okay, because I was sane. When I'm sane, and taking my medication, I'm very sane.

I was sane enough to stop obsessing about Serena Whinn and that dim and distant time of childhood joys and terrors. The lid was back on Pandora's box. If I'd had any hope of finding her, it would have been different, but I knew I didn't, so I put it all away.

At least, I thought I did. Then I was given some notes to type and it all started up again.

Forthcoming adult education classes. Watercolours, conversational French, Photography II, Victorian literature. I was typing up the résumés of the enthusiastic amateurs and retired teachers who'd be running them.

David Lamb. He was the one who'd be teaching Victorian literature, one of the professionals. I looked at the list of schools where he'd taught before retirement – I looked blindly, seeing only letters to be typed, until my gaze flittered across the words Lyford VI Form.

I stopped. End of any work I'd manage that day.

It seemed that David Lamb had taught in Lyford VI Form from 1972 to 1978. I tried desperate calculation. It covered a year when Serena would have attended. There couldn't be any doubt that she'd have gone to VI Form. Lyford was just going comprehensive when we left. I don't know that I understood what it meant at the time, except that I wouldn't have to take the Eleven-Plus. Which was a relief.

Yes, I could remember Serena smiling at my relief. Pleased for me. Not for herself, because the Eleven-Plus wouldn't have been a problem for her. She'd have sailed through that and O levels and surely gone on to do As, which meant the VI Form that was to serve all the town's new comprehensives.

Yes, but what subjects would she have studied? David Lamb had taught English. Chaucer and Shakespeare, Austen and Shelley. That suited Serena. Poetry. I couldn't see her doing physics.

It was pointless, trying to guess, when I didn't need to. David Lamb was here. I had his address. All I had to do was ask him.

He looked a bit surprised to find me on his doorstep. I'd knocked, no reply, but I'd seen a man coming down the street, and I'd waited, on the off chance it might be him, and yes it was.

'Hello. Looking for me?'

'David Lamb?'

'That's me. What can I do for you?' He had his key in his hand but he made no move to insert it in the lock while I was standing there like an expectant mugger.

'You're going to be taking an adult education class in the autumn. Victorian literature.'

'Ah. Yes.' He was opening the door now. 'But if you're interested, you'll need to ask at the council offices. They're producing leaflets. I'm afraid I haven't got any material to give out yet. But of course I'll be very happy to see you in my class.' He wore a corduroy jacket. I wondered if they were obligatory for teachers. I could remember one who wore a shiny black suit and a bow tie, but most of them wore corduroy.

'I'm the one typing the leaflets.' Since I was in one of my sane periods, I was looking reasonably normal. Nothing too wild-eyed or alarming. Just an anonymous council employee.

'Ah. I see. Oh dear. Have I made some terrible slip-up? Split an infinitive?'

I laughed. I wasn't laughing at what he'd said. I was laughing at the thought that I might actually be on the brink of a breakthrough, but he didn't know that. He laughed with me and it seemed that now we were good chums.

'Nothing like that. At least, I haven't noticed any. It's personal, really, why I came. I saw that you used to work in Lyford.'

His grimace was expressive. 'That's going back.'

'I grew up there.'

'Ah. Did I teach you? Sorry, I don't know your name.'

'Karen Rothwell. No, you didn't teach me. I left Lyford before I went to high school, but you might have taught a friend of mine. I've been trying to track her down.'

'Oo.' David Lamb's grimace deepened. 'Names. That was a long time ago. But come in, anyway. Wife's away, so excuse the mess.'

The mess was a pair of shoes not correctly positioned on the shoe rack and an unwashed mug on a coffee table in the sitting room. I laughed again. I could show him real prize-winning mess.

But, time for business. 'Serena Whinn.'

'Yes?'

'The girl I'm looking for. Her name was Serena Whinn.

She's have been studying for A levels 1971 to 1973. And you were there from '72. Do you remember her?'

'Serena Whinn. Serena Whinn.' He was trying the name on his tongue, accessing a mental filing cabinet. 'No. I'm fairly sure I don't. It's hard, you know, remembering all those names, all those years. So many Jane Smiths and Mary Joneses. But Serena Whinn. That's quite unusual. I think I'd remember that name, and I don't. You say she studied English?'

'I don't know. I have no idea.' I sat still, trying not to wail my disappointment.

'If she did sciences, I wouldn't have known her.'

'No.' Clutch at a straw, any straw. If not Serena, what about her archangels? 'Barbara Fulbright?'

'Barbara... Oh. I don't know. I remember several Barbaras. Was one of them a Fulbright? Might have been. Possibly. Sorry. I really couldn't say for sure.'

'Denise Griggs?'

Blank.

'Angela Bryant?'

'No.'

'Ruth Jefferson?'

'No. Sorry, I... Ah. Wait. Ruth Jefferson. Hang on now.'

I sat up, like a dog panting for a whistle. Please. Please!

'That name does ring a bell. Yes! Although I didn't actually teach her. No, that's right. She left. Bit of a to-do. I'd only just started, ha ha, yes.' He was chuckling now. 'The deputy head had been drilling into me what smart, conscientious, well-behaved young people attended Lyford VI Form, and then this girl dropped out because she was pregnant. Seems nothing now, does it? But it was still pretty scandalous, back then. She gave up her A levels and they bundled her off to get married, hastily.'

'Ruth Jefferson? You are sure?' Of all the girls who circled Serena, Ruth was the one least likely to fall from grace, I'd have thought. She wasn't a saint, like Serena, but she was a mouse. Very small, very neat, very obedient. Her father was a monster, keeping her on a leash and terrifying us whenever he turned up at school, which he did most days. She would never have dared put a foot wrong, let alone any other part of her anatomy.

'Pretty sure. Because of the name. Jefferson. American president. A grand name, you might say, and I thought it rather sad – well, funny sad, I'm afraid – that on top of everything else, the icing on her punishment, so to speak, she finished up being called – oh, something. What was it now? No, can't remember, but she married someone with a rather unfortunate name. They did, in those days. Get married if they fell pregnant, I mean. I know…we were way past the Summer of Love and revolution in the streets of Paris, but 1967 got to Lyford the long way round. It's not the natural home of hardened rebels and free spirits, and she certainly wasn't either.'

I could agree with him there. I could picture her father, Mr Jefferson, shouting at her as she cowered, while he pointed a shotgun at the culprit with the unfortunate name.

'Well, sorry I can't help you any more than that.'

'No, that's fine. That's great. More than I had before.'

I excused myself from David Lamb's house before he could press me to tea and biscuits. I promised to consider taking his course.

I didn't need to go to an evening class to read Victorian

novels. I'd probably read them all, anyway. I walked to Gem's Books, wondering what I was to do with the information I'd been given. It was so little, but it was all I'd got. Ruth Jefferson had got married, in 1972 or 3 to someone with an unfortunate name.

My newly self-controlled persona was telling me it didn't matter. I wasn't going to obsess about it. But the worm had already bitten and its jaws were locked on.

Malcolm was busy with a customer when I went in, so I did my own searching. He let me use the place as a reference library. Finding people – how to. I finished up in the genealogical section and discovered that there was no shortage of advice on finding your great grandmother in the 1881 census, or how to trace distant ancestors through parish registers.

Malcolm broke free and ambled over to see what I was up to. He was a nice man, Malcolm. No poster boy, that was sure. In his fifties and getting stout, his ginger frizz – real ginger, not like mine – turning grey, his battered features beginning to sag. But his eyes were always kind, the kindest eyes I'd ever seen. And he tolerated me. The fellow book enthusiast.

'How you doing, Karen?'

'Fine. Frustrated.'

'What you looking for?'

'A girl from school. No, not Serena Whinn.' I'd explained about my fixation with her. Not why the fixation had arisen, because I didn't know myself, but I let it stand, as Charlie had suggested, as a fondly remembered schoolgirl crush. How sweet. What a hoot. 'A girl called Ruth Jefferson. Apparently she married, in the early 70s. I think, according to this, I need to go to Somerset House.'

'Mm.' He rubbed his chin, looking at the elderly, cloth-bound book I was holding. 'Might be a bit out of date. Births, marriages and deaths. All that moved, I think, to St Catherine's House. Then again – not sure, have to check, but I think it may be somewhere else now. Let's see.'

Malcolm had books coming out of his ears, but he had a computer too, and a modem to connect to the internet and Yahoo. 'The Family Record Centre,' he said, rubbing his chin. 'Clerkenwell. Sounds a good Dickensian name, doesn't it?'

We consulted a London A-Z and a map of the Underground, which I studied solemnly, as if going to London was something I did all the time. I think I might have been, as a child, on the train, with Mummy and Daddy. To see the Tower perhaps or the zoo. Lyford had been close enough, so we must surely have done, but it was a blank. I knew I'd been once in an ambulance. I'd been twelve and in no position to take note of the metropolis around me, so the experience was no use now.

I was terrified at the thought of going there now, but if I had to, I had to. My car was in some pound somewhere. It had been scooped up from where I'd abandoned it and the police said it wasn't fit to drive. I couldn't afford massive repairs, so I'd have to go to London by train. That was a relief, at least. I'd managed the motorway to Lyford, but London would have been beyond me. I was mad, but not that mad.

'Do you really need to go?' Malcolm shut the A-Z and handed it to me. A loan. 'There's a website, might help. Supposed to bring old friends together. What's it called now?'

We were back on the internet, and he found it. Friends Reunited. All I had to do was look for my old school. I was dancing in my head, wanting to laugh out loud, it was so ridiculously easy, after all I'd been through. All I had to do was type Marsh Green Junior School, Lyford and…

Nothing.

Hopeless. Two or three names, none of which I recognised. No hint of Serena or any of her friends.

I stopped wanting to laugh. I wanted to cry instead.

'Never mind,' said Malcolm. 'Let's have a cup of tea. There's always births, marriages and deaths.'

There were always births, marriages and deaths. Nothing was going to stop people getting hitched, in their millions, having babies and dropping dead. And nothing was going to stop civil servants diligently making records of it all. Every single one. That's a lot of records. First I had to get to them.

I found myself in London, in the jaws of a city deranged in its busyness, traffic everywhere, people everywhere, everything constantly on the move – except me, the professionally deranged one. Mostly, I was standing still, the A–Z and a map of the Underground in my sweating hand. But I found the centre, in the end, a hedgehog of a building, and after that the fun began.

I knew there would be indexes to consult, but what I hadn't expected was the risk of broken arms, snapped fingers and bruised feet, as I tussled with other researchers. They all seemed determined to wrestle the vast index volumes onto whichever bit of desk I was standing near. Every one of them was wearing hobnailed boots and knuckledusters.

I was lucky that I could narrow my search to a single year. David Lamb had started at the VI Form in the autumn of '72, and Ruth had left, to be married hurriedly, shortly afterwards.

I found her in the fourth quarter of 1972. No mistake. It had to be her. Married in Lyford, surname of spouse…Smellie. Oh Lord. No wonder Mr Lamb remembered it.

I checked, to be sure, under Smellie, in the same quarter. Yes. Russell Smellie, surname of spouse: Jefferson.

If I wanted to know more, I would have to order the certificate and wait for it to come by post, but I couldn't see the need. I had what I needed – Ruth's married name. The nightmare journey was worth it.

Safely home, and after washing the dust and petrol fumes of London from me, I headed for the library and its ranks of telephone directories. It seemed improbable, but I started with Lyford. Smellie.

R Smellie.

Could I really be that lucky? She was still living in Lyford?

I dialled the number, panicked and put the phone down before it could ring. Let's not be impulsive.

On the other hand, what was the point of all my angst, my trip to London, my research, if I didn't follow it up? I took a deep breath, stilled my nerves and dialled again.

It rang, kept ringing. How long could I let it ring before I was justified in giving up? I was just about to when the phone was picked up. A woman's voice said '574881. Yes?'

She was abrupt. Maybe just breathless. Not the squeaky little girl I remembered, but then she wouldn't be.

'Excuse me, are you Ruth…' I couldn't bring myself to say it. 'Jefferson?'

'Was. Ruth Melly now.' That was how she pronounced it. I didn't blame her. 'Who is this?'

'I'm – I don't suppose you remember me. We were at school.

I'm Karen. Karen Rothwell.'

There was silence. It went on so long, I thought we must have been disconnected. But we weren't. Just as I was wondering if I should jab the receiver button and shout 'Operator? Operator?' like they do in films, she spoke.

I heard her say 'Karen,' very faintly, as if she was mouthing the impossible to herself. Then she spoke aloud.

'Shit.'

— 5 —

I was on my way to Lyford again, by train this time, so less fraught, and my mind, thanks to therapy, less kamikaze. Which didn't mean I was expecting an easy, pleasant day. Ruth Jefferson/Smellie-with-a-silent-S wasn't expecting me. Quite the reverse. When I'd suggested that we meet, she'd flapped and flustered in undisguised horror and finished with a firm no. No, because she was far too busy. Today and tomorrow. All this week. In fact, all this year. A meeting just wasn't possible.

I was banking on the hope that, once she'd put the phone down and recovered from the immediate shock of my call, she'd be more reasonable. She wouldn't slam the door in my face, would she?

Maybe she would, but I'd have to try. Something had happened back in 1966, I was convinced of it. It was something I had blocked out, not because it represented halcyon days of innocent normality before the trauma of my accident, but because it had been too horrible to bear. Something worse even than the accident. Something that was creeping up on me at last, slithering around in my memory, waiting to piece itself together, and until it did, I knew I was never going to be right. Even with my medication and my watchful guardian, and my interminable talks with Miles, I was always going to be on the brink of what Charlie called 'an episode.' There was a big black hole, waiting to be filled.

It required a sort of surgery, and that was always painful, whatever the lying doctors promised, but you don't get well without it. At the moment I was sane enough to appreciate that pain was going to be essential, if I wanted to survive. Which proves I was feeling pretty sane. When I wasn't, I didn't want to survive.

I had a street map of Lyford. I knew how to find Ruth's house, in Farnham Drive, on the south side of town, at the edge of the Marley Farm estate. An old lady at the train station told me which bus to catch, which was as well, because the town centre was a mystery to me. I might have been to town on the bus with my mother, but it wasn't this town. Not this pedestrianised way with artistic benches and miniature trees, or this looming mass of shopping centre, or this multiplex cinema of steel and glass. No Lyons Corner House any more. Not even the corner it had stood on.

I caught the 27A bus, and felt easier once I was trundling into a district I'd certainly never known, riding up on to the knees of the downs. If I'd never known it, I couldn't be disturbed by the mismatch between memory and reality.

The ease wore off rapidly as I approached No. 32, Farnham Drive. It was the garden that jostled tiny fibres of memory. A neat garden. A garden I couldn't possibly ever have known, and yet, somehow, I did.

*

'You're to come to tea,' says Ruth.

I follow her, obedient but nervous. Ruth doesn't usually make me nervous, though I puzzle over her. I puzzle over how she's always so neat. Her hair is always parted so perfectly you can see a straight line of scalp, like chalk along a ruler. Mine is always a mess by the time I get to school, but Ruth keeps hers smooth. She has a little comb she carries with her.

Her socks never fall down, either. Mine do. They always finish up looking like ankle socks, even though they're supposed to be up to my knees. I pull them up hastily as we turn in through her gate. I don't want to be shouted at.

I'm fairly sure I will be, though, because that's what Mr Jefferson does. He shouts. It's more like barking, really. He always seems to be at the school, or outside the gate, even though he's not a teacher, or anything like that. He stands watching, ready to bark at anyone who runs or pushes or crosses the road without looking properly. He has very short hair that stands up on end, and a moustache that bristles like a broom when he's barking. And he has a camera. He takes pictures if we're naughty.

'I've got you on camera, boy! What will Mr Cutler say when he sees this photograph, eh? Eh? What do you say to that?'

I think he's called a governor. That's why he's at the school all the time. Must be a bit like being a lollipop lady. It's not just us children who are afraid of him. The other parents who come to the school gate are a bit wary too. My dad sniffs when Mummy mentions him and says, 'Ex-army.'

Meaning Mr Jefferson was in the army in the war. Which is probably true because most of our fathers were in the army, during the war or after it. My dad was. I've seen a photo of him in uniform, by a great big gun guarding the viaduct. That was when he was in the Home Guard, he says. Then he was called up and went to all sorts of places. Catterick. Andover. Barbara Fulbright's father went to Burma. Denise Griggs's went to Italy and got shot. Not properly. Not killed or anything and he's still got arms and legs, but it's still exciting, except that he won't talk about it. None of them want to. My Dad just says, 'Well, you know, that was then.'

None of them want to remember it, except Mr Jefferson. I think he'd like us all to be in the army, everyone drilling, marching, stamping to attention, while he barks orders. 'What you need, boy, is a spell of army discipline. Bring back National Service. That would knock you into shape.'

He wasn't at the school gates today, which means he'll be at home, waiting for us, and I don't really want to go to tea with Ruth but I suppose I have to.

Mr Jefferson is in the garden, holding an inspection of his roses. They are in straight lines, not daring to flutter a petal and the grass is standing to attention. There aren't any weeds in this garden. The hedge is cut like a brick wall. He turns to look at us, shears in hand.

'What's this, what's this? Who have you got there, Missy?'

Ruth looks at me, reluctantly. 'She's Karen, Daddy. She's coming to tea.'

'Oh is she, indeed? And who gave you permission to invite this Karen to tea? Did you ask Mother?'

'Yes, Daddy.'

'Very well, then. But no noise. And no messing up the lawn! You know the rules!' He glances at my school bag. 'What have you got there? Gym clothes, I hope. All children

71

must carry gym clothes. Right, up you go and change, at the double. No wearing best blouses in the garden!'

We go upstairs, but we don't get changed. We don't want to play in the garden. I wouldn't dare because it might mess up the lawn. We don't do anything really. We hover in the bedroom Ruth shares with her sister, and we very quietly look at her dolls of different nations, arranged with great precision on the window sill.

I don't like it there. It's too quiet. I can hear creaking on the stairs, like a monster creeping up, and then I can hear a funny noise, like someone breathing through the crack in the door, and I think maybe the monster's just outside. Ruth doesn't seem to hear, but I stick close to her, just in case.

Breathing.

'Ruth! Your tea's ready. Bring your little friend down.' Mrs Jefferson is twittering up the stairs, and immediately Ruth jumps up as if she can't wait to go down. Me too. We race to the bedroom door and open it, and there isn't any monster there, just Mr Jefferson, with his bristling moustache.

'Hurry up, girls. Don't keep Mother waiting. Have you washed your hands?'

No, we haven't. Mr Jefferson doesn't trust us to do it properly. He follows us into the bathroom and insists on scrubbing our hands for us, holding our wrists. I don't like the feel of his skin. His fingers make me shiver. I want to be out of there. I want to go home.

But then it's teatime, with fluffy Mrs Jefferson in her frilly apron and it's all right because there's jelly and real tinned cream.

*

I only went once. I never dared go to Ruth's door on my own. I might have disturbed Mr Jefferson's regimental roses.

Now I was looking at Ruth's own garden. Not a rose in sight, but there were salvias and lobelia, arranged in brutal, geometric precision. An exact square of perfect grass. Not a hint of moss on the tarmac leading to the garage and the front door. Maybe Mr Jefferson was living here too, with his daughter, in charge of the garden and ready to photograph that salvia if it shifted out of line.

I felt as daunted as I had back then. With better reason, probably. Here I was, after Ruth had specifically ordered me not to come, and I had resurrected a ten-year-old's terror of defiance. I forced myself forward and knocked on the door. A very ordinary door, on a very ordinary house, brick and pebbledash and a bay window.

No response. It was a Saturday, which meant she most likely wouldn't be at work, but she could still be out. The house could be shut up for a week. The family might be on holiday.

I noticed the bell and pressed it. Then I saw, through the bubbled glass, someone coming down stairs. The door opened.

A woman. Forty-five, like me. I wouldn't have recognised her – except that somewhere in that frazzled, middle-aged housewife with the deep-etched frown lines, I could still make out nervous little Ruthie with the precision parting and the purse on a strap and the pure white socks that never fell down.

'Hello, Ruth,' I said.

Her chest rose and fell three times, before she said, 'Karen Rothwell. I said not to come, didn't I? I haven't got time for this.'

'I won't stay long, I promise.'

'Oh fuck it. You'd better come in, then.' With a huge sigh of irritation, she led me through to her living room. 'I might have guessed you'd turn up, whatever I said. Stubborn little cow. Always were.' She was groping for cigarettes, lighting one, offering the packet to me. 'No? Well, go on then. Might as well take your coat off.'

'Thanks.' I slipped it from my shoulders.

'Shit!' She was looking me over. 'You're a skeleton. What's it with you? Some sort of anorexia, I suppose.'

'No, nothing like that. I've been ill. In hospital. I lost a bit of weight.'

'A bit? Christ. So what was it then? Your illness. Nothing serious?' She was asking because it was the way conversation was obliged to go, but she didn't really want to be told. There are many people like that. I could recognise the symptoms at a glance, so I didn't bother her with details.

'Nothing serious. All fixed now.'

'Right.' She sat down, then jumped to her feet again. 'Since you're here, I suppose I'd better make some tea.'

I could recognise the symptoms of prevarication too. She escaped to the kitchen, and I shared the relief. I thought I'd got it all straight in my head, while I was on the train, what I was going to say. But now I was there, I could feel the tell-tale racing of my heart, and the twinges of panic that could turn me into a gibbering wreck on the floor if I didn't take care. I breathed deeply and slowly, looking round the room.

It was like the garden, horribly neat. Nothing out of line on the mantelpiece. Books perfectly aligned on shelves. Magazines precisely stacked under the coffee table.

It didn't make sense, the contradiction. Her father could be in charge of this house, still governing her life, yet little mouse Ruth with her parade of dolls had left school in disgrace and pregnant, and turned into a strangely sour woman, who talked like a fishwife. Rebellion and conformity hand in hand.

But then I suppose life with Mr Jefferson would lead to some sort of collapse, sooner or later. Because he really wasn't what he pretended to be. We could all bear witness to that.

*

'Come here, boy! Yes, you, boy. Come here, I say!'

Mr Jefferson, camera round his red, swollen neck, is roaring, one arm raised, like a German salute, summoning Kenneth Dexter. Kenneth has kicked a hole in the fence. Kenneth is for it now.

Kenneth comes, loping. Other boys lope like that when Mr. Jefferson summons them, dragging their feet because they'd much rather run away, but they daren't. If even their fathers and Mr Cutler, the headmaster, are afraid of Mr Jefferson and jump to attention when he calls, how can they disobey? But Kenneth lopes because that's the way he always runs. Like a wolf.

He runs right up to Mr Jefferson, like he's obeying, and then he hits him. Doesn't stop running, just slogs him straight on the nose, and then he runs on.

Mr Jefferson swells up, and up and up, like a bullfrog, his face dark red and his moustache sticking straight out and he turns to roar at Kenneth again, and Kenneth turns to come back, fists up, right up to him.

And Mr Jefferson collapses, like a burst balloon. He puts up his hands to defend himself and he cringes, with a noise that sounds like a whimper.

We all see it. We hear it.

Kenneth puts his face right into Mr Jefferson's, and says 'Perv!' and Mr Jefferson cowers again. Then Kenneth lopes off, backwards, shouting rude words and laughing.

He's not the only one. There are titters and giggles, from schoolchildren. From their parents too.

Mr Jefferson swells up again, but no one believes in him any more.

*

Ruth must have stopped believing in him too, I suppose. Enough to let her socks drop.

She returned with a tray. Tea and a shop-bought fruit loaf. She handed me a mug and a plate. I felt I was being tested, so I took a bite of the cake. Too dry, too sweet, but I'd finished it, just so that she wouldn't get the wrong idea.

'I heard you married,' I said, swallowing painfully, reaching for the tea to wash it down.

She laughed, not very humorously. 'Yeah, well. I expect the whole world heard. Yes, I got stuffed. The wages of sin, always catch up with you, apparently. Didn't have to be so bloody quick about it, though, did they? We'd only done it once. I ask you. One grope in the bushes for curiosity's sake and the next moment you're up the aisle and stuck with a screaming baby and gas bills.'

She was watching me as she rabbited on. Smoking rapidly. She was nervous.

'How did you hear, anyway?' She carefully flicked her cigarette into a glass ashtray. 'You moved away. Don't know why we didn't. Staying here, in godforsaken Lyford. Stupid, isn't it? Marriage, children, I don't know. Suck the fucking life out of you.'

Fucking. She slipped in obscenities, but it was obvious they didn't come naturally to her. She was forcing them. Playing the hard woman. She drew hard on her cigarette. 'Where did you go? Manchester, wasn't it?'

'Liverpool. Then Coventry. I live in Yorkshire now. That's where my mother came from. She wanted to go back there when my father died, to be near relatives.' I knew she wasn't remotely interested in my life story, which sounded unutterably dull as I recited it, but that was the point. I wanted to play down any drama and reassure her that I wasn't going to eat her. She was watching me as if I might.

'Anyway, I met a man who used to teach in Lyford. At the VI Form. I asked about people I used to know and he remembered you.'

'A teacher? Can't say I remember any. Who is he?'

'David Lamb. Taught English.'

'I didn't do English. How would he… Oh, you mean he remembered the scandal. Well, at least I stirred the place up. Had them all queuing up to tell me what a disappointment I was. None of them came to the wedding. Thank God. Fucking awful. Full humiliation or nothing. Had to be in church but he wouldn't let me wear white.'

She didn't need to explain who she meant by he.

'So you had a child.' I had to say something. What I wanted to say was, never mind you, where's Serena Whinn? but I was sufficiently self-controlled to stop myself. I glanced round the room again for clues, but there were no photographs. None. No weddings, no babies, no holiday snaps or Christmas gatherings. Which was odd, considering we never saw her father without

77

his camera, capturing evidence of all our sins.

'Child! Four of the bloody things.' Ruth stubbed out her cigarette and drew out another. 'You'd have thought I'd learn, wouldn't you. Hanging one millstone round my neck after another. Still got Emma and Lee living here. You'd think once they were adults, I'd be rid of them but oh no. Emma's got herself a job in town, but claims she can't find anywhere to rent. And Lee's just finished uni, so is he out looking for a job? Is he fuck. Can't be bothered to get off his arse. Just plays that bloody guitar all day. Lee!' She was at the door, shouting. 'Keep it down!'

Since she'd mentioned it, I could detect, very faintly, the thump of a bass line. How she heard him was a mystery. Except that it wasn't really a mystery at all. She was just determined to be aggravated about something.

Was it me, doing this to her? Setting her on the prowl, looking for things to snarl about? Perhaps I should try to smooth things over. 'Four children,' I said, lamely. 'How lovely. Do you have photos?'

'No I bloody don't! Why would I want photographs, when I've got the bloody brats themselves? Why does everyone go on about photographs, all the bloody time? Christ, haven't we had enough of all that?' She stabbed her cigarette into an ashtray.

I heard the thump on the stairs, far louder than the music. A cheerful looking boy poked his head round the door. 'Sorry. Too loud?'

'Yes! Can't hear myself think.'

He was looking at me, smiling, brows raised. 'Hi.'

'Hello.'

Ruth flapped a hand in my direction. 'Karen. Someone from

78

way back. No one you know.'

'Not a friend!' He pretended shock. 'Mum doesn't do friends. She hates everyone, don't you?'

'Don't be ridiculous.'

He laughed. 'Anyway, I'm off into town. Do you want me to get anything?'

Ruth sighed. 'Oh, don't bother yourself. Well. Milk. You might as well get another couple of pints. The amount you get through.'

'And you're not made of money and we're eating you out of house and home. Okay. A couple of pints it is. See you!' With another smile at me, he was gone.

Ruth scowled. 'He'll get the wrong sort.'

I was willing to bet that he'd get exactly the right sort. The dynamics of this situation were obviously way beyond my comprehension, but then each insane family is insane in its own way.

'Kids,' said Ruth, bitterly. She lifted the tray to wipe an invisible mark on the coffee table. 'So. Let's get this over with. I don't suppose you really came here to find out about my failed family-planning schedule.'

'Well…'

'You'd better not be here to rake over the past.'

'Um.' What was I to say? That was exactly what I wanted to do. 'Not exactly. I was just thinking about school days. You know.'

She stared at me. 'You are joking.'

It was obviously a negative topic in her mind, but then, everything seemed to be a negative topic in her mind. I couldn't gauge if she was confirming my suspicion that something bad had happened back then, or pouring out bile on life in general. There was nothing for it but to go on as if I hadn't heard. 'School days at Marsh Green. All of us. You know. Angela and Denise and Barbara – and Serena. Remember?'

She was groping for another cigarette, her hand shaking. 'What do you mean, remember? What sort of a stupid fucking question is that? Of course I fucking remember. How could I bloody forget?'

'Forget what?'

'Jesus!' She looked at me as if I were demented. I wasn't. Not yet. But I would be soon at this rate. 'You ask me that? Don't bloody ask, because I don't want to talk about it, right?' As I opened my mouth, she repeated 'Right?'

So what could I say? 'Do you ever see anything of – of any of them?'

'Christ. Do you think I have time to go chasing round after old gangs from thirty-five years ago? You might have, but I don't.'

'I just thought I'd like to look them up.' And hope one of them might be less unhinged.

'If you want to track them down, fine, but it's nothing to do with me. Do whatever you want, but leave me out of it. Can't be that difficult for you, can it? You found me. Barbara. She'll be in a solicitor's directory, won't she? Or something like that. Just don't come asking me.'

'Did she become a lawyer, then?' A painfully obvious question, but I needed to keep calm – keep her calm. Keep talking. I'd had enough people in my life trying to calm me down. My turn now.

'Yeah! Or… I don't know. Something. Maybe. Look.' She

was pacing round the room, then she turned to confront me. 'Why? Tell me. Why have you come? Because if you just want to rake all that business up, that would be just sick. I mean, seriously sick. I don't want to think about it. I'm certainly not going to sit here talking about it. None of it, the murder or any of the rest. So just leave it.'

'Murder!' The word screamed in my head, but nothing came out of my mouth. Black wings flapped around me. The terror pounced back to my shoulder, hissing in my ear. 'Murder!'

My expression must have revealed something. It must have, because I could feel myself cracking, like a windscreen suddenly crazing into a thousand pieces that were just waiting to fly apart. I could feel my heart pumping, the roar in my ears, the sweat on my lip—

But Ruth saw none of it. She wasn't seeing me at all. She was caught up in her own words. 'It's over. Okay, she died. It was horrible. It's over. I don't want to know, right? If you want to—' She stopped. Now she was seeing me. Seeing something that made her turn pale and take a step back.

'Who?' I managed to whisper. 'Who was murdered?'

'Oh for Christ's sake, what d'you mean, who? If you, of all people, don't know…' She was screeching, venting an anger that was a defensive shield for her to hide behind. 'Look, I don't know what your game is, Karen Rothwell, but I want nothing to do with it. Just go, will you? Get out. Asking who – that's sick.'

She was beyond reason and I was beyond pretence. I needed to get out, as much as she wanted me to go. I grabbed my coat and let her usher me out of the house. I walked away, listening for the slam of the door. It didn't come. She must be standing there watching me. I didn't dare look back.

handsfor the chairat the door. It didn't move. She ran the
timeuntil they would reach that dreadful door. Fear stabbed
at herwith pincer-like precision as her... to... the... to...

— 6 —

'Don't slam the door! Christ, you know what it does to my head.'

'Sorry. Thought I'd shut it quietly.' Lee sauntered into the kitchen, glancing at his mother as he stowed the milk in the fridge. 'Friend's gone?'

Ruth scowled. 'What's it look like? She wasn't a friend, anyway. Just someone I knew at school.'

Lee watched her, scrubbing. 'At school. Is this something to do with, you know, Grandad?'

Ruth clenched. 'Why does everything have to be about your grandfather? It's nothing to do with him. Why do you have to keep going on about it?'

'Mum.' Lee took the nailbrush from her. 'Stop it. Your hands are clean. Leave it. Please.' He handed her a towel and a bottle of hand cream. 'You're going to take the skin off again.'

'Leave me alone. You don't know what you're talking about. Go on. Get back to your bloody music. I've got things to do.'

'Okay. Just as long as you promise to stop scrubbing.' He hugged her from behind.

Why did her family have to be so bloody understanding and caring and good-humoured, all the time? Why couldn't they snarl and be resentful for once? Then she would have good cause to bite back. Bite and scratch and spit, and get it out of her system.

She pushed him free. 'You can stop treating me like a bloody child.' She dried her hands, moving away from the sink.

It was enough to reassure him. 'Okay then.'

She watched him trail upstairs, then she retreated to the living room, pulling the door shut behind her. She rocked on her heels for a moment, then picked up the phone.

Put it down.

Picked it up again. Dialled.

'Ruth. Yes,' said a clipped, disembodied voice.

'Barbara.' She stopped to catch her breath.

'Yes.'

'Something's happened. A woman. She came here. I told her not to, but she came anyway. Where did she come from? She's not supposed to be alive.'

'Who? Stop babbling, woman. I don't know what you're talking about, and this really isn't a very convenient time.'

'Oh, but—'

'I am sitting by Mother's hospital bed, waiting for her to pass away. I doubt she'll last the night, so I don't want to listen to babble. If it's something serious, just spit it out.'

'Karen Rothwell. She came here.'

There was a brief pause. 'Good God.'

'Yes!'

'She's dead. Well, obviously not. What did she want?'

'To talk. I can't. I just can't.'

'Calm yourself, Ruth. So she's keen to talk. Well, that makes a change from refusing to open her mouth, at least. What did she say?'

84

'She claims she doesn't remember anything.'

'Very wise. The less remembered the better. What did you tell her?'

'Nothing! I told you, I can't. I don't want to talk about it.'

'Well then.'

'But I think she might be coming to find you.'

Another brief pause. 'Does she know where to find me?'

'I sort of let drop—' Mutterings down the phone.

'Well, I have nothing to hide. But I don't have time for this, right now. A pity you didn't keep your mouth shut.'

'Yes. I'm sorry.' Ruth scrubbed furiously at a fingerprint on the sideboard, and caught her own reflection in the polished mahogany. She winced. 'Sorry about your mother, too.'

'Yes, well.' An irritated sigh.

'I didn't want to speak to her at all. She just showed up. I told her not to come. I don't want anything to do with it.'

There was a short sharp laugh on the phone. 'Sorry, Ruth. Too late for that, don't you think? Too late for any of us.'

7

I sat on the train, quietly disintegrating again, all Dr Pearce's patient work unravelling in a moment. Why wouldn't Ruth say more? Or why had she said so much? One word? Murder. To say that, to open a trapdoor beneath my feet and then deny me any explanation. Electric jolts and sparks were flying within me, trying to make connections. Trying, trying, trying to grasp the memory that wouldn't come.

A child had been murdered. As soon as she'd said it, I knew it was true. I'd always known it. Why hadn't I thought about it, the moment I remembered Serena, back in January? This was the explanation of the dread that had been haunting me. I'd been so obsessed with finding Serena again, searching, searching, finding nothing. Why had it had never occurred to me that I could never find her. Because she was dead.

*

There are policemen standing, legs apart, hands behind their backs, helmets on, all across Aspen Drive. When people come too close, they stretch out their arms to keep them back. People want to get by, though. Adults. They're huddled in the street, some of the mothers looking shocked, pulling their cardigans tight around them, some of them angry, shouting at the police. The men are all angry. All shouting. Some of them are trying to get round, through the part-demolished prefabs. A gang of them, holding sticks, shouting that they're going to string him up and suddenly there are panda cars, bumping over the concrete after them, lights flashing. There's a police van and Alsatians straining at the leash under a nightmare wintry sky.

I am terrified. I watch it all out of the car window...

The car window...

'Tell me about the car. Listen, girl, just tell me. You saw the car!'

*

Tell me about the car.

I could hear the words being shouted at me, but I couldn't see the car. What car? I could feel my chest tightening, my throat sealing itself shut so I couldn't speak. Wouldn't speak. Not to anyone. Not to the man looming over me, shouting at me...

Serena turned and smiled at me, her dark eyes pleading.

'Tell them, Karen. Tell them.'

I felt sick.

I nearly missed my stop. Sanity surfaced just as carriage doors were being banged shut. I looked out of the window and realised I was home and the train was just about to start up again. I flung myself out onto the platform. The train jolted and moved on, and I realised I'd left my coat in the rack. It was raining.

I caught the bus, getting soaked in the process, and leapt off again after two stops, because I decided I didn't want to go home. I wanted to go to Gem's. The bookshop wasn't quite in the town centre. It was tucked away in a side street, relying on regulars who knew where it was, and students from the university who had a nose for anything cheap, and passing bookworms who could instinctively tell where a bookshop might be.

I needed to talk to someone. That was a good sign, that I recognised the need to talk. At least, that's what Miles would have said. But I didn't want to talk to him, or to Charlie. Not to anyone who had a file on me at their fingertips. I wanted to talk to someone who was just a friend. Malcolm.

'Look at you! Like a wet dog,' he said. 'Come in and dry off before you turn into a fish.' He switched on an electric fire, shifting boxes of books out of the way.

'I left my coat on the train.' My teeth were chattering. The fire bars were beginning to glow but I wasn't feeling the heat yet.

Malcolm fetched me a towel. 'On the train, eh? Where have you been gallivanting off to?'

'Lyford.'

'Ah.'

'I found the friend – one of them. Ruth. I went to see her. She said things.'

'What things? Nothing very pleasant, by the look of it. I can see she's upset you.'

'She said things that made me remember…my friend Serena. I know now why I've been so obsessed with finding her. Why she meant so much to me. Why I've blocked it all out. It's because she was murdered.'

'Good God.' He rocked back in shock.

'And I think – I don't know – I can't remember. I have this terrible guilt. I think I should have said something. I saw something and I should have told people about it.'

'Oh Lord, Karen. What makes you think that?'

'I keep seeing her, telling me to tell them. She's asking me why I didn't speak up. If I did, maybe she'd still be alive. I don't know. Ruth got so angry. Said I of all people should know. But know what? I don't know what it is she thought I'd know.'

'And she wouldn't tell you?'

'She threw me out. Refused to talk about it. It really upset her. What if it was all down to me?'

'No, don't think that!'

'But if I'd spoken up—'

'Listen, if your friend Serena was murdered, then it's the murderer who's responsible. Not a little girl who probably couldn't understand how important her words might be.'

'But she keeps looking at me! Serena. She keeps turning to look at me. I hear her saying, "Tell them."'

'Karen.' He took my hands and looked at me with overflowing sympathy. 'It wasn't your fault.'

'If only I could remember.'

'I know. And I do understand, it's impossible for you to let this go, now you've got this far. You can't just leave it hanging, can you?'

'No!' I felt so relieved that he understood, that he wasn't telling me to get a grip and stop fantasising, or was I taking my medication? He wasn't shuffling papers and taking notes and assessing my rambling revelations in medical terms.

'I need to find a lawyer,' I said. 'How do I do that?'

'Do you really need one? Whatever this Ruth implied, no one's accused you of anything, have they?'

'No, it's not that. It's another friend. One of the gang.

Barbara Fulbright. She's a lawyer. I thought, if I could find her…'

'Solicitor or barrister?'

'I don't know.' I tried to remember what Ruth had said, before she tried to unsay it and claimed to know nothing. 'Solicitor, I think.'

'I've got a directory somewhere.' Malcolm mooched off among his tightly packed shelves in the second-hand section and returned with a hefty tome so dark and dire it could only be a directory of lawyers. 'It's about five years out of date. What did you say her name was, again?'

'Barbara Fulbright. Oh God. Of course that's her maiden name. I suppose she's married and she's called something completely different.' I shut my eyes, thinking of another trip to the Family Records Centre, another trawl through marriage indexes, but this time without a clue of the date.

'Don't despair,' said Malcolm. 'Let's look, first. Hm, hm, hm. F. Fo. Fu. Fulbright. Barbara. Yes! There you are.'

I looked, not daring to believe. Refusing to believe. There were probably dozens of Barbara Fulbrights around. How would I know if this was mine? She didn't live in Lyford. According to the directory, she was in Carlisle, which was about as far from Lyford as you could get.

But Ruth had said she was a lawyer.

'You going to try and speak to her?' asked Malcolm, jotting down the details for me.

'I think so.'

'Would you like me to come with you?'

'Oh.' I was taken aback by the offer, far beyond my expectations. But it was the wrong moment. It had been good to talk to him – just what I'd needed. My panic on the train had subsided. But now I needed to deal with this alone. Serena, my lovely Serena, had been murdered, and my overwhelming sense of guilt, despite Malcolm's reassurances, convinced me that I bore some of the responsibility. I was ashamed of what I might discover and I didn't want to share that shame with anyone just yet, even with Malcolm.

Especially with Malcolm.

8

'So. Hello. How are you, Karen?' My sister sounded crisp, as she always did. She had a special tone for speaking to Karen. It was a let's get this over with tone.

'I'm fine,' I said, automatically. 'And you?' Family courtesies, ruthlessly maintained. Fortunately for her, we didn't have to maintain them very often. She only wasted good money on a phone call from Sydney on birthdays and... Oh God, it was her birthday. I should have phoned her two hours ago, at nine o'clock. Which would be six o'clock in the evening, her time. That was our standard arrangement. 'Have you had a good birthday? Hope you got my card.'

'No. Did you send one? You probably forgot to post it.'

I was preparing to argue, constructing a massive and detailed lie, but what was the point? She knew me. I hadn't just forgotten to post it. I'd forgotten to buy it. My mind was in 1966 Lyford, not in Millennium Oz. 'Sorry.'

'And you didn't phone, usual time. If you can't be bothered, fine by me, but I thought I'd better check to make sure that you're all right – hadn't done anything stupid.'

'I'm fine. Sorry I didn't phone earlier, but I was out.'

'Oh yes? Where?' Meaning she couldn't believe I had a social life.

'Oh, just Gem's. I've been helping with a display.'

'On a Sunday?'

'Well, you know. It's the only quiet time.' It was true that I had been helping with a display, though not this morning. A while back, I'd done a dozen sketches of assorted aliens, spaceships and futuristic dystopias for Malcolm when he'd put on a sci-fi promotion and now he'd asked if I could do the same for a fantasy week. I wasn't having any trouble sketching monsters...but Hilary wouldn't want to know about that. 'So how has your birthday been?'

'Great so far. Dave's booked us a table at this new Italian place. The kids are joining us there.'

'How are they doing?'

'Who?'

'Shaun and Hayley.'

'Ah, you remember their names. That's an improvement.'

I held the phone away, so she couldn't hear me sigh. Yes I could remember the names of her children. They probably couldn't remember mine, though.

'They're fine.'

They were fine, she was fine, I was fine. Great. 'Do you remember Serena Whinn?'

'What?'

'Serena Whinn. She went to school with me. In Lyford. Do you remember her?'

'Well I'm hardly likely to forget the name Whinn, am I?' Her hiss whistled down the phone. 'Look, Karen, I didn't phone to chat about your old school chums. You know how much this call is costing me?'

More in effort than in money, I suspected. 'I just wondered—'

'Please let's not start reminiscing, for God's sake. The less said about all that, the better. It was bad enough at the time. I'm not going to wallow in it, all over again.'

'I don't want to wallow, honest. But she was... I just want to know what happened. Before my, you know, my accident.'

'Karen...' She stopped. I could hear her drawing a deep breath. 'Let's stop this charade, shall we? You and I know perfectly well it wasn't an accident. Mum may have wanted to believe you just slipped out of that window, but we both know you bloody jumped.'

I was silent. She'd said this before. She believed it. I suppose she was right. But I didn't know it, because I couldn't remember anything about it at all. Nothing about the fall from a fifth floor, whether it was an accident or deliberate. I'd been over it a thousand times with Miles, but I could only remember waking up in hospital, in pain, physical and mental. Pain that never went away.

'Sorry,' I whispered.

Hilary sighed. 'Look, let's forget it, shall we. I don't want to get hung up on the past. I've got to go. Dave's in the car.'

'All right. Well, enjoy your meal. And, like I said, happy birthday.'

The thing about siblings, is that sometimes they're loving and sometimes they're not. I've known brothers and sisters who'd do anything for each other, and I've known some who won't speak, who find cause for quarrels and bitterness in every quarter, who compete for everything with ferocious jealousy. I'd come to take it for granted that I and my sister were just siblings who couldn't quite get along. Never had and never would. But it wasn't true. There had been a time, long, long ago and far, far away, when we'd been the best of friends.

*

'I want to paddle!' My sister jumps up. Enough of sandcastles. She turns to run, and I laugh because there are two patches of sand sticking to the buttocks of her ruched swimsuit, and a trail of sand all down the back of her sturdy little legs.

'Best go and keep an eye on her, Karen,' says Mummy, adjusting her straw sun hat and gathering up our buckets and spades.

So I run after Hilary, which would be easy because my legs are longer and stronger, but I stop, seeing a crab begin to wriggle out of the sand. I want to see him come out properly, but he looks at me and changes his mind, sweeping the sand up to cover himself again. When I run on, Hilary's already at the foamy line left by the last wave and she charges on, straight into a big churning breaker that knocks her right off her feet.

She's squealing with cold and fright, struggling as the wave pushes over her, then hauls her back. I race, as fast as I have ever run, to grab her out of the water, jumping her up as she splutters salt.

'Don't let go!' She throws her wet, sandy arms around me, and buries her face in my shoulder. 'Don't let go…'

…This one.' Hilary hands me a bauble. It's like a raspberry, all bobbles and each bobble catches the light.

I reach up to hang it on a high branch.

'More!'

95

Three more balls, and then the glass icicles.

Daddy looks round from the football on telly. 'Finished yet, girls?'

We step apart, to let him see.

'Not bad. Not bad at all.'

We think it's better than not bad. We come together again and gaze up at the glory of our Christmas tree, and we grip hands, sharing the build-up of excitement that's so huge, it will never end. Christmas is the best time in the whole world.

*

We'd been the best of friends. Perhaps, in time, as we'd developed our own interests, gone to different schools maybe, discovered boys, argued over music, we'd have grown apart anyway, in a gentle, organic way. But there wasn't any growing apart. There was just a short, sharp full stop, because I had my accident.

I was egocentric, of course, as children and invalids invariably are, but it wasn't as if I'd actively craved to be the centre of attention. I just was. I'd been in hospital, in crisis, the focus of concern, everyone flapping around me, worrying over me, the whole family revolving round me. Hilary must have felt utterly excluded. She wasn't neglected, not in any normal sense, but in her eyes I had it all, because I was ill, and she was ignored, because she was healthy. All that infant affection turned to resentment. I was aware of it, while locked in my own revolving world of treatment and fuss, but I didn't realise how deep it ran until our mother died.

I'd had a two-edged relationship with my mother, ever since the accident. She devoted herself to me, so much so that

I sometimes think she barely registered my father's death, of a heart attack at fifty-nine, except when it raised financial complications. She busied herself with me, fussed over me and let my care rule her life, but it never stopped me feeling that she disliked me. Maybe it was because she knew, despite her adamant disclaimers to the last, that Hilary's story was right. It hadn't been an accident. I'd tried to kill myself and she could never quite forgive me.

I don't know what she imagined Hilary's role was to be. Hilary left home, got married, had children, but she was still expected to be there, on call, to help, to listen to my mother's complaints. To share the martyrdom, I suppose. Hilary did what the world expected of her, seething with silent resentment, but when our mother died, the silence ceased.

'I'm giving you warning now, I don't give a toss about last requests and deathbed promises. She's gone and she doesn't have any say in it any more, so don't expect me to step in as your long-suffering nursemaid for the rest of your demented life! I'm off; so far away you won't be able to screw up everything for me, any more.'

She was upset, of course, letting her grief out as a burst of anger. Her husband Dave had calmed her down, but then he confirmed that they were off to Australia in a month. By the time they flew out there, she was ready to smile and give me a big hug, for appearances' sake, if nothing else, and promise to keep in touch. Which she did, every birthday and Christmas.

She'd forgotten all those Christmases and holidays before the Fall. Of course she had. I wasn't the only one who'd wiped out the past when the world changed. But she remembered the name Whinn. The name of a child who was murdered. Yes, she'd remembered that, but it could hardly be productive to nag her into saying more. She'd only been seven at the time. Too young even to appreciate the full horror, let alone absorb the details.

For those, I would need to speak to Barbara Fulbright, and I couldn't call her office until Monday, so I'd have to sit and endure the rest of Sunday in anticipation.

Such intense anticipation that I only remembered at the last moment that I was supposed to be having lunch with Charlie. She'd booked us a place for a Sunday roast, the full monstrous affair – part of her monitoring attempts to coax me into normal appetite. If I could cope with a roast potato, she'd be convinced I was okay. I didn't want to eat. The gnawing monster that had me back in its grip was telling me I couldn't eat, or drink, or swallow. Much better to simply close down and disappear into a black hole. This was a feeling that had accompanied me for years, sometimes walking a few paces behind, sometimes invading my body and mind to the exclusion of all else. But if I let on to Charlie that it was beginning to get a stranglehold again, she'd step in with one of her interventions and my plans to speak to Barbara Fulbright would be put on indefinite hold.

So I went to lunch, and made a fine show of loading my fork with roast chicken and peas, and sat there looking sane and innocent.

Charlie was delighted. 'This is great, isn't it?'

'You shouldn't be seeing clients on a Sunday,' I said.

She laughed, reaching for the dessert menu. 'Yes, but you're not just a client, are you? You're a friend.'

'Is that allowed? Aren't you supposed to keep us at a professional distance?'

'Not at the weekend. What about crème brûlée?'

'Sounds nice.'

'Good. You're looking great, Karen. I'm so pleased. I think, this time, you're really getting things together.'

Yes, things were coming together. Like two express trains, possibly, but there was no stopping them now.

By Monday morning, I had decided on my plan of campaign. Ruth hadn't wanted to see me and when I cornered her, she threw me out. There was a good chance that Barbara Fulbright would do the same, if I simply phoned and invited myself for a chat. But she was a solicitor. She had an office. She had appointments. She could hardly refuse to see me if I turned up as a client.

I phoned her firm in Carlisle. 'Could I make an appointment to see Barbara Fulbright please? It's a domestic issue.'

'Could you hold the line please?' Brief consultation in the background. 'Hello? I'm very sorry, she's not expected in the office all this week. She's on leave, a family bereavement. Can another of our partners help? Ms Fulbright doesn't actually take many family cases, but our legal team has specialists in all—'

'No, it's Ms Fulbright I need to see. I don't mind waiting. When she's returned to work, that'll be fine.'

'In that case, I'll check her diary. Yes, I can make an appointment for Thursday fortnight. 10:30. Would that be all right?'

'Yes. Thank you.'

'And your name?'

'Karen...' Even as I started to say it, I realised it would be a mistake. 'Garnet. Mrs Garnet.' There must be a million Karens in the world. The Christian name might not alert her, but Rothwell would. I could have used Charlie's name, Freeman, but there was probably a law about trying to pass yourself off as a social worker, so I borrowed Malcolm's instead. He wouldn't mind.

I was late into work as a result of the phone call. Charlie was waiting for me. It wasn't the first time I'd been late and complaints had been made.

'I thought you were doing so well, Karen. But late this morning, and apparently you've been messing them around for the last couple of weeks, not turning up, not doing anything. They're a nice bunch here, Karen. Not like in accounts, but you've really exhausted their patience. Now, are you going to settle down and at least turn up at the office?'

'I'll try,' I promised. Charlie had gone to such lengths, pulled so many strings, to turn me into a fully functioning, working woman. But none of it was relevant any more.

I explained it to Malcolm as I tidied the shelves at Gem's for him, while he plotted where to pin my monster sketches. 'It's so pointless, turning up at an office, typing gobbledegook, coming home again, just so that they can tick a box to say they've employed their quota of loonies and cripples. Mandy feels the same. She's got a maths degree and just because she's in a wheelchair, they treat her like an idiot, a patronised dogsbody, taken on to tick a box. It's meaningless. I can't do it anymore. Here.' I pulled out a handful of books. 'These should be under philosophy, not travel.'

He glanced at them, while pinning a dragon on the shelf end. 'Quite right.'

'I should make an effort, for Charlie, shouldn't I? At least pretend to be normal and sane. But I can't. I've got this thing hanging over me, like a sort of grief that I never worked through properly and until I do, I can't settle. Until I know what really happened, what I should have said or done, I can't just sit there every day, typing pointless lists. But I've got to, for another whole fortnight. Why did I let Carlisle put me off for a fortnight? They could have given me Barbara's address, and let me find her for myself. It didn't really have to be in her office.'

'Well, for a start, they would never have given you her private address. And didn't you say she was on compassionate leave? She's lost someone. You're not really going to turn up on her doorstep when she's just back from a family funeral and start cross-examining her about a murder, are you?'

I wanted to say yes. 'No, of course not. But I can't keep going into that office all day, pretending to work while I wait.'

'Well, I'd say...' Malcolm stood on tiptoe to pin up three sketches in a row. 'The solution is to hand in your notice and come and work here, instead.'

'Don't talk tripe.'

'I'm not talking tripe. You spend half your time here, anyway. The place would go to pot if I didn't have an assistant. And I know you've got this Serena tragedy on your mind. I understand how it's eating into you. But it doesn't stop you getting things right here, does it?' He tapped the philosophy books I was still holding. 'And I need your artistic talents for this promotion... Straight?'

I looked at the three sketches. Yes, they were straight, but did they work? Three elfin warriors. 'I'm not sure about those. I meant to make them look noble, but they're more like homicidal maniacs.'

'No, they're fine. Elves are homicidal maniacs. It's well known. So what do you think? About working here. How about I have a word with Charlotte? I'll get an assistant and she'll get a gold star for moving you into the real commercial world. No need to tell anyone this isn't the real commercial world, is there?'

I was reluctant, sensing well-meaning charity. Which it probably was. Malcolm was religious. Sort of. He didn't make a fuss about it and I don't think I ever heard him mention God, but I knew he regularly attended services, the sort that let you sit and contemplate infinity, instead of requiring loud and busy commitment, so once or twice I'd gone with him. A cathedral choir is always balm to the nerves.

I certainly didn't begrudge Malcolm his religious comforts. He'd had a miserable marriage, I think, and it would probably have ended in separation if she hadn't developed a brain tumour and died. I could understand the guilt and other emotional complexities surrounding the death of someone you really didn't like very much. He could have his cathedral services, but I wasn't sure I wanted to be one of his good works.

But then I wanted to continue working in the council offices even less, so I just smiled and said nothing when he proposed the move to a delighted Charlie.

The council didn't even ask me to work out my notice. Can't think why. And Charlie explained that Malcolm could claim a subsidy for taking me on, which made me feel less guilty about the whole thing. I wasn't going to be doing any more in the shop, really, than I had been doing for years without taking his money, and I didn't want him to be out of pocket.

It was odd, he was quite right, I could continue to obsess about Serena and still function efficiently at Gem's Books. I could enter data on his computer and type up labels without a single mistake. In the office, I'd rarely managed a complete sentence that didn't have to be corrected, word by word. So I was fine. Mostly.

Fine, because of the medication and because of the driving sense of purpose. In the shop, I shared sandwiches with Malcolm. At home, I couldn't face food. I think Malcolm knew I wasn't quite as securely on the sunny uplands as I tried to appear, but he made allowances for me. He'd seen me at my worst.

He probably guessed that when I disappeared into dark corners of the shop, or into the overflowing book den I called home, the obsession would settle quietly at my side, ready to grab me with its ice cold fingers of panic whenever I thought of making a run for it. I'd forget for a moment and sink into a novel, and there she would be, turning to look at me.

Serena.

'Tell them, Karen. Do it for me. Just tell them.'

— 9 —

'You're to come and play with us.' Barbara Fulbright is standing in front of me, blocking my way.

'All right.' I turn obediently towards the corner of the playground where Serena and her friends are waiting.

'Just you,' says Barbara.

She's a big girl and lives in one of the big houses on the edge of the estate beyond the Methodist chapel, and her father has a big car and drives to work, wearing a suit. Her mother wears a suit too, when she comes to the school – a tweedy one – and a hat, not like most of the mothers who wear housecoats and keep their curlers in. She looks more like a gran, really, but maybe she's just old fashioned. Barbara wears a gymslip in the winter. She's the only girl in school who does, and I don't think she likes it, but she never says so.

She's very clever. She always comes top of the class except when Serena does. They take it in turns. Perhaps that's why they're best friends. We're in pairs in Serena's group. People are always in pairs – Mummy and Daddy, Armand and Michaela Denis, Hans and Lotte Hass, America and Russia, the Lone Ranger and Tonto. It makes everything balance. So we're in pairs too. Serena and Barbara, Denise and Angela, and it used to be Ruth and Teresa, but now it's Ruth and me.

Ruth isn't really interested in me, and Denise and Angela don't much care, but we all pretend, even Barbara, who doesn't like me at all. That's all right, though, because I don't much like her. If she weren't always following Serena around, and trying to be nice to people because Serena says so, she'd be a bully. The first years are afraid of her. But none of it matters, as long as Serena likes all of us.

Oh, the ecstasy of knowing that Serena likes me.

'Got her!' Barbara hurries off to Serena's side as soon as we reach the group, to show that's where she belongs. She takes Serena's hand. I'd never dare do that yet.

Ruth sidles up to stand beside me, because that's where she belongs now. Angela gives me a quick wave, too busy jumping up and down to do more. Denise looks impatient because I've taken so long to get there.

None of them really want me there, but it doesn't matter.

It doesn't matter, because Serena is smiling at me, even if Barbara is the only one to hold her hand.

*

I sat staring out of the train window, wondering what Barbara Fulbright would be like now. Not a bitter, nervous wreck like Mrs Smellie, that was certain. Probably still hard and clever and she still wouldn't like me. But it didn't matter, because she'd tell me everything. Barbara was a girl who never held back from telling you what was what, even if you wouldn't like it. Especially if you wouldn't like it.

Now she was a solicitor. I knew two solicitors. One was Mr Wylie who'd dealt with my mother's affairs when she'd died.

He was very ancient, very deaf, half blind, and did a lot of mumbling into papers. The other one was Jim, who worked for the council, lounged around the offices and was what the more generous girls called frisky, and what the less generous ones called a menace who needed castrating. I couldn't pair my image of Barbara with either model. But I'd find out what she was like soon enough.

A crack of dawn journey, one change, long enough normally for me to get lost in a book. I had an Ursula Le Guin to occupy me, but I couldn't read it. For years I had lived in books, but these days my concentration was shot. So instead of reading, I stared out of the window, hypnotised by the wheeze and whine of the train and the images flashing past, blurring, one into another.

Towns, stations, fields, hills – Marsh Green, Serena picking herself up, tears welling in her eyes, such big, dark eyes. Kenneth Dexter, his grey skin turning white as paper, that dumbstruck look of denial…

Kenneth Dexter, laughing, pointing, mocking. 'Ginger. Hello, Ginger.'

Kenneth Dexter, frowning, jaw jutting. 'You watch it! I'll have you!'

I saw him. He blurred. I saw him again. What was this? Why was I seeing him? I didn't mind Serena's face continuously materialising in my head, but I didn't want Kenneth Dexter there. What was he doing?

So quick to threaten. 'I'll have you!' Supposing…supposing he'd killed Serena, and I'd witnessed it. Or seen something, a clue, and I'd been too frightened to speak because he'd threatened me.

But he'd looked so mortified when he'd accidentally knocked into her. He couldn't have done it.

Except that she had been murdered, and there was only one person I knew who had it in him to be a killer. Everyone said he was a born thug.

Doomed to be a thug, I suppose. The sink child of a sink world.

*

The Dexter house, on Austen Road, is dark and grimy.

'Bloody disgrace,' says Mr Treece who lives two doors down, and Mrs Treece pokes him and says, 'Language!'

Mr Treece stops using language but he grunts as he pokes the rubbish that spills out from the Dexters' garden. It's a jungle of long grass and rusting metal. There's always a patched-up old pram by the door because Mrs Dexter's always having babies. There's a Mr Dexter too, but he's nearly always inside. I don't know what that means. He's not inside the house, because I never see him there, but he's inside somewhere.

'See Jack Dexter's inside again.' Parents, at the school gates, sniff and nod and look knowing. 'Don't know why they bother letting him out.'

They don't say it near the house though, because mostly they keep away from it. 'This way, hold my hand, we'll cross to the other side of the street.' They wrinkle up their noses as they steer their children clear. It's because Mr Dexter's 'inside' and because Mrs Dexter keeps having babies.

I heard Mrs Bryant whisper to Mrs Philpot. 'She has men. Shameless. The council should do something. The vicar tried to have a word with her and she swore at him!'

The Dexters' house is just as dark and grimy inside. Full of rubbish, newspapers, broken chairs. Never much food or warm bedding, though, or toys. Mrs Dexter doesn't do much fussing round the house like Mummy. She's always very nice to me, though. Sort of. Just acts as if I'm one of her own. Maybe she thinks I am. It must be difficult for her to keep count. I think it's funny that she swore at the vicar. It was probably because she was drunk. She sways a lot in the street.

'Drunk!' says Mummy, pursing her lips.

'Not surprised, with so many babies,' says Daddy.

There are a lot of them. Kenneth is just one of the middle ones. There's a baby called Baby and Clive with the funny legs and Susan with one eye that looks the wrong way and…

*

My stomach was twisting. Why was I remembering it at all? Why had I ever visited the home of Kenneth Dexter? He may have chased and threatened the rest of the civilised world, but I couldn't recall him ever doing worse to me than call me Ginger. I wasn't worth terrorising. Maybe I was imagining it. But real or imaginary, I needed to get my head out of that house.

I squeezed my eyes shut, dug my nails into my palms and forced myself to look out and focus on the real world. Fields, hills, valleys, smoke.

Black pall of smoke, hanging in the air, billowing. Another in the distance. Then a third. I saw an elderly couple, further down my carriage, look out, then look at each other, shaking their heads, wordless.

The present crashed into my thoughts of the past. Foot-and-mouth. It had been there, a constant droning litany, day after

108

day, along with the eternal diet of atrocities, corruptions and earthquakes. All those TV and radio news bulletins that I had drowned out with thoughts of Serena and this interminable quest. News was never good news, was it? Shut it out.

But now, there it was, reality, death, destruction, grief, horror, walking hand in hand with my elusive haunting. There was no escape. I was looking through glass at black smoke that mirrored the smoke in my head. I couldn't cope with both, not at the same time.

I couldn't cope.

No. Not now, please. I needed to cope. But there it was, that rising tide of panic at not being able to face anything. It was the start. I knew I was beginning to unravel again. Hold on. A bit longer. Long enough for me to find the truth and be able to finish with this thing...

Carlisle. Never been there before. I'll probably never go there again. I wasn't in the best position to appreciate whatever it has to offer, which may be a great deal. All I could see was an urban mass that was hiding my Grail, somewhere in its dark heart. I emerged from a grand station into rain, and wandered with a street map in my hand, ineptly reading it. I nearly finished up in a castle, then realised I was going the wrong way. Barbara probably had a posh house, but not a posh castle.

I wound my way through a terraced maze of Victorian brick and northern stone, as my map soaked up the rain and began to disintegrate at the folds. At last, I found myself dripping at the reception desk of Barbara Fulbright's office, twenty minutes ahead of schedule. The girls at the desk got on with their work busily, smiling at me occasionally. Phones kept ringing, and

I grew tenser each time. Doors kept opening and my heart would race faster.

I'd left too early to think about taking my medication.

'Mrs Garnet?'

I sat there blankly, forgetting the name I'd chosen, until one of the receptionists emerged from behind the desk and stood in front of me. She was summing me up as a pathetically troubled soul. Can't imagine where she got that idea.

'I'll take you to Ms Fulbright's office, shall I?'

'Yes, thank you.' I rose, dropped my coat, dropped my bag and we both crouched to retrieve them, almost knocking heads. I could feel the silent sigh.

'Come in,' said a voice behind a door as the receptionist knocked. A calm, authoritative voice. Barbara Fulbright rose from her desk as I was ushered in, and offered me her hand. 'Mrs Garnet? Sit down. Please. What can I do for you?'

She didn't recognise me. Of course not. She had no reason to suspect anything. I hadn't phoned and blurted out my name as I had with Ruth. Barbara Fulbright probably saw a dozen clients a day and I was just one more sad little woman who'd got mixed up with life's complications.

Besides, I wouldn't have recognised her either, if I weren't on the lookout for glimpses of the girl I'd known. She was solid, this woman. Hefty. Tall and sturdy. She'd been tall at school, but ungainly with it. None of Serena's grace. The weight of age had added a certain gravitas. Her hair was clipped short in an aggressively neat style, dyed a honey colour. It had been longer, curly and plain brown back then. She'd always looked plain, next to Serena. Now she looked – I think they'd call it handsome. Discreetly but carefully made up. Commanding.

All quite different.

Except the eyes. They were still the same. Hazel, watchful, without warmth. It hadn't just been me she hadn't liked. She'd never been very friendly with anyone except Serena.

'I'm sorry,' I croaked. My mouth was dry, sour sawdust soaking up my saliva. 'I'm sorry to intrude at this time – you've had a bereavement, they said. I…'

'Oh. Yes, my mother died.'

'I'm so sorry.' If I could just keep apologising, perhaps I'd get a grip.

'It wasn't a shock. Ninety-three and she'd been ill for several years. Alzheimer's. Didn't know who I was, by the end. So, shall we attend to your business, Mrs Garnet?'

'Sorry.' I swallowed and tried again. 'I'm not really Mrs Garnet. I'm Karen Rothwell.'

Her hands were laid flat, eighteen inches apart, on her desk. They didn't move. Those hazel eyes surveyed me without expression, while my skin crawled.

Then she sat back and looked up at the ceiling, leaving me to study the stretched skin of her throat, wondering how long she could stay like that.

At last she tilted forward and folded her arms. 'Karen Rothwell. Of course. Ruth said you'd surfaced. Warned you might be on the prowl.'

Warned. Did she need to be warned? I must be a monster.

'Said you were anorexic, too. Yes, I can see that. I should have guessed when you came in. So, you've made an appointment. Do you really need legal advice or was that an excuse?'

'An excuse. I didn't know if you'd want to see me, otherwise.'

'Why wouldn't I?' She made my suggestion sound utterly

absurd – why would she have any problem seeing me? But I could feel the aggressive defiance in her. She was in control, she was trained to deal with things – but that was what she would be doing: dealing with me. 'You realise you'll have to pay for the consultation, anyway.'

'Yes, of course.' I had a cheque book. Whether it had funds in it to cover the fee was another matter.

'All right.' She glanced at the clock on the wall. I was to have my allotted quota of time. 'So no legal ramifications still stalking you. But you felt this subterfuge was necessary.'

'I saw Ruth. She didn't want to see me. She got in a state, so I thought…'

'Oh Ruth.' A short, scornful laugh. 'Still finding ruination and despair round every corner. And if you were round the corner, well of course she'd scream blue murder. Everything is a catastrophe to Ruth, an insufferable imposition, not to be borne. As you doubtless observed. This is what happens when you have a dictator ruling your life, telling you what to do and think, and suddenly he's hanging from a lamp post.'

'Her father? Was he hanged?' Hanged. The word wound itself round my vocal chords with a shudder of panic.

'What?' Barbara looked at me as if I were a complete idiot. 'No, of course not. I meant metaphorically. All that humiliation, with the photographs. Public exposure. Ridicule. It was probably worse than hanging, for him. They had to move, you know. To the other side of town. I'd say that was what sent her over the edge. Good girl Ruthie suddenly became bad girl Ruthie who missed class, smoked behind the bike sheds, tried a bit of petty larceny. And got herself pregnant, of course. Almost a joke, really. You wouldn't know about that,

I suppose. You'd been hustled away from Lyford long before.'

Pulse racing again. We'd moved, yes. A new factory for my dad to work in, a new place for us to live – a flat in a tower block – new schools for Hilary and me. It must have involved upheaval and disruption, but I had no recollection of it. And why did Ruth have to move too? What was this humiliation over photographs?

'I'm sorry. The truth is, I don't remember being hustled away. Were there photographs? I don't remember anything. That's why I came. I can't stand it anymore. I need to find out. All I can remember is Serena. Serena and…' I shut my eyes.

'Yes.' Quite expressionless, her voice. 'You would. Everyone would remember Serena.' Her one special friend. I don't suppose Barbara Fulbright had ever had another. She wasn't the sort of woman to have friends. She'd had one, and that one had been murdered. Dear God.

I opened my eyes, expecting to see her distraught, but her face was as expressionless as her voice. Unmoved, or just frozen.

She studied me for a moment, and then shrugged. 'Funny that you can't remember, because it was all anyone talked about for weeks. The murder and the photographs. They weren't actually connected, as it turned out. Inadmissible evidence, you might say. Even so, it was all mixed up in one very distasteful mess. I expect Ruth chooses to think of herself as a victim. Never one for taking charge, even of herself. Too accustomed to being quiet and doing what she was told.'

'What happened?'

'With the photographs? You really don't remember? After the murder, the police were everywhere, of course, nosing into all our lives. Everyone and anyone connected with the school.

They must have had a tip-off. After all, I'm sure someone, somewhere, must have suspected. They searched the Jeffersons' house and found photographs. Stacks of photographs. All of children.' She laughed, a short, sharp laugh. 'Ever go round Ruth's house? Told to get changed? He probably had a spy hole. I expect we were all in those photos. No idea how extreme or explicit they were. Maybe just lots of little girls stripping down to their knickers. But they were lewd enough for the police.

'God!' She laughed again. 'These days, he probably would be strung up on a lamp post. Lynched by an angry mob. We do love our paedophiles. Back then, it just got him labelled a dirty old man, which is all he was, don't you think? Wouldn't ever have dared touch any of us up. Too much of an ineffectual coward, under all that bluster. But in the circumstances, with a murder on their hands, the photographs were enough to make him a suspect. There was obviously a sexual motive. I can see that now, although, back then... What were we? Ten? Eleven. We had no idea about these things, did we? Nowadays, I imagine most ten-year-old girls have tried it all and could write a book on it. Not us. The worst we ever imagined was Black Jack Coke stealing our undies.'

She was still looking at me, waiting for a reaction rather than a response. I didn't know how to react.

She shrugged. 'Well, however innocent we were, adults could imagine a lot more, even back then. A little girl on the estate had been molested and murdered, and here was a dirty old man with stacks of pathetic kiddie porn. He was hauled in for questioning. Flashing lights, handcuffs, full scale arrest to scandalise the neighbours, oh the dishonour. But then it turned out he had a watertight alibi, a governors' meeting or something, that put him out of the running, so they let him go. Besides, he couldn't drive, and they'd identified the car by then and thought they had the real culprit, so Jefferson walked.

'Never got his reputation back, though. Very wise of him to move. Unfortunately, Ruth had to move with him, which is when she started to go off the rails. She just wasn't very good at it. Could have gone the whole hog and joined some revolutionary terrorist gang, but no, she just gets pregnant and finishes up as a housewife, complaining about the ironing.'

I don't think Barbara took her eyes off me once, while she was speaking. She spoke not so much to communicate as to pin me in place while she examined me. Judging how much of an irredeemable wreck I was.

'I don't remember,' I repeated. 'Any of it. Photographs, murder, any of it.'

'Not even her getting into the car? No? Well, that's very odd. You wouldn't talk then, and now, I suppose, you can't talk. And yet you were the one who saw it.'

I was shaking inside, and the trembling was beginning to work its way to the surface. Car. There was an image, almost. But not quite. A car, Serena getting in... but it wasn't real. It was an image I was constructing. I couldn't... It wouldn't...

'So it looks as if we'll never know the truth. I suppose it's hardly surprising that you blocked it out. Only way to get on with your life. Did you? Get on with it, I mean?' Her gaze flitted forensically over me. I didn't look like a woman who'd got on with her life. At least I could explain that away.

'I had an accident, after we left Lyford. I fell from a window. I spent forever in hospital. I think that became such an all-consuming part of my life that I never really thought about

115

what had gone before.'

'Mm-hmmm.' She took the explanation, without apparent doubt or sympathy. 'Career? Family?'

I shook my head.

'Not married to a Mr Garnet then?'

'Oh, no! No, he's my boss. I just wanted to use another name.' A long pause. 'You not married then?'

'Was. Divorced. Went back to my maiden name. Just the once was enough for me. Not like Angie. She never seems to learn. Three divorces, I think? Don't suppose there'll be another. Too drunk to stagger down the aisle or up the register office steps these days. Hasn't had an exhibition in years, though she keeps talking about it. Probably can't hold the camera steady any more. And Serena, - not divorced, of course, but still got through two husbands. Hers just died. Funny, when you think about it, that Ruthie, who complains non-stop about what a shit it is, trapped into marriage and babies when she was just a kid, is the one who's made a long-term success of it. Unless you count Denise, who's married to Christ, and He'll be on His knees and begging for a divorce before she releases her talons.'

She was talking, but I couldn't really hear, because my head was buzzing, aching, trying to understand. Serena was widowed? Twice?

So she couldn't have been murdered in 1966.

Serena turned and smiled at me, tears in her big brown eyes. Tears of sympathy and disappointment, because I—

I couldn't breathe. 'Who?' I gripped the desk, trying to get control. Fighting to speak. Barbara sat there, watching me, emotionless. 'Who died?' I managed at last, bile rising with the words. 'Who was murdered?'

116

Those hazel eyes widened. The glossed lips pursed. 'You are honestly telling me you don't remember?'

'No!' I bit my fist.

'You seriously don't remember them finding Janice Dexter?'

The name was carried away on the roaring of my blood. My brain wouldn't hear it.

'Janice Dexter,' repeated Barbara, coldly. 'And you were her best friend.'

I threw up, staggering to my feet. Somewhere, in the raging storm of my brain, I could hear Barbara sigh and press an intercom. 'Julie, could you send Mr Cox in here, to clean up a mess.'

And then I was outside, walking, like a drunk, people swerving to avoid me. Somehow I must have found my way back to the station, because I was on a train, getting away. Away. Away.

Except that I couldn't get away. The images came with me.

— 10 —

Barbara Fulbright stared out of her office window. The room stank of disinfectant, now the janitor had done his work. Better to open the window, clear the air.

She forced her fingers to move. Cold air swept in. She turned back to her desk, seeing and not seeing the neat papers, the files, the pens arranged in regimented order. The calendar. Ridiculous cute touch in an office so dedicated to hard-nosed legal efficiency. A calendar of cats. Today's cat stared at her in unblinking accusation.

Abruptly, she turned the calendar around, sat down and picked up a pen. Work to do.

She sat staring at a blank sheet. Work to do.

She picked up the phone and consulted her address book, rearranging her pens as it rang and rang. And rang.

At last it stopped ringing. 'Yeah? What?'

'Angela, is that you?'

'Well, I'm never too sure about that. Looking around, can't see her anywhere else.'

'You're drunk again.'

'S'right! I am drunk again.' The voice faded as if the speaker had forgotten the need to speak into the phone.

'Is Denise there? I thought she'd taken you on as her mission, now the convent's sent her packing.'

'Oh yes, a mission. That's what I am. And she's out shopping for healthy goodness.' A pause. 'Hello?'

'Yes, hello, Angela. Concentrate. It's me. Barbara Fulbright.'

'Yes, yes. That's right. Barbara full of brightness. How's your mother?'

'Dead. I've just had a visit from Karen Rothwell.'

'Ah! Ah. She's a ghost, is she?'

'No, she's not. Just a basket case. She's seen Ruth and she's seen me. I'm just warning you, she'll probably come looking for you and Denise.'

'Oh. Well. If she finds me, perhaps she can tell me where I am.'

'Somewhere at the bottom of a bottle of Scotch, by the sounds of it. Anyway, there you are. I've warned you.'

'Should be Serena you warn. Spoken to her?'

'What do you think I'm just about to do?'

'Ah well, that's good. Leave it to Serena. Serena always sorts it out. Everyone and everything. Lovely Serena, Serena my—'

Barbara put the phone down. Took a breath, took a sip of water. Then she tried a second number.

—11—

'Janice wet her knickers! Janice wet her knickers!' The boys are chanting, and some of the girls with them.

Janice is standing in the playground, looking forlorn, waiting for me.

I come running up and take her hand. 'Go away!' I shout. 'Karen Rothwell's pooped her pants!'

'Have not!' It makes me angry and my eyes sting, but Janice just squeezes my hand. Children have been shouting and taunting her since we started school and she knows there's nothing she can do about it. They shout at me because I'm friends with her. Sometimes, I secretly think that if I stopped being friends with her, they'd stop being nasty to me.

But she is my friend, my very best friend, and now that school's over for the day, we can get away from them all.

My mother's waiting at the school gate. Hilary is already with her, having her mittens pulled on straight. Mummy sees us and looks annoyed. 'Oh. I suppose you're going off with that girl.' She always calls Janice That Girl. 'Is That Girl staying to tea? I can't feed the five thousand, you know.'

Janice doesn't mind. There's no point minding.

'Don't be late for your tea,' my mother warns, and leads

Hilary off.

Hand in hand, Janice and I start off down Manor Way. We start to run, then stop and just walk, because Mr Jefferson is on the prowl, watching us, and we don't want him bawling at us again, promising spankings.

Once we're out of Manor Way, we can safely run, past the playground and the bus roundabout and the Parade, with the post office and Co-op and butcher's shop and hairdressers, on round Aspen Drive. It's downhill in places, not very much, but enough to have us flying, squealing as we go, hair streaming. We can fly!

In Aspen Drive, I can turn left towards Linden Crescent and Janice can turn right towards Austen Road, but that's for later. What we're really running for are the empty prefab plots off Aspen Drive, because that's where we have our den. One of our dens. The world is full of dens. We have one among the kingcups in the Rough and one on the Allotments, among the raspberries, and we have one on the plot that used to be No. 12 Brontë Road, when the prefabs were still here. There's a blackcurrant bush that didn't get squashed by the bulldozer, and a pile of rubble that used to be a coal bunker, but the front bit's still standing, with a hatch you can pull up, and behind it we've got a treasure chest that used to be a biscuit tin. It's for special things.

Janice needs somewhere to keep things, because her home is so crowded, and the little ones make off with anything she leaves lying around. She hasn't really got much, except the doll Kenneth got for her. It used to belong to Jacqueline Winstanley, but Kenneth took it. He shouldn't take things, but I don't care because Jacqueline was being horrible to Janice and pinching her. I'm scared of Kenneth, even though he never takes things from me because I'm Janice's friend.

They are both in my class, Janice and Kenneth, but they're not twins like Gordon and Guy. It's because Kenneth was born in September and Janice was born in August, so they're in the same school year. Janice likes him but I'm glad he never comes to play with us. Too busy fighting other boys.

'Come on!' Free from adult eyes, we race to our den and lift the coal bunker hatch, and lie down to peer into the cave in the rubble behind.

'Is he here?' Janice lifts up a mixed-peel carton that's jammed next to the biscuit tin. It's waxed paper and printed to look like a little house. It's empty.

'Oh.' I'm as disappointed as she is. We'd found a mouse and we wanted him to live in the little house, but he's gone. It would have been nice to have a pet.

Crouching down in the concrete corner, out of the wind, the smell is getting a bit pongy.

'Did you really wet your pants?' I ask.

'A bit,' Janice admits.

'Oh well.'

*

Once more, I was sitting on a train, staring out of the window blankly, seeing nothing. Not hellfires, this time. Not cities, or stations or fields. Just Janice, my very best friend.

Tears were pouring down my cheeks, my chin, my neck. How could I have done it? How could I have betrayed her by forgetting her?

Janice Dexter. The saddest girl in the world, it sometimes

seemed. You didn't get to be joyful if you were a Dexter. Everyone called her names, said she smelled, said she had nits. I expect she did. We all did from time to time, queuing up to face the terror of the nit nurse. Janice was as undernourished as all the Dexters – I realise that now, it being an issue I've come to know a lot about. Back then I thought she was just small, like a fairy. Or maybe a pixie, because she wasn't pretty enough to be a fairy. How could she be pretty? Her face was never washed, her hair never combed, her clothes were always grubby and had holes. My mother despaired of our friendship. What she wanted was for me to play with the nice girls, the ones who went to Sunday school, who wore blazers and hairbands and whose mothers walked upright, without falling over. But I wasn't in with the nice girls, not till that last year. I was with Janice. My friend. My very best friend ever.

We used to play every day. Sometimes at her house or mine. Mostly hers, because her mother didn't mind. Or we'd disappear from adult eyes into the private kingdoms that only we could discern. Those demolished prefabs were a godsend for children like us. We could roam freely, hand in hand, where adults wouldn't even notice us, let alone bother to prise us apart. Me and Janice Dexter.

She'd been murdered.

I could remember the fact, now, but not the images that should accompany the fact. That must have been when I'd started blocking things out. What could be worse than having your best friend murdered? Now, at last, I could see her as clearly as I'd started to see Serena Whinn. Janice – Janice smiling, gaps in her teeth, flaking skin, thin fair hair straggly and knotted, always a scab of dried snot under her nose. Janice in that thin, limp, yellow gingham dress that had been handed down through four older sisters and was splitting at the seams because it was too small for her. Janice, tongue between her teeth, threading a daisy chain through my hair. Janice looking wide-eyed in delighted wonder when I brought the cardboard mouse house to our den. Janice, one shoe scuffing the other and shoulders hunched as she stood in the school corridor, in disgrace about something, eternally sad – but then smiling as soon as she saw me.

Janice looking up, face wet with tears, mouth open, blubbing, scared—

The image hit me with a force that was almost physical, winding me, lifting me out of my body.

Janice with blood on her face.

I huddled, trying to hide from the image, but it wouldn't go away.

What had I seen? I didn't know. I didn't know!

But there had been a murder. I had watched, from a police car, the gathering mobs in the street, the huddles of worried mothers – Mrs Dexter struggling to get through, bawling her eyes out, a whale in tears, and no one came near her, no one offered comfort or help.

'Well, what can you expect?' people whispered.

Her boys, Kenneth and his older brothers, one of them already a man with half a beard, gathered like an army ready to charge, swearing foul-mouthed vengeance.

And somewhere in it all was my utter misery because Janice was dead. Murdered.

There was a car. I remember. There was a car.

I'd tried to picture Serena getting into it, and I couldn't.

This was why. It hadn't been Serena, it had been Janice.

'Tell them, Karen.' Serena, holding my hand, pleading with me to speak. 'Tell them what you saw.'

What did I see? I felt a compulsion, that cattle prod, stinging me, urging me to picture Janice getting into a car. I couldn't. I knew it had happened, but still my mind kept blanking it out. I could only see myself in a car. A big police car.

Why was I in a police car?

I fought to make sense of it all. Was this the source of my guilt? I'd watched my friend getting into a car, and I hadn't stopped her. Even though we'd been told repeatedly, warned with that ominous voice adults used when they wanted to terrify us to death, that we should never, ever, get into cars with strangers.

Because if we did…

We didn't know what would happen if we got into cars with strangers. It was a mystery so dark and terrible that parents wouldn't spell it out. It was like Black Jack Coke.

Another name I'd forgotten, till Barbara mentioned him. Black Jack Coke. He was evil and misshapen and black with coal dust, and he lurked in the slime and mud under bridges, so you had to run across them or his fingers would creep up over the edge or through the planks and grab your ankles. Boys would laugh and taunt us with shouts of 'Black Jack Coke will get you,' and we would huddle together, in case he was round the corner.

Everyone knew about Black Jack and everyone knew he wasn't real. Not really. Maybe one of the coalmen who delivered to our houses was called Jack and that had started it, but Black Jack Coke had grown into the monster who had to be out there somewhere. In another age, we'd have invented a troll, or a dragon. Our age invented Black Jack. None of us knew what he would do to you if he caught you, but rumour had it that he'd steal your knickers. That would probably be what strangers in cars did too.

Then we found out what strangers in cars did. They killed people. They killed Janice Dexter. Molested, Barbara said. Obviously a sexual motive. There it was, then. My best friend, ten years old, had been raped and murdered. Oh God. I wanted to be sick again, but there was nothing left to bring up.

What had I seen? I pressed my forehead hard against the unyielding glass of the train window, trying to force memories to coalesce.

No good. I couldn't see anything except Janice's upturned face, snotty, howling, open mouth red. Blood red. Blood.

What blood? How? I couldn't understand. I couldn't cope.

I just wanted to block everything out.

Unravel me now, please.

'Karen, oh Karen, what are we going to do with you?' Charlie had picked me up from the station. 'Oh dear, look at you. I was going to offer to take you to lunch first, get something inside you, but you're obviously in no state for that.'

'No.' It was kind of her, coming to meet me off the London train. That was where I'd finished up, the day before. I'd got on a train, any train, in Carlisle and disappeared into a black hole. I don't remember the train arriving in London at all. I suppose I was in a state, embarrassing people, causing a palaver. Wouldn't be the first time. Over the years, I'd made quite an art of it.

I spent the night somewhere institutional. I think it might have been a police cell. It's difficult to say. Doubtless they, whoever they were, found enough clues in my bag to figure out who I was, where I'd come from and who to contact. In the morning, dosed up with sedatives, they'd put me on the train back north, and Charlie was waiting for me.

'So what happened? I thought you were doing so well, Karen. What's sent you off the rails this time?'

'I remembered my friend. From school.' The sedatives were still at work and I was in a dreamlike state, hearing my answer as if it came from someone else's mouth.

'This Sally, Sylvia – no, Selina person again?'

'Serena. No. Not Serena. She's important. She's terribly important, I know that. But it was my other friend. She was killed. Janice Dexter.'

Charlie did an emergency stop. A van, up her exhaust pipe, hooted, and manoeuvred round, deliberately close enough to joggle the wing mirror. She wound down the window. 'Sod off!'

A finger was raised, in the van.

'Sorry about that.' Charlie drove on again, sedately, eyes looking diligently at every road sign and traffic light, which meant that her thoughts were elsewhere. 'So. You've remembered Janice Dexter.'

'Have I remembered her before?'

'No. Never.'

'But you know her name.'

'Yes. She's in your notes.'

'Oh.' I watched shops flashing by. Beginning to take things in. Dogs. An old woman with a walking frame. I wished I was

127

an old woman with a walking frame. No one would notice me then. I could fall down and die and no one would notice. Old women didn't count. I wasn't quite old enough, that was my trouble. 'What do they say, my notes?'

Charlie licked her lips. 'That you were, you know, distressed. Traumatised by her death. You were having trouble talking about her. Or rather, to be honest, you refused to talk about her. It was like you couldn't hear her name if someone said it.'

'I see.'

'Miles says you – well, he can explain it. You'll talk to him this time, about it, won't you? He's waiting to see you.'

'I suppose.' It wasn't as if I'd ever had a choice. 'Will you tell me what happened to her?'

Charlie was very busy at a junction. By the time we were round and in the right lane, she'd decided that it was all right to reply. 'She was murdered, I know that much. She was found in a drain in a wood, I believe.'

'Was she raped?'

'Maybe. Yes, something like that. Look, don't discuss this now. I really don't know enough about the case. Miles will talk to you.'

'He won't, though. Miles doesn't talk. He gets me to talk, and that's no good. I can only talk about the bits that are already there, in my head. I want to know about the missing bits. I want to know what I did. Or what I didn't do. She was murdered, and I saw something and I should have told people, but I didn't.'

'Well.' Charlie slowed, as a bus pulled out in front of us. She took a deep breath. 'The little girl was abducted. Apparently, you saw her get into a car with – well, presumably with her murderer. You told someone but I suppose it was just shock setting in. When the police questioned you, you wouldn't speak to them. Wouldn't say a word. Switched off. I think there's a term for it.'

'There's always a term for everything about me. Millions of terms. Like amnesia. Post-traumatic stress. Hyper-arousal. Bipolar. Dissociative identity disorder. Blah blah blah. They're all pointless. It's just doctors picking labels at random to stick on people, so they sound as if they know what they're talking about. But they don't really. I like nice proper terms, like "away with the fairies," or "stark raving mad" or "out of my tree". Much better.'

Charlie glanced sidelong at me, with a smile. 'You're sounding more awake.'

'Yes. I am. I am poised on that pivot between being drugged to the eyeballs and being a gibbering idiot, so please, while I'm still functioning, tell me the rest. I wouldn't talk to the police…'

'You wouldn't talk to anyone, not after you'd first mentioned it. But once they'd found poor little Janice and what had been done to her, they knew the story must be true. She'd been abducted and you must have witnessed it and they were desperate for you to describe the car or the man or anything. And you wou— couldn't. That's all. I think some people got a bit upset about it.'

*

'What did you see?' An angry face in mine, shouting, spittle spraying my face. There's a door behind him. I want to run through it but I can't. I have to sit in this chair while he bends over me, shouting and spitting.

'Tell us, girl! Enough of this dumb insolence! Tell us what you saw!'

*

'Yes. They were upset. I wet myself.'

'Well, I'm not surprised. You were only a child.'

'Sorry. I think I've done it again.'

'Never mind,' said Charlie, bravely, handing me tissues. 'Let's get you in to see Miles.'

'So Janice was murdered and she was your best friend. How did that make you feel, Karen?'

'Guilty.'

'Why were you guilty?'

'I should have said something.'

'Did you feel responsible for her death?'

'Yes!'

'And do you still feel responsible now?'

Did I still feel…? The trouble with talking it through with Miles was that he was totally missing the point. He was missing it in a way that should have been flattering. Yes, we'd gone through the story over and over again, piecing together my fragments of memory until they made sense, and I could figure out what had happened.

I'd walked home from school with Janice, I'd seen her get into a car with a stranger, and no one had ever seen her alive again. Three days later she was found in a drainage ditch. I'd told my story to a friend, but after that, I'd clammed up and the police couldn't get a word of confirmation or denial out of me. I'd locked myself up in a private torture chamber, from which I'd never emerged, even when our family moved, to start afresh, away from it all. I'd fallen and perhaps it was a suicide bid, born of the guilt I carried. But I really wasn't to blame, and if I could just talk it out, I would see that and be on the road to recovery.

It was all about me. Miles didn't give a toss about what had happened to Janice. 'Why don't you draw Janice for me?' he kept suggesting, but why should I? He wasn't interested in what Janice looked like, how she sounded, what she must have felt. She wasn't his patient. I was his only concern. I was to vomit up the truth in order to feel better about it all. Janice Dexter was merely a thing in the story. She was of no importance to anyone.

He wanted me to understand that I was not to blame. I wasn't responsible for Janice's death. My silence had been unavoidable and understandable, the reaction of a traumatised child. I couldn't have saved her, or brought her back to life, so I must learn to cast away the guilt.

Yes, Miles, I wasn't guilty of her death. But what about the guilt of betrayal?

I'd been friends with Janice ever since we'd started school at five. Two little forlorn waifs, terrified in a roaring crowd of strangers. If we ever fought, it was only in the way kittens fought, all forgotten the next day.

But my friendship with Janice didn't stop me gazing with awe and longing on the divine Serena and her select coterie. I watched and admired from afar, never dreaming of joining them. That was far above my unworthy ambition – until that last year. Until Teresa Scott left Marsh Green Junior, because her family was moving to a different town and then, out of the blue, they were all over me. Barbara, Ruth, Denise and Angela.

As if they'd had a committee meeting and, after reviewing all the candidates, had selected me. I don't think any of them had even spoken to me before, but now they chatted, they walked with me, they called me to join their games, to sit with them in the playing field, knotting elastic bands for skipping, or folding paper games that would reveal immortal truths – like favourite colours.

Serena didn't change towards me. She had always spoken, sweetly and gently, when chance had brought us together. She'd often smiled at me, she'd invited me to join her team when I was left, unwanted, on the side. But now her seraphim, who had studiously ignored my existence, suddenly took me up as one of theirs and I became a golden girl.

I was almost paralysed by the honour. I wasn't overwhelmed by Ruth's obedient declarations of friendship, or by Barbara and the others, but the thought of being allowed to trot in Serena's golden wake every day made my heart swell and my heels lighten.

My mother was delighted when Ruth came home with me, instead of Janice. She never called Ruth 'That Girl'. We had tea, with proper china. She was even more delighted when I, with Ruth and the others, was invited to the house of Serena Whinn. It could have been my coming-out ball. I was being presented at court.

And there was Janice, on the sidelines, watching. Not angry, not resentful. Just a bit wistful, as if she knew she didn't have a hope. I didn't give her up. I tried to involve her, bring her into our games, but without much success. Serena smiled on her, but the others froze her out. Still, we walked home together. Ruth was a bit annoyed, one day, because I hadn't chosen to walk with her, which was silly, since she lived on the opposite side of the estate. She cried about it, and Serena put her arms around her to comfort her. I felt like a monster.

But still I walked with Janice, down Aspen Drive, among the weedy, whistling remains of the derelict prefabs. We walked together on the last day of Janice's life. Somewhere, along that road, where no one lived any more, and only stray cats scuttled in and out of the shadows, a car pulled up, and I watched Janice speak to the driver and get in. I didn't stop her. I didn't shout a warning, even though I knew it was something we should never do. Black Jack Coke was in that car, and he took Janice away and killed her. She went missing – and then she was found, dead, battered and drowned, stuffed into a culvert among the leeches and the rats, her knickers ripped off.

And I said nothing. Except to Serena. I was as sure as I could be that it was Serena I must have told, and she had explained it all to the police. Yes, of course she would, because Serena's father was the policeman in charge of the case. Inspector Whinn. That was why my sister could remember the name Whinn. It was his angry, impatient, desperate face I could see, spluttering at me, commanding me to identify the killer.

But I wouldn't.

I expect Miles was right. I was simply traumatised from the moment Janice got into the car, my brain cells already conspiring to deny it. Once I'd offloaded the terrible secret on to Serena, I couldn't bear having it in my head any more, so I'd thrown it out. Completely.

Which was why, even now, going over it again and again with Dr Pearce, I could only state it as a known fact, not as a genuine memory. I could no longer see the car, or its occupant.

'That's all right, Karen. You're doing fine. Now tell me again, about Janice.'

I told everything I knew about her. Not really to him, just to any ghosts on the wind that might be willing to take note. I told them about the scab on her knee that never healed. About her giggle and the way she could go cross-eyed to make me laugh. About the dead mole I'd taken into school so proudly, and Miss had said, 'Very nice, Karen, but maybe we should bury it,' and how I'd been mortified and Janice had crept out after class and dug it up again for me. About the bedroom she shared with four siblings and how we had to pick our way through bedding to get her other jumper – her best one, the one with fewer holes. About her youngest brother, Clive, who wore callipers – I think he had rickets. About her doll, her one toy, stolen for her by brother Kenneth and when she cried because it had an eye missing, he filled the hole with chewing gum. About our finding three caterpillars, on the playing field at school, and deducing, as proto-scientists, that they were mummy, daddy and baby caterpillars, because one was much smaller than the others.

Miles, of course, only wanted to know about me knowing about Janice. He nodded and smiled as I talked, because he thought it meant I'd broken through some mighty concrete blockage. I talked, because it was all I could do to bring her back to life. But still I could not remember the car.

No one was asking me to, any more. Why would they? They might have been desperate to know, thirty-five years ago, but no one cared now. It was forgotten. Was anyone ever caught and convicted? Maybe. I was out of it from then on.

Charlie was hugely pleased with me. 'Miles says you've been going great guns. Leaps and bounds. I really think you might have turned that big corner, Karen. It's all coming back to you, now, and you don't have to hide from it any more.'

Malcolm was pleased too, when they let me back out into the big wide world. 'Thank God for that, Karen. Gem's is going to pot. Can't manage without you.'

'Yes you can,' I said, though it was nice of him to say so. 'The last thing you need is a resident lunatic, messing up your shop.'

'Well, you know what they say. You don't have to be mad to work here, but…'

I gave a fake smile. No, it really didn't help to be mad.

I wasn't mad now. I was sane. Cured. I went back to work and for a month it was as if I really had turned that magical corner back to normality. The mystery and the horror I'd been nursing all these years was Janice. Her absence had been sending me round the bend. I'd transferred my anxieties and obsession on to poor Serena Whinn, but now I knew the face I should have been remembering. I had Janice back.

I told Malcolm all about my childhood, those early years before my accident, or whatever it was, in Liverpool. I described to him, ruefully, my recent disastrous meetings with Ruth and Barbara. Not much chance of meeting the others. All I knew about them was that Serena was twice widowed, Denise was religious, and Angela was a photographer, several times divorced, who was too drunk to hold a camera any more.

As it happened, Malcolm found Angela. Just by chance. He had contacts with other bookshops, of course, and he was on mailing lists. He received some bumph from a place in Hay-on-Wye, not a bookshop, but an art gallery, and somewhere on one of the leaflets was a photograph by Angela Bryant, local artist. He showed me. We agreed it could be her. The leaflet mentioned she had a studio somewhere near Brecon.

Interesting. Nice to know. That was all. I was no longer in the grip of a mania, no longer craving for more. I had Janice and though I might not have filled in all the squares, I had enough to make sense of what I was. And what I was now was fine enough.

Then the glass moved.

—12—

It was just a glass beaker.

Malcolm and I had shared a mid-afternoon lunch – sandwiches and a can of Fanta. No rush. It was a Sunday, and the shop was shut, but after visiting the cathedral to listen to the choir singing matins, we'd come back to do a bit of tidying up, weeding out and repricing. He was going to spend the rest of the day drowning in accounts and I was going to make a couple of deliveries to favoured customers. I suppose most people would have regarded it as a day of rest, a chance to shut the shop door and forget about business for once, but as Malcolm and I both loved books, there was no better way to spend a Sunday than in the midst of them, in undisturbed tranquillity.

When he'd chewed the last crust and drained the can, Malcolm went off to fetch his papers and I took our crockery out to the kitchenette to rinse under the tap. I left the plates propped up in the sink and the glasses upside down to drain. Then, the way wet glasses sometimes do, a beaker began to move across the board.

*

'You all have to put one finger on.' Barbara is bossing us, as usual. 'No, not really hard, Angela. Ruth, you've got to, or it won't work.'

Ruth hangs back, all little mousy in case we're doing something that isn't really allowed. But Barbara says to do it and when Barbara gives orders, it's always best to obey, so she places one nervous finger on the upturned glass, as if it might bite her. I obey because I don't know what there is to be nervous about. I am taking part, that's all that matters. I helped cut up the paper and write some of the letters and words. I belong.

There are six fingers resting on the glass, some plump and pink, some short and stubby. Mine is a bit grubby. Janice and I had been decorating our den with paste and glitter before I came here, and I forgot to wash.

'Sit back, Denise! You're pushing the letters.'

Denise is round and short. Reaching across to place her finger on the glass, her belly is squishing into the table and bits of paper have shifted out of the perfect circle we made. She reaches again, trying to breathe in and going very pink in the face.

'Right. Now. Is there a spirit in the room?'

We wait. Nothing happens, except Ruth's finger begins to tremble on the glass.

Barbara's impatient. 'You try.'

'Is there a spirit in the room?' asks Serena, very gently, and perhaps it's because she doesn't sound as if she's going to smack the spirit, like Barbara did – the glass shifts.

Instant squeals. Two fingers snatch back from the glass.

'Stop it!' says Barbara. 'Put your fingers back!'

So we all settle down and concentrate, terrified and lapping up the terror.

'Is there a spirit in the room?'

This time we're ready for the sensation as the glass glides across the table to the word YES.

'Are you a good spirit?'

The glass gently bumps the word again.

'What is your name?'

P E T E R

'Oo! Like Peter Pan!' squeals Denise. We're all going to see *Peter Pan on Ice* after Christmas – the car factory's arranged it.

'Sh!' orders Barbara.

'Sorry.'

'Do you have a message for any of us, Peter?' asks Serena.

As the glass begins to judder, the door swings open and we all jump and shriek. But it isn't a creepy spirit called Peter, it's Mrs Whinn, with a tray of Corona and chocolate biscuits.

'Here we are. And what on earth are you doing there, girls?' She's leaning over to look at the table, the glass, the circle of letters. 'Oh, that silly game. I'm not sure I approve. Well, make sure the glass doesn't scratch the table, won't you?'

Serena smiles sweetly at her mother. 'It won't, I promise.'

'All right then. I'll leave you to your ghouls and ghosties.'

She bustles out, leaving the tray on another table. Serena's mother is very nice, but things are a bit flat when she's gone. Like a balloon has gone bang.

Angela pushes some of the letters back into place, then we look at each other, waiting for the magic to return.

'Draw the curtains,' suggests Serena.

Barbara gets up and lumbers round the room, closing the curtains, and it's all spooky again because we've just got the fairy lights on the Christmas tree.

'Are you still there, Peter?' asks Serena.

YES

'Do you have a message for any of us?'

YES

'Who?'

B A R B

'Barbara?'

YES

Barbara opens her mouth to say something, then stops. She's pretending that she's just impatient, but I can see her finger trembling as the glass moves from one letter to the next.

C A T

'Oh!' Barbara begins to cry. She's not a crybaby, but she blubs.

Serena lays a hand on her arm. 'Maybe he means you are getting a kitten for Christmas after all. Do you mean that, Peter?'

YES

Barbara sniffs, appeased, and tries to pretend she just got something in her eye.

'Do you have another message?'

YES K A R

'Karen?'

'Me?' I squeal. So eager. I never though a spirit would waste time on me.

AND J A N I C E

'Karen and Janice?' asks Serena.

YES

'Janice isn't here.' I feel guilty pointing it out. Of course Janice hadn't been invited to the Christmas party at Serena's home. I could hardly have expected Serena to invite her.

T E L L H E R.

'You'll have to tell Janice Dexter,' orders Barbara. She's forgotten about crying because she's got me to concentrate on now. 'Give her the message.'

'Yes, go on.' My eyes are fixed on the glass, eager for more. Ruthie can't take it and pulls back with a whimper, but the rest of us stay, our fingers glued to the glass as it slides and judders.

O N E W I L L K I L L T H E O T H E R

This time, three fingers leap from the glass as if it's shattering and stabbing us with splinters. I sit staring at it. Because it can't be right. It must be going on to say something else. Like 'Ha Ha Joke'. But it doesn't. The glass stops moving.

Someone starts crying. It's me.

*

I didn't tell Janice about the spirit message. Barbara did. We'd met in the street, on Christmas Eve, to take presents to a new, sizeable mouse that seemed willing to hang around in our presence.

On reflection, I think it was a rat. There were a lot of them around the demolished prefabs. He ate the mixed peel wax-paper house, so we'd put a cornflakes box for him in the abandoned coal bunker, and the cheese we'd left there had been eaten. Not surprising really. All the vermin and creepy crawlies on the estate must have made a beeline for it, but we were convinced only our mouse Christopher would find it.

We'd been hoping he'd be there, waiting for a Christmas surprise, but by the time we met as planned, I didn't care about the mouse any more. I'd come to the den as arranged, drenched with guilt and fear, and Janice, unaware of what had upset me, was trying to cheer me up, when Barbara came along Aspen Drive from the Parade, with sheets of Christmas wrapping paper and, of course, at sight of us, she had to bustle up to join us.

* * *

'Have you told her?'

I can only shake my head.

'What?' asks Janice.

'A spirit told us one of you would kill the other one.'

'No! Don't!' I don't know if I'm pleading with Barbara or Peter, who is not a good spirit, whatever he claimed. He's an evil spirit.

'It's true,' says Barbara. 'If a spirit said it, it must be true.'

'It's not,' I insist, beginning to cry again. Janice catches on and cries too. It isn't fair. We look at each other, wanting to gang up against Barbara and spirits and the whole world, but what can we do? Besides…

A spirit had said it. I can't escape from it, the thought and the new, creeping, chilling fear. I don't want to kill Janice, so does that mean that, secretly, she wants to kill me?

And I see the self-same doubt and terror in her eyes.

* * *

It had been a game. A stupid game, something to keep the girls amused by candlelight, around the Christmas Tree. Just a fun

142

game. I don't know whose idea it was. Barbara seemed to be in charge, but then she always did step in, like Brown Owl, no matter who suggested anything. If she had set it up, did that mean it was her finger secretly moving the glass? Someone's finger was, but the other five of us never suspected a thing. You can't possibly cheat with such things, can you? We were gullible and innocent, and open to all the terrors of the world.

Whoever it was, it must just have been a joke. A very sick joke. We'd been telling ghost stories, trying to frighten each other and loving the thrill of exquisite fear, but this was on a different plane. The terror that it planted, first in me while we played the game, then in Janice, thanks to Barbara's officious interference, was something that couldn't have been undone, even if the culprit had come clean. I could remember that Christmas, now, as the moment when my life began to crumble, and the shadows started creeping in.

*

'Karen! Come back down here now. Look at this mess. Karen! It was just a glass of squash. If you didn't want it, there was no need to throw it across the room. You've ruined poor Hilary's dress and it was brand new!'

I don't care. I just want to hide under my quilt. I don't want orange squash. I don't want a glass of anything.

'Roy, you try and do something with her. I've had enough.'

My father's turn to have a go at me. 'Now come on down, Missie, and stop all this silliness, or I'll just have to pack up those presents and send them back to Father Christmas. He only gives presents to good children, and I don't know what he'd think if he could see you now.'

143

'I don't care! I don't want them!'

My sister is in the bedroom doorway, her face screwed up, crying her eyes out because it's Christmas and I've spoiled it for her. But I can't help it. Everything is spoiled, forever.

*

That was just Christmas. After Christmas, it was January and in January, Janice died.

'Okay?' Malcolm poked his head round the kitchen door. 'Karen?' He looked me over with a practised eye. 'Will you be okay to take that delivery? I can do it later, if you like.'

'No. No, I'm fine. Just thinking.' I went through the artificial motions of appearing to pull myself out of a reverie, smiling, wiping my hands dry. 'I'll take it now, shall I?'

'If you're sure.' He tossed me the keys to the elderly van he kept for business. I'd done a few deliveries in it, because he said I needed to keep my driving hand in, until we figured out what to do about my impounded car.

I started the motor, made a big show of driving the van out of the yard, down the road, round the corner, then I stopped. I needed to sort this out.

That stupid game…

I didn't do it, did I?

Or did I? Before she could kill me?

There was still this big black hole in my memory. The hole that Dr Miles Pearce didn't seem to worry about because I was talking so freely about Janice that I must be all right. He knew I still couldn't conjure up the car that she got into, but that didn't matter, because it wasn't something the police would be interested in any more. It didn't contribute to my condition.

But here was the real reason. I couldn't conjure up the car, or

144

the murderous stranger in it, because there was no car. I'd told Serena there was, apparently, but I'd made it up, to conceal the truth – that I had killed Janice. Because I couldn't stand the fear any more. I couldn't cope with waiting for her to kill me.

I don't know how I'd done it, except that I had that one horrible memory of looking down on Janice's upturned face, smudged and smeared with tears and snot and terror.

I must have done it.

But didn't the police find who did it? Isn't that what Barbara told me? They'd found the car and the culprit, even though I'd refused to tell them anything. Or did she say she *thought* they had? Or *they* thought they had. Maybe, for all these years, some innocent man had been in prison for a crime I'd committed.

All that questioning by the police. I could remember it vividly now, questions over and over and over, pleading, shouting, the thumping of tables, and all the while, my brain commanding me to block them out. Perhaps it wasn't the helpless reaction of a traumatised child, after all. It was the panicking reaction of a child murderer, trying to conceal her crime from the rest of the world.

What had I done? Who had paid?

Barbara would know. I'd rushed out without waiting for her to give me the full story. I could go back.

I couldn't face her again…the office I'd left sprayed with vomit, the unpaid consultation bill. And no point going back to Ruth, who'd thrown me out. But I could find Angela. She had an exhibition in Hay-on-Wye. The gallery leaflet said so. I could go to Hay.

I was splitting in two again. Half of me knew that I was being stupid, that I needed to deliver these books for Malcolm and then go home, get some sleep, talk it through tomorrow, maybe, with Charlie. Make another appointment to see Miles.

The other half was already screaming at me that I had to resolve this now. I had to know. I had to put right what could never be put right.

So I drove to Wales.

—13—

Yes. I know. I shouldn't be allowed on the roads. Many had said it and wondered how I'd ever been allowed behind a wheel. It was why I hadn't made more of a concerted effort to haggle with the police about getting my car back. If they'd stopped to take a closer look at me, I'd probably have had my driving licence taken away.

I had it in the first place because I did occasionally manage long spells of apparently perfect sanity. Charlie had persuaded me to try for it, because she thought I'd have a better chance of turning up to work on time if I drove. Sane or not, I had a habit of missing buses. So I learned and I passed. And I was mostly not too bad, on roads I knew. Other drivers might never suspect I was a dangerous lunatic. I'd been feeling so sane recently, that if Malcolm had asked me, the day before, to make a delivery to Wales, I would probably have managed it without any problem. Or at least with no more than the problems naturally involved in finding a place I didn't know, on roads I wasn't sure about. For a start, he would have given me a map.

But today, thanks to a moving glass and all that had spilled out of it, the mental safety harness had snapped and I was in chaos again, driven by compulsions that made no allowances for my geographical delusions. I just drove. I think that once I got going, from that side street where I'd paused to finish cracking up, I must automatically have taken the route towards Lyford. In the motorway furball below Leeds, the cattle prod jabbed, to tell me I didn't want to be going south. I should be going west. So I did.

I recall a lot of horns blasting and brakes screeching, and swearing from lorry windows high above me. Changing lanes on a motorway was a major triumph of will over sheer terror for me. It was a miracle I didn't cause a serious pile-up with multiple fatalities. Perhaps the spirit in the glass was watching over me, determined to make me drink, to the full, the cup of gall that was waiting for me in Wales. So I found myself travelling towards Manchester, not London.

At least I was aware enough, this time, to notice the petrol light coming on. I just made it to a service station as it started to flash in panic.

I needed to fill the tank. It would cost the earth and I couldn't remember what was in my bank account but I knew it was next to nothing. My debit card would probably be refused.

Malcolm's jacket was in the van, flung across the passenger seat, along with some unopened mail and an empty grease-stained paper bag. Wincing with painful guilt, I checked it over. Malcolm's credit card was in his pocket, along with a helpful note reminding him of his own pin number. I think this was why Malcolm was always so sympathetic to my hopelessness. He was just as bad.

I used the card, because I had no choice, but at least I had the decency to feel ashamed. To steal, from Malcolm of all people. It was selfish, mean and despicable. But what else could I do? I'd already stolen his van. No use telling myself I'd only borrowed it. I was supposed to be delivering some books to an address a mile from the shop and instead I was driving to Wales. I had taken without consent. Malcolm would probably have the police on my tail by the end of the day.

No, not Malcolm. He wouldn't do that to me. But it was probably the end of his willingness to employ me, or offer any sort of refuge at Gem's Books. He couldn't employ a thief. But then, I was worse than a thief. I was a murderer. Future employment would not be an issue if I spent the rest of my life in prison. Because, of course, once I was sure of the truth, I would confess. The notion of a trial and a life sentence was a strange comfort. It would solve everything. But first I needed to establish that truth. I needed to find Wales. How hard could it be?

I managed to avoid finishing up in Liverpool. I was on the M6 and going south. Surely I needed to be going west by now. I stopped again at the next services and bought a road atlas. The cheapest on the WHSmith shelves and I used my own money this time. My card was accepted. I sat in the van, studying the map. So Wales was there. And there was Hay-on-Wye. And Brecon. Yes. I really didn't want to be on the M6.

So I got off it and headed west, with the atlas on my knees. I must have gone in circles a few times, lost my bearings completely, came perilously close to getting back onto the M6, heading north, nearly found myself in Birmingham, and finally, deep in the middle of nowhere, in pitch darkness, I accepted that I was lost and there was no point in struggling on. Apart from anything else, no one was going to open their doors to a madwoman in the middle of the night. Better to stop now, and try to find Hay or Brecon at first light. So I pulled into a lay-by – more of a farm gateway, really, and switched off the engine. No help for it but to wait till morning.

I didn't think I'd sleep, but I did.

*

First day back at school. The weather is raw, the sky grey and I am miserable. Our mother packs Hilary and me off together every day, and we don't usually part company until we meet up with her friends. Then she runs off with them and I go on with Janice. But today, Hilary runs off as soon as we're out of Linden Crescent and Mummy can no longer see us. She's had enough of me, over Christmas. She hates me and won't speak to me ever again. She runs, pigtails flapping, to be away from me, but she needn't run. I am dragging. Dreading the meeting with Janice at the prefabs.

I see her. She's coming along Brontë Road, dragging just like me. Perhaps, she's hoping, if she goes slowly enough, I'll go on, up to the Parade, and miss her. I think she must be thinking that because I'm thinking the same. Let her go past first.

But we're both dragging so much, it's pointless. We give up the struggle and come together like we always do. She looks at me sadly, scared.

I'm scared too. It's not fair.

'I won't kill you if you promise not to kill me,' I say.

Wide-eyed, she just nods.

'Cross your heart and hope to die?'

She nods again. 'And you.'

'Cross my heart and hope to die, I promise.'

We hold hands and walk on, our entwined fingers

gripping like vices, clinging on for dear life.

Cross my heart and hope to die.

*

I woke with a crick in my neck and one leg so numb there was no feeling whatsoever. I struggled into a sitting position and pushed the van door open onto a fresh, sparkling morning. I was surrounded by fields, some lush, some newly harvested. The trees were heavy with dusty summer, aching to turn. A line of blue-purple hills rimmed the western horizon.

I stood up, supporting myself against the van until blood and sensation returned to all my limbs. I was thirsty. There was a half-consumed bottle of water in the door pocket. I don't know how long it had been there. Quite a while, from the stale taste, but I drank it anyway. I found a cereal bar in Malcolm's jacket. He was a perpetual nibbler. I ate it. I didn't want it, but I didn't want to reach Angela and be diverted by endless comments about anorexia and self-starvation. I hadn't been starving myself for the last month or so, but I was still thin. More than thin by most people's standards. I couldn't afford to arrive looking transparent. My present mission took precedence over my desire to be invisible. That could wait. I could be invisible for evermore in prison.

It was seven o'clock and cars were beginning to pass. That was good. The day was waking up and I'd be able to knock on doors without causing a major panic. I studied the map again, but it didn't have a helpful sticker saying, 'You are here.' I drove on until I reached a junction with a signpost. I thought it might give me a clue to where I was, but it did better than that. It pointed to Hay and Brecon. I could breathe again.

I'd always wanted to go to Hay-on-Wye. The book town.

I'd fantasised about moving there, and disappearing into an inexhaustible kingdom of books. It was living up to the fantasy in my mind: I had to cross a drawbridge to reach it and bribe the guardian of the gate. Or at least cross a wooden bridge and pay a toll. The town itself was a bit of an unglamorous disappointment. Just brick and concrete and tarmac like any other. Warehouses, yards and car parks. A supermarket. I don't get that. Why would anyone want to buy food when they've got bookshops?

A lot of bookshops. But I wasn't in search of books, I was in search of Angela Bryant.

I parked up by a clock tower. Still too early, I realised. People were on the move but the shops weren't open yet. I wandered the streets, looking for the gallery that had advertised Angela's work, and found it, still dark, locked. A couple of her photographs were displayed in the window – a river in a deep gorge, black and white, which made it ominous and dramatic, and a fish, in weed, the colours so mingled you had to stare hard to see which was which. I thought they were quite good.

I carried on walking, up and down the streets. Mothers began to appear, taking their children to school. It was September. New term. Some looked reluctant and sullen, going back to the grind. Some, the tiniest ones, looked terrified. I don't remember being terrified when I was five. Only when I was ten.

Doors began to open, signs appeared on pavements. The gallery opened at last and I went in.

There were still a few of Angela's photographs on the walls, but a new exhibition was being installed. Paintings, this time. As I stood there, staring round, looking for inspiration, a young woman asked if she could help.

'Angela Bryant, the photographer. I need to see her. Do you have her address?'

'Oh, sorry. We can't give out addresses. But I can give you a leaflet. She has a studio, I think. Or she did. Where are they, now?' She unearthed a bundle from behind the counter, and handed me one.

'Thanks,' I said, and found a quiet corner in which to scrutinise it. *Angela Bryant grew up in Lyford and attended...* yes, yes, yes. *She has exhibited in....* Go on. *Her studio near Brecon.* Oh very helpful. How near Brecon? There was a photo of the studio in the leaflet, mountains rising behind it, Angela standing in front of it. It was a carefully posed photo, of a woman looking arty and mysterious. I couldn't say I recognised her. I peered closer at the picture, hoping to detect a house name, or even a number. A road sign? Nothing. I could hardly drive round and round Brecon, waiting for that mountain and that slate-roofed studio to appear. Why couldn't they just give me her address?

While I watched, unobtrusive in my corner, the young woman unhooked a couple of Angela's remaining photos, took them to the counter, and started to wrap them in tissue. The first went into a crate, standing ready. She was interrupted before she'd wrapped the second, by the doorbell as someone came in. Not a customer, but a local, because they were immediately in deep gossip. I sidled up to the counter and peered round at the crate. It had a large label.

Angela Bryant, Holly Cottage, Llanyfain, Brecon.

Enough.

I took my leaflet and headed back for the van.

Llanyfain wasn't much of a village. A scattering of stone houses along narrow lanes. Holly Cottage stood on a rise at a point where one of the lanes finally petered out into a grass-grown track. The man at the garage on the nearest thing to a main road had directed me, and once I reached the gateway through the towering, untrimmed hedgerow, I could see the house and recognise the studio illustrated in the leaflet.

I walked up to it, but stopped short of the door. The studio was an old barn that had been converted, with skylights and French windows, through which I could make out some packing cases, a table and a lot of cobwebs. Whenever the conversion had been done, it was long enough ago for nature to have begun to reclaim it. Moss was peeling off the paintwork, and brambles, invading from the nearest hedge, were tugging at the lower slates. Nettles had virtually engulfed the door, and I couldn't see any point in fighting through them. It was obvious that the studio had been abandoned. The photo in the brochure must have been taken years ago.

I turned to the house, which looked a little more lived in. Paint was peeling on the woodwork here, too, but there was a lot less moss. A milk crate outside the front door was filled with empty bottles. Whisky rather than milk.

No response to my knock, but I could hear, distantly, a radio. I went round the back, pushing aside unpruned buddleias, and found a small weedy patio. Two mugs stood on a rusting cast-iron table, and a kitchen door was ajar. I could hear the radio louder now, and a woman's voice, raised, not in anger, but shouting to another room.

I knocked on the open door.

A woman bustled into view. Nothing at all like the Angela

Bryant in the photograph. That was because she wasn't Angela Bryant. She was short, round-faced, with an upturned nose and a childish look that hadn't changed one bit in thirty-five years.

'Hello, Denise.'

Denise Griggs stared at me, opened mouthed for a moment. 'It's her,' she said. She clasped her hands together and shut her eyes, her lips moving in silent prayer and then she crossed herself.

'Her, who?' said Angela, appearing in the inner doorway, looking at me without a glimmer of recognition. But then Angela Bryant probably wouldn't have recognised her own mother, from the look of her. She was either on very heavy medication, or she was nursing a very heavy hangover. Judging by the empty bottles, scattered round the kitchen, it was the latter.

'Karen Rothwell,' I said.

'Oh yes. Right. Of course you are.'

—14—

Angela Bryant looked twenty years older than her studio picture. Nothing artistic about her. She was dishevelled and gaunt. At school she'd been tall and lithe, athletic, the exact opposite to the short, round Denise. They'd made a comical pairing, but they hadn't given a damn. Thirty-five years on, Angela was still tall, but she stooped, or was it just that she had trouble standing upright? Her hair was unbrushed and she was wrapped in a dressing gown. Partly wrapped. It kept falling open and she'd grab at it and miss. 'Karen the Undead. Best come in. Where are the fags, Denny?'

'Where I've hidden them. Go and get dressed.' Denise shooed Angela away and then turned back to me, drawing a deep breath. 'Yes. Karen. We've been waiting for you. You saw Barbara, didn't you? We need to talk, of course we do. There's so much we all need to clear off our consciences. Only that way can we hope to find peace. To be cleansed. To be pure again.'

I don't know what sort of greeting I was expecting, but it wasn't this. I couldn't think of any reply, so I let her usher me into a sitting room. It looked tired, tidy enough but it smelled stale.

I watched her busy herself with opening windows, removing a bottle, plumping cushions, like a woman with a mission.

156

Slightly hysterical in every gesture. I remembered her as a rather gushing, officious child, always eager to remind us what Teacher had said, what we had agreed to do, what we were supposed to be wearing. She was the one who'd tell on other children. Never on us, Serena's disciples, because Serena's unspoken rules of love and loyalty wouldn't permit that sort of intimate treachery, but anyone else was fair game for this one-girl Stasi.

She told on Janice once. I can't remember what Janice had done. It wouldn't have been difficult for Denise to identify some transgression and carry it on a silver platter to Miss Hargreaves. I saw her go up to Miss as busily as she was now tidying up the living room, and Janice was hauled off for a five-minute torture session. I found her later, in the corridor, crying. I think I would have hated Denise, but I didn't know how to hate someone who was Serena's friend.

There was something desperate about Denise, as if she too had been taken off by teacher and left crying in the corridor. Chastened. Her hair was cut short, in a pudding basin style that made her face look even rounder. No make-up. She wore a matronly blouse, a high-necked navy cardigan and a plain grey skirt that might have looked elegant on someone Angela's height, but on someone as dumpy as Denise it almost reached her ankles and made her look as if she had a stout tree trunk instead of legs. No jewellery except for a crucifix, which she touched every few seconds.

I'd forgotten she was a Catholic. There hadn't been many of them at Marsh Green Junior, but we all knew who they were; they didn't come in to assembly with us, because they had a different god. Like Jonathan Gold, who was Jewish. Denise had worn a crucifix back then, too. A cross with a writhing figure. She busily encouraged us to do the same. 'If you don't wear a cross, you'll go to hell. It's true. It says so in the Bible, so there.' Angela, who hadn't worshipped anyone, unless there was a God of Running and Jumping, had started to wear a crucifix after that, just to be on the safe side.

'Would you like a cup of tea, Karen?' Denise spoke like a nurse. I wondered if she was one. It would explain her presence.

'Please.' I said it to get her out of the room, while I tried to get my own head straight. I'd come prepared to beg for answers from an alcoholic, who'd probably want nothing to do with me. I hadn't prepared myself for a reception committee.

Angela shuffled back into the room, dressed in an old jumper and older jeans. She still hadn't combed her hair but she had found her cigarettes. I noticed a limp as she walked. Perhaps it wasn't just alcohol that made her unsteady. She slumped into a sofa. 'So then. Karen Rothwell.'

'Yes.'

Her eyes fixed on me, and through the alcoholic haze there was a brief flash of clarity. 'Come to play parlour games, have you?'

Six fingers on a moving glass.

'No,' I said. 'No parlour games.'

She appeared not to hear the second part of my answer, her eyes wandering off again. 'Where's that crazy Denny?'

'Making tea.'

'Oh Christ. Not more tea. Did you know you could reach a state of grace by the eternal swilling of lukewarm tannin? Isn't there a war on, somewhere? She could be out there, making tea for the troops. Ever in the service of others, our Denny.'

To be honest, I am paraphrasing. I actually caught about one blurred word in two.

'Wanted to be a nun, you know. But the convents wouldn't have her. Kept going in as a postulant. Pissy postulant. Then they'd chuck her out again a month later. They thought she had suspect motives. Not a vocation so much as an immolation. I don't think they go in for self-flagellation any more. Or hair shirts. Now she just pretends to be a nun and devotes herself to impossible causes. Like me. I'm the next best thing to a hair shirt.'

'I see.'

'But you saw Barbara, so I suppose she told you all about us.'

'Not exactly. She said Denise was married to Jesus.'

'Yeah. That's about it. Bride of Christ. Or maybe just the first mad Mrs Christ in the attic. So what did our Babs say about me?'

'That you were a photographer. That you'd been married a few times…'

'Three. We don't count Warwick, do we?' Angela raised her voice to let Denise hear. 'Don't think that one was strictly legal, he being already married and it being bigamous and all that. So three proper ones. Average life expectancy of marriage to Angela: two years and one month. Or was it one year and two months? Babs worked it out. It's only that long because Trev stuck it out for nearly eight. Don't know why they can't cope with me. Any ideas?'

It seemed pointless to state the obvious, so I said nothing. She did it for me.

'Because I can't cope with them. Five minutes of marital bliss and I have an irresistible urge to start throwing things at them, and then get very, very drunk.'

'Yes. Barbara said – something about…'

'My being a lush? A dipso? A sot. Imb – imbiber of the fruit of the… Oh, anyway, however she put it.'

'I can't remember how she put it.'

'But she put it. Always to the point, our Babs. Sad old cow, isn't she? Just as sad as me, but I know I am and she pretends she isn't. Look at her, up there all alone in Cumbria, writing wills. Her speciality, wills. Poking around in the dusty relics of the imminently dead. Negotiating the inheritance rules for Granny's teapot.'

'I suppose someone has to do it.'

'And who better than Babs, the imminently, but not quite, dead.'

'Is she ill, then?'

'No. Not Babs. Doesn't drink, you see. You have to drink to be ill.'

I could think of a few other ways.

'Our Babs just lives to be dead. She's made her own will, you know. She told me. Quite proud, like it's her life achievement, making her own will. I suppose that's because she's minted. Must be. Ever met a poor solicitor?'

'No.'

'And do you know what she's going to do with all her millions? She's going to leave everything to a cat charity. Can you imagine that? A cat charity.'

'Now, now.' Denise bustled in with a tray. She placed a mug carefully on a coaster in front of Angela, which seemed utterly pointless, since the table was scored and scuffed and acid-burned by cigarettes and whisky. Then she pressed a mug into my grasp, folding her hands around mine and gazing at me with pained sympathy.

The mug was burning hot. I flinched free and put it down.

Denise seated herself, knees together. 'I think it's the best thing any of us can do, to leave our worldly goods to charity. As the Bible tells us—'

'Bloody cats? I'm not leaving mine to stinking moggies.' Angela burst into harsh laughter. 'Not that I've got anything to leave.'

'Oh but all your lovely photos,' said Denise.

'You think they're worth something? Great. That means there's a chance for me to cause chaos by dying intestate. In-tes-tate. Lovely word.'

'No it isn't. It's a horrible word!' Denise had to rise to everything Angela said.

To Angela's satisfaction, of course. 'Can't you picture it? All your relatives clawing their eyes out over your treasures when you've snuffed it. Ah, but nobody's going to argue over my crap. Do they still do pauper's funerals?'

'Stop it!' said Denise. 'Don't talk about dying, Angela. You're not going to die for years and years.'

'Will if I want to.'

'I'm not going to let you!' Denise's response was shrill and demented. It's always interesting to observe insanity in others if you're insane yourself. She switched an internal button and calmed down, back to being bossy ward sister. 'You're doing very well, and things are really beginning to pick up.' She turned to me. 'She has an exhibition, you know. In Hay.'

'Yes, I saw it. The gallery was just packing it up.'

'Anything sold?' Angela shrugged. 'I doubt it. Denny

organised it. It's called "Getting Angela back on track." Quite delusional. She unearthed all my tired old shots. Haven't taken a picture in years. Why should I? I never wanted to be a photographer. I was going to be an Olympic medallist.'

'That's how I remember you. Always running and jumping.'

'But she had a little bit of an accident at college,' confided Denise.

Angela's gruff cackle drowned her out. 'Three o'clock in the morning and I decided to take on the hurdle track. Which seemed perfectly sensible, as I was pissed as a newt. The hurdles won. Quite decisively. Think I've still got a bit of one in this leg. I carry it round as a keepsake.'

'I'm sorry.'

'Yes, well, don't suppose I'd have really made the grade. Anyway, there was nothing for it then but to do something harmless, like photography. At least it had one benefit. It got right up Ruth's nose. Can you imagine, her hearing I was taking up photography? I do believe she actually foamed at the mouth. Never forgiven me. I offered to photograph her kids when they were young. Thought she'd have a seizure. So easy to wind her up. I never do kids. Or adults, for that matter.'

'Yes you do. That beautiful one of pensioners on a bench by the sea.'

'That wasn't a bloody portrait. It was a study of wrinkles. Done it. Don't want to do it any more.'

'Now, now,' said Denise. 'You mustn't deny your God-given artistic talent. It's in your soul. Still there, Angela. You'll find it again as soon as you pick up your camera. It was always there, just waiting for the opportunity to come out. In fact, I think, maybe that accident was just God's way of guiding you to your real vocation—'

'Oh for Christ's sake.' Angela grabbed her mug, took a desperate swig, realised it was tea and put it down in despair. 'You don't half talk total bullshit, Denny. Karen here was the artistic one. You an artist, Karen? Whatever, I don't suppose you made it all the way here, into the wilds of sheep-shagging country, just to hear about my professional hiatus.' Her incoherent babbling was becoming even more slurred as her eyes began to droop. She looked as if she might fall asleep mid-sentence.

'No, of course not.' Denise looked at me with brave expectation. 'Karen came here to lance the tragedy of the past.'

'Lance away,' muttered Angela. 'Squeeze all the pus out.'

It was exactly why I'd come. I decided not to prevaricate in case Angela passed out before she could answer my question.

'1966. What happened? I can remember some of it, but not all. I haven't been well.'

Denise nodded understanding, encouraging me to go on.

'I know Janice was murdered. I know – I think I know she got into a car. I think I told Serena. Is that true?'

Angela's eyes didn't open wider, but her fidgeting stopped. She froze.

Denise shut her eyes and crossed herself again.

'Yeah, you told Serena you'd seen it,' said Angela.

'What exactly did I say?'

'Just that. I don't know. Was there any more? It was all the police were interested in, anyway. Inspector Whinn. Serena's father. In charge of the investigation.' She managed another humourless cackle. 'Must have wished he wasn't. My God, he must have. Got pilloried for the way he handled it. Cocked it up from start to finish. Not even a court case to show for it. I suppose, officially, it's still an open case.'

Denise gave a whimper.

Angela ignored her. 'I reckon that's why he buggered off to Hong Kong. Colonial police. We never saw Serena again for years.'

'But you've seen her since?' I was on the edge of my seat.

'Oh yes.' Angela's eyes shut. I thought I'd lost her. Then they opened again a slit. 'Saw her. Didn't speak about it though. None of us wanted to resurrect it, did we. Not until you turned up.'

'I see,' I just managed to say.

'Want to know more, go ask her. Not that she'll remember. It was all years ago. Years and years and years ago. She's probably forgotten all about it.'

'No!' Denise gave a little scream, like a mouse in agony. 'Not that. None of us can forget!'

One moment the kindly nurse and the next a mental patient. I could tell her exactly how she was feeling. Her nerves were jangling, like metal girders beginning to come apart, the edifice beginning to shake. Share the love, share the insanity. 'Do you know where she is?'

'Serena Whinn-Davison-Canterbury.' Angela folded her hands, piously, as she slumped further down the sofa. 'Our globetrotting saint and merry widow. Yes, she's back in Blighty, rich as Croesus. That's what you get with two wealthy hubbies. Why weren't mine ever millionaires?'

'Yours aren't dead, Angie. That's horrible.' Denise was verging on fierce tears. 'I think Serena would rather be poor and have them alive than have to go through all that. She didn't deserve it. And she is wealthy, it's true, but there's no one better that God would entrust wealth to. She's so generous to everyone. She supports all sorts of charities.'

'Yeah, yeah, the Blessed Serena.' Angela shrugged grudgingly.

'She runs a counselling service, you know. Helps people with phobias and motivational problems and that sort of thing. I want Angela to go and see her.'

'To hell with that.'

'You're still in contact.' I didn't want to hear about her wealth, her dead husbands or her business plans. For months, Serena had been turning towards me, waiting for me to come to her. Why couldn't they just shut up and lead me to her?

'We chat on the phone, don't we, Denny? Let her give us little pep talks. Little embraces of encouragement. And we've visited. Oh yes. Denny insisted on dragging me back to Lyford to see my brother Colin and do family penance. So we took a trip out to Serena's grand estate and were served lapsang souchong by the butler.'

'Now, now,' said Denise. Her favourite phrase. 'She has a very nice house, that's all.' She was back to being ward sister, though every few moments she compulsively bit her finger. 'It's complete nonsense about her having a butler. She made us coffee, and lunch in the garden. She said she has a lady who comes in once or twice a week, but that's all. She helps out at the local school and the old people's home.' She gripped Angela's arms with a sudden surge of earnest enthusiasm. 'That's the sort of thing you should do, Angela. Get involved in the community. Be of service. It's a reward in itself. To serve God and our fellow man.'

Angela pulled free, stuck a finger down her throat and

pretended to retch.

'So she's living in Lyford again?' *Just tell me where, please!*

'Not *in* Lyford.' Angela attempted a pantomime posh accent, which failed because she was slurring far too much. 'One does not live in Lyford, darling. One's cleaner lives in Lyford. One lives over the hill where Lyford is not quite visible.'

Denise bit her finger again. 'She lives in Thorpeshall. You know it?'

I shook my head.

'One of those lovely villages on the downs. And why shouldn't she, after all she's been through? It was terrible, you know. Tragedy after tragedy. Tony Davison, her first husband, died in a plane crash, out in Australia. Left her with a business in chaos and she didn't know anything about running a business, so she had to sell up. To his bitter rival, which made it even worse. She felt so guilty about that, on top of everything else. Then back in England she married lovely Jack Canterbury – they worshipped each other, and he was diagnosed with cancer and he…' Denise's voice was rising to hysteria pitch. 'Took his own life. Truly terrible. A mortal sin.'

'Especially since it turned out he didn't have cancer after all,' said Angela, staring into her mug of cold tea. 'Bit of a bummer, don't you think?'

'Serena was distraught. So awful. So many deaths.' Denise's frantic wittering subsided into a sob.

'Yes,' said Angela. 'So many deaths. Starting with little Janice Dexter. But not including Karen, apparently. That's a turn-up for the books, isn't it? Karen still alive.'

I chilled at her words. They were too sinister to be comfortable, not sinister enough to be malicious. 'Sorry?'

'Word got round, you know, that you were dead too. You and Janice, both. Would have been nice to think the bastard in the glass got it wrong.'

A sharp intake of breath from Denise. Her eyes turned up as if she were about to faint. 'That Ouija board. That was it. Holy Mary, Mother of God have mercy on us. It was Satan at work.'

Angela choked on her own attempt at laughter. 'It was a crap game, you silly cow. It wasn't real, was it?' She stared at me for a second, with blatant accusation. 'Was it, Karen?' Then her eyes flickered away again. 'How come they decided you were dead? Must have been because no one heard from you. Not a peep, all those years. Until you popped up like the Ghost of Christmas Past on Ruthie's doorstep. So.' She leaned forward to stub out the remnant of her cigarette on the table. 'What's really brought you out of the woodwork, at long last?'

An apple, rolling into a drain…

'I started to remember things. I don't know why. I've been ill.'

'So you said.' They looked at each other. I didn't need to say more on that score – thanks, Barbara.

'I remembered Serena first, and then – Janice – the murder, but…' I clasped my head. I was trying to keep calm, just to get the simple information out of them, but my inner unravelling was running out of control. I was grabbing at threads, slippery as spaghetti. 'I just can't remember what I – what happened. I can't remember!'

'Seriously?' Angela shrugged. 'So you don't have any revelations, after all? Can't tell us what really happened to Janice?'

'I don't know what happened!'

Denise knelt in front of me. She took my hands in hers and looked up into my face with tearful eyes.

'Karen. Look into your heart. You know the truth. Tell us. Get it off your conscience now. Be washed in the blood of the Lamb. Confess.'

'Yes, I would, I will, but confess what?' I got up, desperate to get away from her.

They looked at each other. Why did they have to be so bloody oblique?

I pushed. 'They knew the man who did it, is that right?'

Denise did one of her about-turns on a pinhead again. She clasped her hands to her lips, less in prayer this time than in panic, and started shaking, with a low moan. One moment recommending the virtues of confession and the next a quivering wreck at the thought of what she might hear.

Angela was equally disturbed. She stood up suddenly, walked to the open window and leaned out, breathing deeply. Then she turned back and faced me.

'They had a name, all right. But not a body to go with it. Leastwise, not intact. The 4:22 saw to that. So no one even got to question Nigel Knight.'

—15—

Nigel Knight follows us home from school sometimes, laughing, lolloping like a great big dog. He doesn't laugh like the boys at school, mean and sneery. He laughs like everything's just funny. He's big, Nigel, bigger than most of the men on the estate. But then he is seventeen. He's not at school any more. He lives with his dad on Cherry Way and he works on his dad's allotment, on the other side of Foxton Road. He doesn't have a proper job because he's a bit simple. That's what my dad says, but Mummy says he's not normal and a menace and they ought to put him somewhere. He's not really a menace. He just stands in the road sometimes and the cars have to brake, and the drivers shout and honk their horns. He follows us because he really wants to play. Sometimes we let him come to the swings with us, but he's much too big. Grown-ups usually warn him to clear off…

*

How could anyone have accused Nigel Knight of anything – of this? And yet, in the seething whirlpool of my mind, memories float to the surface. Memories of his name being snarled, of angry voices, dogs barking. And then whispered voices, shoulders shrugged defensively. Mr. Knight, his father, standing in the road, looking just as bewildered as his son had ever done.

'Not Nigel,' I whispered.

'That's what the police thought,' said Angela, turning back to the window, groping for another cigarette.

'It was me!' Denise wailed. 'It was me. God forgive me, I did it! Because you wouldn't talk. You wouldn't tell them. I knew what you'd said to Serena. She told me. I had to tell them, you see. I had to make them believe. I shouldn't have done it. I'll be punished all my life!'

'Oh for Christ's sake, always the histrionic guilt-trip,' said Angela. Denise, still on her knees, was trying to beat her head on the carpet. She was too stout to manage it with ease. 'Silly bitch, how's that going to help?'

I grabbed Angela's tea and swigged it, because my mouth was too dry to speak. I cleared my throat and croaked. 'What was it you told them?'

'I told them I'd seen Janice getting into the car with Nigel. Like you told Serena. Except that that's not what you told her, was it? You just said into a car with a stranger. It was because Serena – you told her something about it being a dark car, like, you know, purple, and about bits of wood? So I thought, well, it had to be Mr Knight's car, didn't it? You know, the maroon Morris Traveller. With the wooden frame. And he used to let Nigel drive it sometimes, didn't he, round by the prefabs? When no one was watching? I wanted them to be sure, that was all, so I told them I saw it too. From way down Aspen Drive. I told them it was Nigel Knight.'

Whatever it was I'd told Serena, I could not conjure up an image of Janice and a Morris Traveller. I couldn't conjure up an image of Nigel Knight. It was wrong. All wrong.

'What happened to him?'

There was silence as Denise and Angela exchanged glances.

'The police went to arrest him. Well they had to, didn't they, because of what I'd told them!' Denise wiped her eyes, then her nose, groping in her cardigan sleeves for a tissue. 'Mr Knight, wouldn't let them in the house. He said everyone was always picking on his boy and Nigel was harmless and wouldn't hurt a fly. Well, he wouldn't, would he?'

'No.' Angela and I spoke together. It was the one thing we were all certain about.

Denise blew her nose loudly. 'Nigel must have been frightened by all the racket. He ran for it. The police got a big search going. All those policemen, banging on dustbins, knocking on doors, swarming everywhere. And the dogs. And all the people on the estate up in arms, threatening to burn Mr Knight's house down, and… It was horrible.'

Another silence. We could all hear the baying mob.

'Anyway, they finished up at the – the allotments. They'd got the idea—'

'All right!' Angela threw herself round the room like a tiger trapped in a small cage, flinging open cupboards, searching. 'Where's the fucking whisky? You cow, Denny. You've hidden it again. Yes! All right. They went looking on the allotments because I told them to.'

'Nigel's shed…' I could see it, plain as day.

*

The allotments are our playground at weekends, and on weekdays for anyone who bunks off school. There are always whiskery old men around, planting their peas and hoeing their lettuces, or sitting in their wooden sheds, sharing a Thermos of tea, ready to shout at us if we run too near to their precious dahlias or beanpoles, but there are so many allotments, squeezed into the wedge of land between Foxton Road and the railway line, there's always somewhere for us to run shrieking, without anyone to mind.

Most of our dads have patches here, so no one dares to order us off, in case we're carrying messages or sandwiches. Dad has a strip and he grows cabbages and I hate cabbage, but sometimes I go to his wooden shed when he's having a break, and help him wind twine or count beans. Mostly, though, I go with Janice up to the far end, where a lot of the strips are just weeds, and there are empty sheds, and one of them has fallen down. Helped down. Kenneth Dexter and his gang did a lot of pushing and jumping on it. They carted bits of wood off somewhere, and burned the rest in a great big bonfire, and they got thrown off for that.

Other boys bring their go-karts and bikes here and whizz around between the strips, really fast, so we keep clear, Janice and me. We've got our hideaway among some old raspberry canes. When the raspberries are ripe, no one comes to pick them, so we eat them. Angela and Denise come up here sometimes too. Angela's always going to be in the sports races at school and she practises running in the straight bit down the middle of the allotments and Denise times her by counting out loud, because she hasn't got a stopwatch like Miss Jones, the games teacher. I came up here with Ruth once, too, because we're supposed to be friends, but she didn't like it. She said it was too muddy. It's only muddy when it rains.

Nigel Knight comes here. His dad has a strip, down by

172

the gates, really neat and full of veg and flowers, but he's got another one too, now, up among the weedy ones, for Nigel to work all on his own. Nigel likes things like digging. He goes a bit wild sometimes, digging really deep holes, but his father helps him fill them in. He's been given lettuces to plant. He looks after them really well, like they're his babies.

He hasn't been given a shed. I think the other whiskery men are a bit annoyed about having him there, but they don't like to argue with Mr Knight because he's too nice. Nigel's found a shed all of his own. It's one of the really rickety ones that no one else uses any more, and there are apple trees in front of it, that have grown really big and straggly, so you don't even notice it until you're right up to it. Nigel has a chair in there. One leg's broken short but he props it on bricks. He keeps comics there. He's shown me some of them. He always laughs and comes out when we're around, and then we watch him digging more holes, and we clap and we laugh with him.

*

'It was a game,' said Angela. 'Hunt the thimble, hide and seek, hunt the bloody Nigel. Christ, I was a child. We were all bloody children. How were we supposed to understand? Even the murder. They said Janice Dexter was dead. We didn't get it, did we? We didn't really know what death was, or sex or any-bloody-thing. Murder was a thrill. The man hunt was a thrill. So I told them about Nigel's secret shed. I just wanted to see the dogs go for it. All those bloody Alsatians, straining at the leash. I wanted to see him run. Didn't everyone love running? Fuck it!' She slammed the cupboard door and leaned on it, face screwed up.

Denise sobbed.

'He ran,' I said.

'Of course he ran. Wouldn't you? Seeing a hundred policemen and snarling dogs charging at you? He must have been scared shitless. But he was trapped. Those pig sheds, you know. They blocked his way out, so there was only one way to go. Onto the railway line. Rolled down, straight onto the track.'

The railway track. It ran straight as a plumb line east of Foxton Road. At the south end it was up on an embankment. Then it levelled out and by the time it reached the end of the allotments, it was in a chalky cutting. I'd ventured over the wire fence once, for a dare, I think, and a couple of men had come racing from their radishes to shout at me and haul me back. You don't go on the railway track.

Of course you don't. When the trains roared through, they sucked the air out of you, and the ground trembled under your feet. They were thundering dragons who sent you flying.

Kenneth Dexter climbed onto the track once. Men shouted at him too, but he didn't listen. He ran across and off the other side and he didn't get killed.

But Nigel did. I couldn't remember the precise fact, but I could remember, even locked in my room, hiding from everyone's sight, the squeals and clanks echoing through the winter air, the dragon screaming, as the train screeched to a long, squealing stop.

I could remember the general shock, my mother's face screwed up in horrified disgust.

I could remember the ringing of an ambulance and Mr Cartwright, our next door neighbour, in the front garden like

174

everyone in the street, straining to hear, and saying, 'Don't know why they're bothering with an ambulance. A shovel and bucket's what they'll be needing.'

'Stupid fool,' said Angela. 'Stupid, poor, pathetic, innocent fool.' She came unsteadily to stand before me, and looked down at me, swaying. 'And you really don't remember what you saw?'

'No.'

'You lucky, fucking cow!'

She was shaking. Denise was at her elbow, trying, solicitously, to guide her back to the sofa, but Angela pushed her off, angrily. 'Why can't that happen to me? Why can't I forget? Ever seen someone dismembered and disembowelled by a train? It sprays, you know, right up in the air, and a head can roll—'

'Don't!' Denise screamed, covering her ears. 'Don't talk about it. It's horrible!'

'Yes, that's exactly what it was. Horrible. The sort of thing you'd really like to forget. Only I can't! But lucky old Karen has the magic gift. She has forgotten what she saw. Assuming, of course, that she really did see it at all.'

They both turned looks of accusation on me.

'I don't remember any car. I don't remember Nigel. I don't remember what I told Serena, but I think I must have made it up.'

A mutual glance of satisfaction.

'All I can remember...'

It shot straight back into my vision, the image of Janice, looking up at me, howling with fear.

'I remember blood on her cheek. Janice. I remember water.

175

Dark water. That's all! I don't know what I did! I remember being so scared. Terrified of that spirit message.'

Denise moaned. 'You see, it was the Devil at work. Punishment for us toying with satanism.'

'Jesus! It was a bunch of kids larking about, having fun!' said Angela. 'Stupid fun. I don't know who moved the bloody glass. Someone who didn't stop to think how scared you'd be, Karen. It wasn't me, but it had to be a joke. It was stupid, but we were kids. We're not responsible.'

'Yes; we are,' whispered Denise, beating her breast.

'Anyway, what were you doing, hanging round with Stinky Jan? You were our friend. You had us. You didn't need her. You should have told her to push off then—' For a moment it was the child, Angela, speaking. We were all back in 1966.

*

'She was supposed to come with me.' Ruthie is crying. Snivelling into her handkerchief. I wonder what she'll do with it, because Ruthie's hanky is always dead clean.

I am guilty, but there's nothing I can do about it. I was supposed to go round Ruthie's house. I don't know why I was supposed to go there, but I went to the allotments with Janice instead, like I always do on Saturdays.

'She's always with that Janice. She doesn't really like me.' Sob, sob.

'I do!' I'm not just guilty but ashamed now. It's true. Secretly, I don't like Ruthie very much, but she's Serena's friend so I really ought to love her.

'I don't know why you keep bringing Janice along,' says Barbara. 'You're our friend, not her. Serena doesn't want her tagging along all the time, do you?'

Serena smiles at me, a sad smile. 'I don't mind,' she says, and puts her arms round Ruthie, resting her lovely cheek on Ruthie's hair. 'Poor Ruth.'

'I'll go next week!' I promise. Cross my heart.

*

'We were all just children,' repeated Angela.

But none of us felt that was exoneration enough.

'Did you really like her? Janice Dexter, I mean. Or were you just trying to wind us up. Because I can't see why anyone would really want to be her friend. Smelly, flea-ridden didicoi.'

'Shut up!' said Denise. 'Don't pretend to be all horrible and callous, Angie. You know it made you sick. You cried like anything. Poor Janice, poor little girl. We should have been nice to her, like Karen...' She turned towards me as she spoke, and then dried up.

'I was her friend.' I didn't say it defiantly. It was simple truth. Janice was my friend the way Angela and Denise and Ruth and Barbara never were and never wanted to be. 'I loved her.'

'Then why did you kill her?' asked Angela.

'We don't know that!' said Denise.

'She does, though,' said Angela.

'I don't. I don't know anything. I think I did kill her. I must have done. I can see her face. But I can't remember.'

Silence.

'Well,' said Angela at last. 'It's all irrelevant now. You may have told Serena some hogwash about a car, but you never said another word. We never saw you again. You didn't come back to school, and you'd moved away by the end of term. Someone told us you were dead and it really didn't seem all that surprising.'

I breathed deeply. 'I was, nearly. Dead, I mean. Still am.'

'Not dead, just gaga.'

Not the only one, I thought. Just the only one diagnosed. Officially, medically, certifiably gaga.

'What are you going to do now?' asked Angela, slumping back. The lancing was over for the day.

'I don't know,' I said. Except that I did.

So did they. 'She'll be going to see Serena,' said Denise.

'Yeah. Of course she will. Serena, the fount of all goodness, knowledge and hope. Good luck with that.'

I cleared my throat. 'Do you have her address?'

'Oh, I don't know – I'm not sure – I think…' Denise fussed in a fluster.

'Give it to her,' said Angela.

Denise faced her in tearful defiance for a moment, then ran from the room. She returned with an address book, but she was reluctant to pass it over.

'For God's sake, Denny, give her the fucking thing,' said Angela.

Trembling, Denise held it out, open, so that I could copy down the address.

Inisfree, Braxton Lane, Thorpeshall.

'Thank you.'

178

—16—

'Eat the soup. It's lovely soup.' Denise was sobbing into it.

'It's not. It's shit. Eat your own bloody soup.' Angela opened the bottle and topped up her whisky with an unsteady hand. 'Just get off my back, for God's sake.'

'I made it especially for you.'

'I didn't ask you to. Why can't you just leave me to rot quietly, on my own?' Angela sank down on the sofa, and pulled a cushion over her eyes. 'I don't want saving.'

'I have to pay…' wailed Denise.

'You can't. I can't. Maybe she can. Karen Rothwell. Pay our debts for us. What d'you reckon? We could offer her up as a sacrifice. All our sins around her neck.'

'Don't say such horrible things! Wicked things!'

'I think we should. Tie her down and cut out her heart.'

'How can you even think of such horrible ideas?'

'Wasn't that exactly what we did?'

Denise stared at her, without replying.

'Anyway.' Angela pulled the cushion tighter over her eyes. 'In case you hadn't noticed, she's gone. Must have got tired of us. Can't think why. She's gone to Serena. Maybe she's on the run from your soup.'

Denise bit her knuckles. 'We should warn Serena.'

'You warn her.'

'I daren't. Serena's had so much awfulness to deal with, in her life. She doesn't want to live through all that again. I don't want to be the one to open things up.'

'It is open! Idiot. Creaking open wider and wider by the minute. And when Karen gets to Serena, maybe it will be blasted wide. She talked to her once, didn't she? God knows what she'll do, this time. So someone had better warn Serena there's a psycho on the way.' Angela lowered the pillow and met Denise's eyes.

'Barbara,' they both said, together.

'Yeah, sick it onto Barbara. She'll know what to do. Let the cold cow deal with it. Not me. Not me.'

'Table for one?' The waitress, on automatic pilot, looked round to see if there might possibly be a vacant table.

There was. Every table was vacant, because they'd only just unlocked the doors and the café – diner – whatever it called itself, was totally deserted. It was a minute or two after six, on a dull, grey morning. Parked up nearby, I'd watched a couple of bleary-eyed boys pulling on kitchen whites as they stumbled to the back door and then, a short while later, the waitress had been dropped off by her boyfriend. I'd given them five more minutes, to get things switched on, then I'd headed for the door.

Still, without thinking, she checked for an empty table. It might have helped if she'd laughed, on realising her folly, but she didn't. She wasn't paid enough. She came in at dawn, went through the motions, served her time and then went home to real life.

I recognised the symptoms of brain-dead work mode. She was me in the office, just younger. So I followed her solemnly to the table she selected, in the sea of empty tables, and settled myself, while she adjusted the dish of sauce sachets and handed me a huge, laminated menu.

'I'll give you a minute, right?' Her voice was sing-song as

she repeated the line she'd be spouting a hundred more times that day.

I nodded and let her retreat to the privacy of the till and whatever occupied her there. Then I resolutely applied myself to the menu. As far as I could tell, every item seemed calculated to turn my stomach. Fried bread. Black pudding. Pancakes with maple syrup, sticky pastries. My instincts screamed 'Run!' But I was going to conquer my instincts. I was determined to eat.

The young waitress sauntered over as soon as I laid the menu down. 'Ready?' She had notepad in hand.

'Orange juice, scrambled egg, coffee, toast…and jam.' I forced myself to go the whole hog.

She shrugged in reply and sloped off to the serving counter, where the boys were already busy frying. No need to call in reinforcements, she was probably telling them. Just a mini-breakfast for this one.

She couldn't know – how could she? – what a monumental milestone this was for me. I was going to eat. Voluntarily.

I'd reached the stage of eating fairly normally when I was with Malcolm or Charlie, but left alone, in my flat, I'd quietly unleash my revulsion for anything that threatened to add substance to my physical existence. Doctors and helpful acquaintances talked about anorexia nervosa, but that was just one of their much-loved labels. I have no idea what anorexic people are seeking, but I knew what I'd been seeking for thirty-five years. Nothingness. I wanted to be nothing. That's why I ate nothing.

But today I needed to be strong and sane. Not buzzing, not giddy, unable to concentrate or see straight. I needed my blood sugar levels up, my energy level static, my pulse steady.

And one meal would make no difference to my substance. It was the last meal of the condemned. Execution time. I was going to Serena, who only ever told the truth, who would never scoff or toy with me or dismiss me as the others had done. She would tell me precisely what I had said and how I'd said it, thirty-five years earlier. Not as later reported and reinterpreted by over-fertile imaginations, but my actual words, with all they conveyed and betrayed. It never occurred to me that she might not remember as accurately as I was hoping, or that a few precise words might not provide the complete explanation I needed. I was convinced that they would. Very soon, I would remember exactly what I'd done.

I hadn't really eaten since Malcolm's cereal bar, the morning before. The moment I'd made it clear I was determined to be on my way, Denise had reverted to gushing hospitality, insisting I stay to lunch. All, ultimately, to no purpose, beyond giving me further insight into their fractious relationship. Denise produced a wholesome, glutinous soup, so wholesome it had no salt or taste, and bread that had the texture of sawdust and possibly no yeast. Angela declared it all to be inedible shit, opting for a bottle of whisky instead, which Denise tried to wrestle off her. While they were struggling over it, I made my escape.

The abortive luncheon party meant it was mid-afternoon by the time I drove out of Llanyfain. I decided to head across country, instead of trusting my frayed nerves to the motorway. A labyrinth of country lanes, interspersed with city centres designed by the Devil, and I had to stop every few miles to consult the atlas, but I still managed the usual mix-ups. I realised I was passing through Aylesbury for the second time.

Or possibly the third. I was beginning to recognise a certain roundabout, even though I kept approaching it from a different direction, and it was then that I acknowledged I simply wasn't functioning any more.

I was going to have to stop. I couldn't afford to face Serena with my mind on a merry-go-round. Better to pause, take time to breathe, and clear my head. So, since the sun was already down and the light fading fast, I found another lay-by and switched off, engine and brain.

Not quite the brain. I slept but I had more dreams. More visions of a bloody Janice. More vision of Serena, pleading with me to speak. Once more a sense of drowning, as I struggled and failed to pull myself out of dark water. But this time, when I woke, stiff as before, my head was astonishingly clear and calm.

Sense ruled, as it had never ruled with me before. I'd start by getting myself physically on track. I'd have breakfast.

When it came, the orange juice helped me force down the eggs. The coffee washed down half a slice of toast. After that, I accepted defeat. It was enough for my purpose. I could feel my metabolism finding first gear. The hum in my ears ceased.

Before paying, I made my way to the Ladies. A couple of early-bird lorry drivers had rolled in, wanting the works, and the kitchen was suddenly clanking with substantial orders. A delivery boy with the day's newspapers was occupying the waitress, so I was able to creep to the toilets without anyone clocking my precise movements.

I needed time. And privacy. I'd slept two nights in the van. What I really needed was a shower, but I'd have to make do. I looked at myself in the mirror, something I usually avoided at all costs, to assess how Serena was likely to react when I turned up on her doorstep. Badly, if she were at all normal. The scrambled eggs were beginning to work but I still had that haggard, half-dazed look that came with hunger. I was skeletal and hectic with it. My freckles looked like a ferocious attack of measles. I had nothing on me to tone them down. My hair was a tangled mess. Not just sandy, it looked as if it had sand in it. It urgently needed washing, but there was no hope of that. All I could do was drag a wet comb through it, till it hung straight and limp.

I pulled open the neck of my blouse and sniffed. Bad news. There were no towels to use as a flannel, just an inefficient hot-air hand dryer. And an equally inefficient soap squirter. These places don't make allowances for mad women on a mission.

I mopped myself down as best I could with toilet paper, but there was nothing I could do about my unsavoury clothes. I had no others to change into. Damp, but slightly less pungent, I paid the still indifferent waitress and headed back to the van.

I'd used Malcolm's card again to refill the tank. The guilt was still alive and kicking, but I found it easier to stifle it, this time. He'd have the van back, soon enough, and for the rest, there was nothing I could do about it.

I took one last look at the atlas. No need for continuous reference to it from now on. I could see the route I needed and my head was clear enough to make sense of the necessary turns.

It was gone eight by the time I found myself driving up the steep scarp of the downs and over the crest into the lush woodlands and gentle slopes where Thorpeshall lay, a few miles and a whole world apart from Lyford, whose grey miasma had been visible as I climbed. Nothing grey about Thorpeshall. This was where you lived if you could afford it. There were old farms that had prospered comfortably for centuries and new detached residences with sweeping drives, swimming pools and a deal of expensive oak timbering. There was a quaint gastro-pub with picnic benches, a small flinty church in a manicured graveyard, and stables where sleek, snooty horses grazed. Even the rows of workers' cottages, with their warm brick and intricately carved little porches, looked as if they'd been acquired by bankers and turned into bijou weekend pads.

I stopped at the triangle of green in the middle of the village, and wondered how likely it was that anyone living here would allow me across their threshold. Unlikely. I was one of the great unwashed. Literally. They'd have to be a saint, even to open the door. But then that was what Serena had been, and from the way the others spoke of her, she surely still was.

I knew who I wanted her to be. Galadriel. The benign, lovely lady of light, offering me a mirror in which I could see the truth. She wouldn't be like the others. I had tried to fit them into character roles, Ruth, Barbara, Angela, Denise, but somehow they all came across as versions of Miss Havisham.

Serena wouldn't be Miss Havisham. She couldn't be.

I'd find out soon enough.

Three roads led from the green in Thorpeshall, and one of them was Braxton Lane. I followed it, slowly rolling along a leafy tunnel, peering through wide gateways and round exotic shrubberies to identify the house called Inisfree.

It wasn't one of the most extravagant ones, when I found it. An L-shaped bungalow, 1920s or 30s perhaps, sizeable enough as bungalows go, in a gracious garden backed by a stand of silver birches, but modest by Thorpeshall standards. It stood on a bend in Braxton Lane, so that with the two houses on either side, it formed a secluded little close. Their gates shared a gravel lay-by where the postman could park and deliver to three mailboxes.

I hovered in the lay-by for a moment, summoning up the courage to go in, and knew one of the neighbours was observing me as he trimmed his hedge. He might be pretending to concentrate on the laurel, but I could feel his beady eyes taking diligent note. This place screamed Neighbourhood Watch.

I turned in, before he could arrest me, and found I wasn't the only visitor at Inisfree. A decorator's van was parked in front of the garage, and a young man in overalls was up a ladder, whistling softly as he painted the woodwork under the guttering. He glanced round at the sound of my engine, raised a friendly paintbrush, then went back to work.

I parked up just inside the gate, and got out, feeling the buzz begin, the pulse start to race. Breathe. Deep. Keep calm. I started to walk along the gravel, as the front door opened.

Serena Whinn came out.

Serena Canterbury, as she now was, but she would forever be Serena Whinn to me. I had hesitated over the others, searching for a resemblance to the ten-year-olds I had known, but there was no hesitation here. She was exactly the beautiful woman the beautiful child had been destined to become. She was Galadriel in a haze of golden light.

She was carrying a tray, with a mug and biscuits, talking to the painter, smiling up at him, and he was smiling back, slipping his brush into his paint can and starting down the ladder.

'Let's hope the rain keeps off,' she was saying, as I approached, blood thundering in my ears. Never mind the utterly mundane words. Her voice was still exactly as I remembered it. Soft. Mellifluous. Maybe a little deeper, more mature, but that was all. 'Time for a coffee, surely, before you get properly started.'

At the sound of my footstep, she turned from the painter towards me, questioning, but still smiling.

I couldn't speak.

I was ten feet away when realisation dawned on her. She recognised me. I could see it. Her dark eyes widened slightly, her lips parted, but there was no appalled surprise, no disgust. She stood for a moment, then reached out, her arms wide, to gather me in.

'Karen. Oh my poor Karen.'

I flew to her, flinging myself into her embrace.

'There, there.' She smelt of roses. I daren't think what I smelt of, but she didn't flinch. She turned to the painter once more, who was down off his ladder now and wiping his hands, before picking up his mug. 'An old friend, Gary. A very dear old friend. I can leave you to it, can't I? Just call, if you need me.'

'Sure thing, Mrs Canterbury. Should be finished by lunchtime.'

'Wonderful. Karen, come.'

She led me into the house.

It was odd how I felt as if I were stepping into warm sunlight. Odd because the sky was cloudy, and there were no lights on within, or heating. In any other circumstance, I'd have thought it chilly, but I could only feel the radiance from Serena. Galadriel. Morning had broken, like the first morning, and the glow clung to her.

'Sit down, darling,' she said, guiding me to a sofa. 'You look exhausted. Let me pour you a coffee. I've just made a pot.' She brought me a mug, delicate bone china, and a glass of water for herself. With one finger, she gently stroked my cheek, her eyes brimful of compassion. 'You have come a journey, haven't you?'

She knew. She understood. I had come a journey in every sense.

'Did you know I was coming?' I managed to croak.

She smiled gently. 'Barbara told me you'd been to Carlisle. She said you were in a terrible state. That was months ago, wasn't it? Now I feel guilty. When she told me, I meant to look you up and see if I could help in any way, but she didn't have your address, and I'm afraid one thing after another got in the way and I never managed it. But here you are, and you've found me. I'm so glad.'

Her tone was so soft and sweet that I barely listened to her words. I simply floated in honey.

'So many years, Karen. More than thirty, isn't it, since we were at Marsh Green School and then you vanished from our lives, and word got round that you'd died.'

I shook my head. 'I had an accident, but I didn't die.'

Her smiled broadened into a gentle laugh. 'No. You didn't. You're a fighter, Karen. Strong will. That's good. You've come through it all.'

'Not very well.' Was that what I was? A fighter? I had flailed wildly at Miles and given him a black eye, and there had been an incident with a policeman's nose that nearly led to an assault charge. I'd probably done even worse things over the long years of insanity, so perhaps I was a mad pugilist. But I

189

wasn't the sort of warrior any general would want in his army. 'I haven't coped with anything very well, ever. I'm a mess, I know, and I always have been.'

Serena squeezed my hand. 'I can see you've been through the wars, Karen. Life must have been so very hard for you. It leaves its scars on all of us.'

'You don't look scarred! You haven't changed at all.' I gazed on her, drinking in the perpetual reassurance of her beauty, inner and outer. She had matured from child to adult, but she still had the same willowy figure, the same rippling fall of dark hair, the flawless peachy skin, the dark, dark eyes, gleaming with sympathy and understanding. And yet... I reminded myself that she had been through as much as me.

'Oh but you've suffered too, haven't you? You lost two husbands, they said, Denise, and Angela...'

There was an instant gleam in her eyes but tears didn't fall. Her throat constricted for a moment, then she nodded. 'Tony, my first love, died in a plane crash. It was a terrible time, traumatic, but good friends helped me through it and I was able to remake my life. And then Jack. Poor, poor Jack. Such a terrible waste. If only he'd let me help him. We could have faced it together. He'd always said he couldn't bear the thought of a slow decline into a painful end, but if he had only waited for the diagnosis to be confirmed.' She turned away hurriedly, raising her glass of water to her lips. She brushed a hand across her eyes, then she straightened her shoulders and turned back to me, with a brave smile. 'But the moving finger writes. There's nothing I can do to turn the clock back, is there? If only we could, but we can't, and there's nothing for it but to soldier on. So tell me, about your tragedy. It was a

190

terrible accident, I hear.'

'Oh. Well. That was a long time ago. I fell from a window. They'd put us in a flat, in a tower block, while we waited for a house to become available. Fifth floor.' In the face of Serena's bravery, how could I mention Hilary's claim that I had jumped, not fallen? I didn't know for sure that I had, so I stuck to the official line.

Serena's eyes widened in horror as I spoke, then she winced. 'How awful. For you, of course, but also for your poor parents. They must have been distraught.'

'It was miserable for my sister too. I was too ill to understand it then, but I realise now how much she felt left out. In a way, I think it damaged her as much as it damaged me.'

'Yes, it must be very hard on siblings. I remember your little sister! A sweet girl, with plaits. You used to walk to school together sometimes. And then you moved away.'

'Yes.'

'Of course I was only in Lyford for another year after you left. My father took a posting with the Hong Kong police, and I was whisked off to the Far East.'

'That must have been exciting. So exotic.'

She smiled, sadly. 'Perhaps. It was certainly a change from Lyford. But it wasn't a very happy time. We'd only been there three years when my father had a heart attack and died. Of course there was the natural grief, but one feels so alone, too, when that happens, on the wrong side of the world, among strangers. Mummy and I moved to New Zealand – she had a cousin there who was very kind to us, but it was a horribly stressful time for her. For both of us.'

'Oh, I'm sorry! How awful for you.'

'Well, we came through it. And New Zealand is a beautiful place. That was where I met Tony, my first husband. A whirlwind romance. I was very young, but utterly enchanted. He took me off to Australia. Sydney – he had a business there. It was an idyllic life for a while. A few short years.' She sighed. 'Then he was killed and I really wasn't a business woman. I did my best to hold things together for him, but I couldn't bear to see his achievements fall apart around me, on my watch, so I sold up. And then my mother passed away too, and I decided it was time to come home. Start afresh once more. Fate was kind. Kinder than anyone could deserve, because I met Jack. He was a professor at Oxford and we were blissfully happy. If it hadn't been for that mistaken diagnosis…'

She turned away again, hurriedly, and after giving a little shake, she concentrated on straightening a picture. It was an oil painting, genuine, not a print, almost abstract, but I could recognise silver birches. The birches at the bottom of her garden.

'That's a lovely picture,' I said, lamely. 'Did you paint it?'

'This? No. I was always hopeless at art, don't you remember?'

I shook my head. I couldn't remember Serena being hopeless at anything.

'Well.' She laughed. 'Not hopeless, maybe, but nothing like you. You were the artist in the class. No, this is a Daniel Pettifer. I'm so fortunate, I know. A group of us were trying to set up art sessions for some prisoners – as a sort of therapy, part of their rehabilitation – and we were lucky enough to persuade him to come and give a demonstration. I offered to put him up overnight and he painted this while he was here. Isn't it lovely? He insisted on giving it to me as rent, which is outrageous, but

I liked it so much, I couldn't bring myself to refuse. I hate to think what it's worth.'

'It is a beautiful picture.'

'Silver birches and beech trees on the downs. I've always loved them. An image of innocent youth, I suppose. I remember all those Sunday walks along the downs, after church. So, after Jack died, I came back here. A homing instinct, maybe. We seek our roots for comfort. It must be a desire to return to the cradle.' She gave an embarrassed laugh. 'I know, I know. If I wanted to go home, I should have bought a place in Lyford, shouldn't I? I did look, but I just couldn't face it. Does that make me an awful person?'

'No, not at all. If you had the choice of Lyford or Thorpeshall, who would choose Lyford? This must be a lovely place to live.'

'It is. If you're up early, you see deer, sometimes. And my neighbours are sweet. So, you, Karen. Where do you live now?'

'Oh...' In Yorkshire, I could have said. Or in a garden flat with rotting windows. Or in a cavern of books, and the fantasy lands and times they contain. 'I don't really live anywhere. I mean, I don't think I really live.'

'Then we must put that right.'

I felt, at that moment, that if she put her mind to it, she could do it. She had been through so much, herself. She had travelled the world – the real one. She had known love, she had known grief, and stress and joy, adventure and determination. And all I had done since my accident, since the age of eleven, was flounder in a cesspit of confusion, creeping into dark corners to escape whatever was out there. But now, with Serena to hold my hand, I would rise up!

Then she put her empty glass down. Upside down. On the

tray where my mug stood.

An upturned glass, waiting for six young fingers to bring it to life.

—18—

It was only when Serena put that glass down that I remembered why I had come. It wasn't the tragedies and triumphs of her life story I'd come to hear her tell me, but the stark truth underlying my own.

I sat motionless as she returned the tray to the kitchen, staring out at the garden, the silver birches beyond. Six silver birches, tall and shimmering. And one lone rowan, tawny berries glistening. Like blood.

Serena returned. She was smiling, then she saw my face and all the pity returned. She pulled up a chair so she could sit in front of me and hold my hands.

'Tell me,' I said.

'It's Janice, isn't it? That's what's been haunting you.'

I nodded.

'Poor little Janice. I always felt so sorry for her. I don't suppose she would have had a very happy life if she'd lived. The world can be so ungenerous, and some are just marked out for misery. I'm horribly afraid all the Dexters were destined for the abyss, without a single hand to help them. I've seen it, so many times. Life is cruel to such people. But for it to end the way it did with little Janice, that's more than cruel. So young, so helpless.'

A tear rolled down Serena's cheek. I watched it through the veil of my own tears. 'What did I do, Serena? What did I tell you? I have to know. I know it was bad. I am crippled by guilt, but I don't know what about.'

'The girls said you couldn't remember anything at all. Is that right?'

'I remember bits. Flashes of this and that. The Christmas party – I remember that. That was when it all… It was all to do with that Ouija game, wasn't it?'

'Ah.' She winced slightly and took another deep breath. 'Yes, of course it was. You're quite right. It was, and I feel so guilty about it. I should never have let Barbara organise it. But we'd played it at her house, you see. Her aunt came to visit and she was into that sort of silliness, palm-reading and so on, so she had us all playing it.

'I think Mrs Fulbright disapproved, but I thought it was just a parlour game. Magic, of course. I was young enough to believe it really was magic, but still a game. Any number of daft messages came through. The spirit said he was Henry VIII and he wanted to marry Mrs Fulbright. Just daft, innocent fun and everyone was laughing. So when Barbara suggested it at our Christmas party, I never thought, for one moment, that there could be anything more sinister involved. But, oh dear God, that terrible message…'

'Who made the glass move?'

'I suppose Denise would tell us it was the Devil.'

'Yes, but somebody's finger was doing his work for him.'

She hesitated, then raised her chin and faced me. 'Truthfully, I don't know. But I've always suspected it was Barbara. It was so horribly bald, wasn't it? So direct, like Barbara can be. Don't hate her, Karen! I know, it was a ghastly thing to do, but she couldn't possibly have predicted the consequences. We were so very young. We couldn't understand.'

'What about the cat?'

'Cat?' For a second, she was taken aback.

'The first message was for Barbara and it said C A T and she got really upset. If it was her moving the glass, why would she upset herself?'

'Heavens,' said Serena softly, lost in thought. 'You know, I had completely forgotten that. You're right. Poor Barbara. She'd found a dead cat in the garden. It had been shot with an airgun or something – you know what boys are like – and she was terribly upset. I've never seen her so upset over anything. She adores cats. So... Someone else must have been moving that glass. And all these years I've been falsely suspecting my dearest friend. Oh Lord. Now I feel even worse.'

'Then who was it, if not Barbara?'

She shook her head. 'I don't know. Perhaps it really was the Devil. I'd thought... Barbara wasn't over-fond of Janice, you know. She can be – I hate to say it, but she can be very adamant in her judgement. She just didn't like Janice. She didn't like the way the poor girl hung around with you. That's why I thought the message must be her doing. Trying to break you up in a horribly clumsy way, but then Barbara has never been the most sensitive or tactful of people. If it wasn't her, I suppose, it had to have been Angela or Denise or Ruth. Unless...' Her eyes held mine for a moment, the question hanging between us.

Could I have done it? Subconsciously? Because I was torn between my old friendship for Janice and my new friendship with Serena and I wanted to break free? That was a possibility

I'd never considered till now. It seemed impossible, when I remembered my own terror at the message. But then, I had learned, in the long painful years that followed, that I could split and shift and do things utterly alien to my sane self. Perhaps I had always been mad and it wasn't the accident that had triggered it. Perhaps I had been born Dr Jekyll and Miss Hyde.

One will kill the other.

Serena shook her head in sympathy. 'Whoever, whatever, it was a horrible thing and it taught me never to have anything more to do with that sort of thing.' She smiled. 'I won't even read the horoscopes.'

Nor did I. I had no need of a horoscope to tell me the future. I just needed to know the past, now, quickly, before I split into a thousand pieces again. I snatched my hands from Serena's embrace and clenched my fists, resisting the urge to beat my head. 'What did I do to Janice? What did I tell you, Serena? It's the key, I know, and I can't find it!'

Gently, she took my hands again, pressing them into my lap. 'Perhaps, Karen, in a way, it would be better for you if you didn't remember.'

'But I can't go on like this. I have to know, once and for all. Did I tell you I saw Janice get into a car? I try and I try, but I can't picture it. If I saw it, why wouldn't I tell the police?'

She took a deep breath, scanning my face intently. 'All right, Karen. I can see that not knowing is worse for you that the truth could be, however bad. And I bear some of the guilt too. I thought I was helping, but I obviously managed things so badly for all of us, I think I only made things worse. Perhaps it's as Denise keeps telling us: confession is good for the soul, and we'll both be cleansed by having it out in the open.'

She bowed her head and pressed her hands together, fingertips to her lips.

All right, children. Hands together and eyes closed.

Thank you for the world so sweet, thank you for the food we eat, thank you for the birds that sing. Thank you God for everything. Aaaaamennn.

Grace. Give me some grace, for God's sake.

'Yes,' said Serena, finally. 'I'll tell you. You came to me, the day Janice disappeared and you said…' She took another deep breath, then started again. 'You told me that you had been walking home together.'

'Down Aspen Drive.'

'Yes. Yes, I suppose you must have done. Because then you'd gone down the lane. You remember? Sawyer's Lane? It led up to Foxton Road by the woodyard. You often went that way home. It came out quite near your street, didn't it? And Janice went with you, like she often did. I remember, you used to play in the allotments after school.'

'Yes. We did.'

'You told me…' Serena took my hands again, squeezing them, 'you told me you and she got into a dreadful argument in the lane. There was a bit of a tussle, I suppose. Children do fight. It doesn't mean anything, half the time. But maybe it did on this occasion, because you told me she ran off, up past the woodyard, and a car stopped. Janice was upset and crying, and when the car door opened she got in.

'You really don't remember?'

'No!' I didn't. But at least I had an explanation, at last, for why I'd blocked it all out. The source of all my guilt. I'd fought with my best friend and I'd scared her so much, she'd fled from me, to her death.

I covered my face with my hands. Serena said nothing, letting me take it in.

I looked up again. 'Did I say it was Nigel Knight?'

'Oh, no. No! That was all such a ghastly mistake. I don't know how it happened. You never mentioned poor Nigel. All you told me was that it was a dark car, on Foxton Road, by the woodyard. That's what I explained to Denise, but she started adding two and two and finished up making God knows what. She somehow equated a dark car and wood with Mr Knight's Morris Traveller and then— She was always rather alarmed by poor Nigel, which was sad, because he was a completely harmless soul. But not the norm, I suppose, and that's enough to frighten some people, isn't it? And then Denise...' Serena sighed, clearly chiding herself for uncharitable thoughts. 'I'm afraid Denise was always rather too enthusiastic for her own good. So keen to be helpful. Especially with adults.'

'She told tales.'

'It wasn't a very attractive trait, was it? But I suppose it spoke to her need for approbation. She needed praise. And that awful year – with poor Janice, when you wouldn't...' She pressed my hands together, leaning closer. 'I do understand, Karen. Whatever had happened, it must have been so traumatising for you. I remember how terribly distressed you were, when you told me about the car, and your quarrel with Janice. You could barely speak, even then. Once you'd got it off your chest, I think you just couldn't bring yourself to speak of it ever again, even to the police.'

'Your father.'

'Poor Daddy was very good with hardened criminals, but he had no idea how to deal with children. He didn't understand that being angry with you would only deepen your terror and make you shut down still more. These days, I'm sure the police have a better grasp of psychology, but back then, well, we were still in a society built on deference. They assumed that little girls would automatically do as they were told by policemen. They didn't understand that a child in shock simply couldn't respond. It must have been horrible for you.'

'Tell me!' That look in Mr. Whinn's eyes. So angry. So appalled…
I said nothing, acid burning in my stomach at the memory.

'I had to tell Daddy about the car, you do understand that?' It was Serena, begging me for forgiveness.

'Yes. Of course you did.'

'I didn't tell him about your row with Janice. I didn't want it to look bad for you, you see. So I just told him you'd seen her get into a car. I thought the quarrel didn't really matter, so it was something they didn't need to know. I suppose that's why I didn't tell the others, either. I knew that Denise would blurt out anything I told her, and embellish it if she could, in order to earn Brownie points. But I never imagined that she'd claim to have seen the car too. Or fix on Nigel Knight so emphatically. Such a tragedy. All I'd said was that you'd turned off Aspen Drive, down Sawyer's Lane and a dark car had been hovering by the woodyard. Meaning on Foxton Road, of course. But she mixed it all up. Nigel's father used to let him take the wheel sometimes, didn't he, on Aspen Drive? Round and round all those bulldozed side streets. That's what she must have been thinking of.'

'Yes. Of course.'

'He was a lovely man, Mr Knight, and he adored Nigel. He'd do anything for him. So sad. If only...' Serena looked down guiltily. 'I shouldn't say it, not with Daddy being in charge of the investigation, but if only the police had acted with more tact, if they'd just been gentle, instead of swooping on the Knights' house with sirens blaring and lights flashing. That must have scared Nigel almost to death. He was such a simple soul. He wouldn't understand. Of course he ran away to hide.

'And I should have spoken up and told them Denise had got it all wrong, that it couldn't have been Nigel, because it must have happened on Foxton Road. But you see how it was. She was my friend.'

'Of course.'

Serena smiled her gratitude at my understanding. 'And she wasn't really a liar, was she? At least, not a malicious fabricator, with evil intent. Just a little girl who was too keen for praise.'

'I suppose so.'

'I think, maybe, she'd talked herself into believing her own story, I couldn't come out and call my friend a liar. But it was such misguided loyalty on my part.'

'You weren't to blame! None of it was your fault, Serena. Not the message on the Ouija board, not my silence, or Denise's lie, or Angela guiding the police to Nigel's shed. Not Janice's abduction or Nigel's death. None of it.'

'Thank you, but a sense of guilt isn't an easy thing to shrug off, is it? It can be unbearable.'

'Absolutely.' How I knew it. How it had twisted my life from that day. 'I am the one who was really to blame. I was the one who quarrelled with Janice, and made her run. I

202

don't remember the quarrel, but I do know I was scared. We both were, because of that spirit message. We believed it and suddenly we were terrified of each other.'

Sawyer's Lane was a gloomy place, overhung with trees. An old farm track that lingered on long after the farm had disappeared under the growing estate. There was a carpet of bluebells under the trees in spring, but at other times of the year, there were just shadows. Still, I often took it as my route home, because the alternative, along Capstone Way, meant passing Tommy Renton's house, and he delighted at driving his go-kart straight at passing girls.

Janice and I had skipped down Sawyer's Lane countless times, together and unafraid, on our way to my house or the allotments. But that last January – I don't imagine there was any skipping. Maybe it had been the sinister gloom of the naked trees that had re-awakened our terrified suspicions, despite our determined promises to trust each other. Somewhere along that lane, it had all come bubbling up to the surface, with such force that Janice had fled.

I could picture her running, down that last kink in the lane that ran beside the high fence of the timber yard, out to the bright light of Foxton Road. The dark nose of a car edging into view, stopping, a sinister shape within leaning across to push the passenger door open. Janice, peering back at me in tearful panic and then scrambling into the car.

The image was vivid. So vivid I could feel my chest rising and falling with a child's confused emotions. And yet, I couldn't honestly remember it. There were times, when I was seriously mad, when I couldn't tell the difference between reality and whatever fantasy I'd conjured up. But I wasn't seriously mad now. I wasn't even light-headed with hunger. And I knew the difference.

'It's strange that I don't remember. Still, even now, I can't really remember the car, any car. All I get are little flashes. Instead of a car, what I actually see…' I screwed my eyes shut, wishing I couldn't see it. 'All I see is Janice, looking up at me. Blood on her face. In dark water. Why? Why do I remember that?'

As I spoke, I could feel Serena's gentle grip on my hands loosen and pull back. I opened my eyes and saw her face, white with shock. She pushed her chair back, stood up, walked to the window, a hand at her throat.

'What is it?'

She shook her head, trying to get a grip.

I stood up. 'Tell me. Please.'

She took three deep breaths, then turned back to me. 'Karen…'

'Tell me! There's something more, isn't there? Something you haven't told me. Something worse.'

'I…' She bit her lip, then laid her hands on my shoulders, sitting me back down on the sofa, before she resumed her own seat, carefully stroking out the folds in her skirt. 'I promised I'd tell you all, Karen, so I will. Not what I know – honestly, I don't know, but I've always wondered. I've suspected. I've feared. That's all. Please understand, I am not swearing this is the truth, but…

'When you came to me, that day, after school, after walking home with Janice… You came running to me. You were in a terrible state, sobbing and – and you had blood on you. On your hands. You were gabbling like a mad thing. If you'd come into the house, if my mother had spoken to you... Oh, why didn't I call her? But you found me in the garden and we sat and talked there, and I thought – oh dear God, I genuinely thought I was protecting you.

'You told me you and Janice had fought, in Sawyer's Lane. Really fought. You'd hurt each other. You said she'd hurt you and then you'd badly hurt her. You were scared, acting so strangely. Hyperventilating, I suppose it was. I didn't understand hysteria. I just knew you were upset. Then, when I asked you what happened next, you told me this story about the car.'

She stared at her hands. 'I had a suspicion, even then, that you were making it up. It seemed so improbable, didn't it? A car just happening to stop, at that moment, and on Foxton Road, of all places. It's such a busy road. Someone would have seen. And it was just after Mr. Cutler had given us that talk, about being wary of strangers and not getting into cars and so on. We'd been talking about it in the playground – about how none of us would ever do it. And then, within hours, there you were, claiming you had seen Janice get into a car...' She stopped.

'What?'

'You told me it was Black Jack Coke in the car.'

'Oh.'

'We'd been talking about him. How we would never get into a car because it was bound to be Black Jack, the bogeyman who lived in drains and under bridges and so on. We all knew he was just a fictional monster, so when you said it was him, I thought – well, you can imagine what I thought. I didn't want to believe it. I told my father about you seeing the car, but I didn't mention Black Jack. And then, when was it, a few days later? When they found her. It was where they found her, you see, Karen... I understood why you'd mentioned Black Jack. She was in that culvert, you see. The stream that ran through the woods by Sawyer's Lane – it disappeared into a culvert under Foxton Road and the railway, do you remember? And that's where they found her, just inside.'

It was as if an army of panicking soldiers in my head, who had been careering around in screaming chaos, not knowing which enemy to attack, had suddenly started to align themselves into order, and were marching, inexorably, towards a black chasm. I couldn't move. I had never been able to remember the alleged car, because it had all been a lie, but I could remember that culvert. I could see it, opening up to swallow me. I could feel water flowing round my feet. I could see blood in that water.

'It was so close, you see, to where you admitted you'd fought with her. I thought – I really didn't want it to be true, but I thought – think – you must have killed her, Karen. I'm sure it was an accident. You fought, just as you said, and somehow, in the struggle, she died, and you were terrified, so you hid her body.'

'I don't know. I think – I think I must have done. But...' I was biting my fingers again. 'She was raped. Wasn't that what they said? Why would they say that, if I killed her?'

Serena sighed. 'I don't think she was raped, dear. I think it was just an assumption that she'd been sexually molested. You see, when she was found, her panties were missing. And that was part of the Black Jack myth, wasn't it? When we'd talked about him, we'd concluded that the terrible thing he did was steal people's panties. I suppose you must have been trying to make people think it was Black Jack.'

'Oh God. Oh my God.'

'Karen, honestly, all this is just supposition – based on half-forgotten stories and bad dreams. I don't know what really happened. I have never mentioned those suspicions to anyone, I promise you. I couldn't do that to you. I'd never have mentioned them now, if you hadn't remembered seeing blood on Janice's face and water. I can see how much it's torturing you. Perhaps it's time for the truth to come out. Was I right to tell you? I think maybe I shouldn't have said anything. You've been ill, and you were always so sensitive, weren't you, Karen? I should have kept quiet.'

'No. I have to know.'

'I have another confession.' She looked up at the ceiling this time. 'When you moved away, and we never heard from you, I thought... I was the one who said you were dead. Because I thought you must be. You see, I was nursing this terrible secret, imagining what you were going through. I knew how guilty you must be feeling. You'd killed your best friend. It must have been too awful to bear, so I thought you must have killed yourself. It's what I'd have done, what I would do, I think, if I'd killed my best friend.

'I know what suicidal impulses are like. When Tony died, I blamed myself so much for letting him fly when we knew a storm was brewing. He was such a daredevil, but still I should have tried harder. When they told me he'd crashed, I nearly – well... It's just that I understand the impulse to do away with yourself. I thought you'd have done it. You were so hurt, so broken up. But you were stronger than that. You dealt with it in other ways. You got over it. And now I've opened it all up again. Can you forgive me?'

'Forgive you? Forgive you! I am the one I can't forgive. I should be dead. I should have died years ago. You're right. You understood perfectly and you're right, I did try to kill myself. My sister is forever claiming that that's what I was doing when I fell out of the window. She was there, in the room with me.'

*

'Karrie?' I can hear Hilary's voice, but it's not real. I can see her, the expression on her face, crumpled with fear, but she's not real. It's like I'm looking at her through water. Or as if she's a picture, not a person. She's not real, nothing is real, except this thing inside me. This pain and fear, this big black thing that's trying to eat me up and I can't escape.

I turn away, look out through the open window instead, over a grey city that I don't know, under a grey sky that is coming down to smother me, suck the air out of me, and I can feel the invisible ropes winding round me, tightening, strangling me with grief and a turmoil of guilt.

'Karen! Mummy, Mummy, come here, please. Karen's being silly!'

There's such urgency in my sister's sobs, but it's all a part of the bad dream. I just want to be out of it. Not to have to do any of it any more – eating, breathing, waking, remembering. No more remembering.

I'm kneeling on the windowsill, the catch biting into my knee, but the pain isn't real either. It's left behind, as I topple forward, and there's nothing but the whistling wind and, far behind me, my sister's hysterical screams.

*

'She watched me do it. Jump. And no one would believe her.

No wonder she hates me.'

'Poor Hilary.' Serena's voice was almost a whisper. 'She must have been so confused.'

'Yes. And angry, not being believed. By her own parents. Because they did believe her, really. They just couldn't bring themselves to admit it. They spent the rest of their lives watching me.'

'But you didn't die.'

'No. Humpty Dumpty was put together again. It took, I can't remember, fifteen operations, I think. To put the body together again. Not the head. The mind. They've never managed to put that right. That's still in a million pieces.'

'And you jumped from a window. Oh God. That would scare me. Heights. I don't think I could ever do that.' She was staring into nothing again. 'Awful how we think these things through, isn't it? How to end it all. Knowing that we shouldn't even be thinking about it.'

'You don't!'

'Oh I do. Or I have. Even since I've been here in Thorpeshall. When Jack died, I felt such guilt that I hadn't seen it coming. He was such a decisive person. I did think, maybe, one day, if the cancer proved truly unbearable, he'd go through with it, just as he'd said he would and I'd dissuade him for as long as I could, but I'd be with him. I'd nurse him, care for him, do whatever he needed. But he didn't wait. I knew him and I should have known he wouldn't wait. My poor Jack. Sitting here, alone, afterwards, trying to figure out how I could shoulder that guilt and yet carry on, starting a new life – there were nights when I thought, why should I carry on? Why not follow him? There's a canal at the bottom of the downs. A lock, deep water. Fill my pockets with stones and just sink into darkness.'

Her gaze, which had been distant, came back to me and she looked at me with horror. 'What am I doing? I don't know why I'm telling you any of this. I shouldn't even be thinking it, let alone talking about it. I'm sorry, Karen. Forgive me. Please.'

She was desperate. A part of me wanted to reach out and comfort her, or offer some sort of reassurance, however lame, but I couldn't. I couldn't move or speak or think, except to visualise, so vividly now, that dark, dirty culvert, deep in the woods by Sawyer's Lane, where I had hidden my friend.

The friend I had murdered. There was the truth I'd been hiding from for thirty-five years. No hiding now. It stared me in the face, the finger of accusation boring into me. *Murderer.*

I stood up. Did Serena flinch? All the time that she had been offering me sympathy and consolation, she must have been afraid too. Surely. She knew what I was capable of and she was alone with me. I could rescue her from that fear, at least.

'I've got to go,' I said. My tongue felt as if it had swollen up to fill my whole mouth. I stumbled towards the door.

'No, Karen, no you can't go like this. Forget everything I said, about suicide, about the lock. Please, let me help you. You're in shock. Wait. I should never have said anything. You'd wiped it out. That's how I should have let it stay.'

All I could say was, 'I've got to go.'

I made it out of the front door, God knows how. I trudged, like swimming through treacle, across a vast desert of gravel to the van, willing my limbs to move.

'All right?' Gary, the painter, moving his ladder, paused to look after me. I must have been floundering like a drunkard.

'All right,' I managed, and fell into the driver's seat. He

210

didn't want to know me. I was a murderer. Go back to your painting, boy, or you don't know what I might do.

—19—

Somehow I turned the van and drove out of Serena's gate, back through Thorpeshall, back the way I'd come. I didn't have a destination in mind, but the instinct to go back was overwhelming. Back and back and back.

Clearer and clearer, I could see Janice's bloody face staring up at me, pleading.

I drove down the steep scarp slope of the downs, beeches arching over me like judges gathering to condemn me, their leaves ashiver with disgust and rejection. Banks of chalk, bone white, hemmed me in, channelling me down and down and down. I swerved. Did I do it deliberately? The van caught the bank and bucked, slewing across the road. But I didn't crash. I pulled the wheel round, and went on.

Down. How much deeper could I go?

The road levelled at last, running out across rolling fields, to the faint blue of tamer hills, the dark green of woods, the distant smoggy haze of Lyford. I passed through another village without noticing, until speed bumps round a school entrance woke me to the fact that I was among people. People who didn't know I was a murderer.

I drove on, weaving along the snaking road, unaware of any other traffic till I reached the bridge. A cramped humpback bridge that would only allow one vehicle at a time. I'd come this way – I remembered the lurch of the van as it had tipped over the brow of the bridge. There was more traffic around now. A small convoy of three cars were coming the other way and I had to hover, waiting for them to pass, before I could cross.

But having stopped, the adrenalin of flight that had been driving me drained out. I couldn't go on. I couldn't cross that canal bridge. I couldn't do anything anymore, except sit there and stare at the bridge. A car behind me hooted and, when I did nothing, it edged past, the driver mouthing angrily at me.

I was in the way. I didn't mean to be. I shouldn't be in anyone's way. I put the car in reverse and edged back onto a wide section of verge. People could pass now and give me no heed. I could be invisible.

The canal bridge rose up before me like a cobra.

Canal, Serena had said. That was where she would go, to end it all.

I got out of the car. A towpath followed the canal, tangled with brambles and nettles. Was there a lock, as she had said?

I walked up to the brow of the bridge. No traffic for the moment, queuing up to edge its way across. Just me. From the brow, I could look up the canal, past rushes and a moorhen swimming, to lock gates, creaking and blackened. They oozed water, and ferns spouted from their rotting joints. The heavy iron gears and shafts were rusting. I could sense, beyond those gates, the weight of black, slimy water. The deep, dark water of my drowning dreams. That was where I belonged. Smothered in slime.

Fill my pockets with stones and just jump in, sinking into darkness.

I pictured myself on the brink of the sheer, narrow chasm, ready to step in and disappear forever. I leaned forward, over the parapet of the bridge, as if practising the move, and looked down.

The green water below barely moved. Its surface was smooth as glass, mirroring the bridge. A perfect mirror image of reality, I saw myself staring up at me, black against a white sky, leaning forward, straining to touch my other self. Then the reeds along the bank began to rustle and bend. A gust of breeze swept along the canal and the green glass broke into a thousand ripples, a jumbled confusion of light and dark. I was leaning over a parapet, looking down into crazed water, and nothing was clear any more.

Just a moment earlier, I'd known everything. I'd known what I'd done, and what I was going to do. Soon, it would all be finished. But now, in a flash, I knew nothing. It was all wrong.

What it was that was wrong, I didn't know, but it had something to do with Sawyer's Lane. There'd been a bridge in Sawyer's Lane. Not an arch of stone like this bridge. This bridge was…where?

For a second, I couldn't think where I was or how I'd come to be there. I thought I was in Sawyer's Lane, and it wasn't right. There was something missing from the picture. It wasn't as Serena had said – except that it must have been, because she'd watched it, hadn't she?

No. I surfaced enough to remember that Serena hadn't been there. She hadn't told me what she'd seen, only what she was guessing had happened. A wise and intelligent guess, based on my hysterical guilt, my garbled lies, the blood on my hands, but she hadn't got it quite right. Something in the story wasn't right. I just couldn't... I couldn't quite grasp—

A lorry came over the bridge, miraculously fitting itself between the parapets, tooting me to squeeze clear. I did, as the great beast rolled past, millimetres away, drawing air deep into my lungs. Oxygen and exhaust fumes rushed to my head. How long had I been holding my breath before the lorry came? It passed, leaving me dizzy.

My head spun. Like a roulette wheel, spinning slower and slower, till it stopped and at last the ball stopped careering round and dropped into its slot. The ball said Janice, and the slot said Sawyer's Lane. That's where I needed to go. To see it once more, and figure out for myself what was missing.

I didn't need the atlas to work out the direction of Lyford. I'd seen it in the distance. I just followed my nose. The first road signs I passed merely directed me to the next village or two, but when I came to a main road, signs in large letters pointed to Lyford. I came to a roaring ring road, which saved me tackling the town centre and whirled me quickly round to the north side of the town.

I recognised the roundabout I had circled when I'd left the motorway on my first visit. I took the turn that led me to Foxton Road. No confusion now. The twists and turns, the old and new estates, were all familiar from my visit in early spring, although the area had transmuted from hard grey to technicolour, with the trees in full weary leaf and gardens in belligerent bloom. I turned into Linden Crescent, as I had before, and parked up, out of the way.

It was only now, back at my old address, that I remembered how confused I'd been in the spring, by the overwhelming changes, the plethora of new houses, new roads, the greedy expansion of the estate. If entire farms and fields had been swallowed up, what chance was there that Sawyer's Lane would still be there? It had been a relic of an older world even in 1966.

Only one way to find out. I got out and walked up to Foxton Road. I turned right. There was a bend in the road, and just around it should have been the timber yard, with the wood and the lane just beyond it.

No timber yard. No whine of saws behind high wooden fences. A block of flats stood there instead, in a pool of neatly clipped shrubs. And beyond, where the corner of ancient woodland should have been, stretched new houses. The old world had been rubbed out.

Not quite. Over the roofs of the houses I could see trees. Substantial old trees that must butt on to their back gardens, meaning that a stub of the woods remained. And there, between the flats and the first house, was Sawyer's Lane. Not as I remembered it, a dark, muddy track, overhung with branches, but a neatly paved lane, with a decorative street lamp, straight out of Narnia. It was wide enough for two mothers with pushchairs to walk abreast – they emerged, chatting, as I watched.

I turned up the lane, determined to try and track down my past, but feeling hope dribble away. How was this place going to jog that final clinching memory? This ruthlessly gentrified pathway was nothing like the lane I'd known. I passed the houses, and gazed into the remnant of the wood that stood behind them. A dozen trees perhaps, carefully lopped of weakened branches and tidied of unseemly undergrowth, where there had once been a tangled and impenetrable forest. It made me think of a poodle, clipped and beribboned, when I'd been expecting a wolf. Not even a chihuahua on the right side of the path, when the old trees that had once sheltered swathes of bluebells had been cleared away entirely, to make way for open, neatly mown grass – a miniscule park for pensioners, with a couple of benches, fronting a stretch of the brook that had been cleansed of junk and planted with irises to give an illusion of rural tranquillity in the midst of urban sprawl.

All this remodelling and neatening had been done a long time ago. Probably so long ago that no one else could remember the way it used to be – the old, truly rural Sawyer's Lane and the deep, dark wood. A pale, bare track had been worn across the level grass, where locals must have been cutting the corner for years. The benches were weathered and greying. An old man was seated on one of them, reading a newspaper. I sat on the other one, wondering what to do next. I was still nursing a surging sense of expectation, but I had no idea how to fulfil it. Go on? Go back? There was nothing here that I could relate to.

It was only when I stood up that I noticed the plaque on the bench. The ground shifted under me.

This bench, donated by Cpl Kenneth Dexter, is dedicated to the memory of his beloved sister Janice, 1955 – 1966.

'You touch my sister, I'll punch you in the face, I'm warning you.'

I stepped back, stung.

How could I have thought there was nothing here? There was everything here. I returned to the paved path, which crossed the brook on a quaint footbridge.

There had been a bridge on Sawyer's Lane. Nothing like this new pseudo-Japanese one, which had steps and decorative railings. The old had iron poles as rails and rotting planks, gaps between them big enough to catch high heels – not that our mothers ever came this way much. They kept to the neat hard pavements of the estate streets. Only children opted for the muddy gloom and fantastic possibilities of Sawyer's Lane.

I stepped up onto the bridge, no danger of my heels catching, and I paused to look down.

At a pipe.

I did a double take.

Everything else had changed, everything had been neatened and paved and trimmed and smoothed, but there it was still, the old pipe that I had forgotten until this moment. I suppose it was simply too solid or too important to be tidied away.

It was a huge thing of cast iron, with massive riveted joints, crossing the brook in the shadow of the footbridge. What was it? I have no idea. A sewer, maybe. Wafting all the shit of Marsh Green through this pleasant little park. It had been painted a pale gloss green, but the paint was worn off in places and the pitted iron showed through.

It had been rusty brown, back then.

I looked down at the brook flowing beneath it. In among the trees, the banks rose, gathering the stream into a dark channel that poured, at last, into the maw of a low, black culvert.

Which hadn't changed at all. Except that the water was cleaner. It hadn't been clean on January 12th 1966. It had been dark and muddy, foam and filth piling up at the lip of the culvert, and threads of crimson in the water.

Threads of crimson blood.

—20—

Cross my heart and hope to die, I don't want to kill Janice. And I'm sure she doesn't want to kill me. Almost sure. I think.

Even so, I hesitate at the school gates. I always wait for her, or she waits for me, and we walk home together, but today I'm there first, and I think 'Shall I just go on? Maybe she's gone without me. There's no point waiting, if she has. I could say I thought she'd already gone.'

But it's too late to claim that because there she is, coming through the gates. We look at each other, both of us hesitating, uncertain. Then she smiles. Or maybe I smile and she smiles in return. We walk on together, because we always do.

Every so often there are tiny snowflakes, drifting out of the grey sky and it's whistling cold, the sort that eats through your head. I have a knitted bonnet that buttons under my chin and mittens attached to the sleeves of my duffle coat on elastic, so I can't lose them, but Janice just has a coat that used to be a lady's jacket and it's got no buttons and the lining's torn out. I can see her ears turning blue. We run a bit to keep warm, then we stop at the Parade, and peer in the window of the general store, to see who's buying marbles or sherbet flying saucers or threepenny chocolate bars. We don't go in. I haven't any pocket money left, and Janice never has any, except when Kenneth gives her some he's taken off someone else. But he's not around today.

So we walk on, dawdling, and by the time we're passing down Aspen Drive, among the empty prefab stands, we've almost forgotten that one of us is going to kill the other.

'Shall we go to the 'lotments?'

'Yeah!' Where better on such a cold, gloomy day? Mr Colley, one of the whiskery old men on the allotments, has a fire in a brazier to keep himself warm and sometimes he roasts chestnuts on it. If you get him in the right mood, and don't run wild among his leeks and Brussels, he'll give you some, throwing them and laughing as you catch them and squeal because they're so hot. Then you sit on the bank by his compost heap and squeal some more as you pull the scorched shells off.

So we'll go to the allotments.

Then I see her.

I'm dancing round as we walk, and looking back I see Serena Whinn, coming down from the Parade. I know it's Serena, because she has a hat, not a bonnet, and a proper coat, not like the duffle coats and gaberdines most of us wear. She never looks cold. Or hot. Or heavy. She walks like there's air under her feet. I can't take my eyes off her, she's so beautiful.

She'll be turning off soon to the footpath that leads to Rowlands Avenue. But no, she's stopped. She's looking along Aspen Drive, to where Janice and I are mucking around, and she waves.

I wave back. Suddenly, everything is complicated.

Janice is my friend, my best friend. She always has been. But Serena is…Serena. To be Serena's friend is to be lifted up on high. To walk on clouds.

I can be both, can't I? Serena's friend and Janice's? But somehow it never really works. I don't understand why. Serena is always very nice to Janice. She smiles at her, and never calls her sing-song names like Angela does. She never pushes her out of the way like Barbara or tells on her like Denise. She doesn't sulk if I talk to Janice, the way Ruth does.

But Janice is always very quiet when Serena is around. I suppose it's because she knows she doesn't belong, because Serena hasn't chosen her. Janice can never even dream of being one of the golden girls, so she shrinks whenever Serena comes near.

That's what Serena is doing now. Not just waving. She's running down Aspen Drive to join us. To join me. She's smiling.

'Hello.'

'Hello.' I can feel my cheeks blushing red with bashfulness. I've played with Serena and the others, visited Serena's house, with the others, shared Serena's secrets with the others, but I've never been alone with her before. She's never picked me out for sole attention before, to the exclusion of the others, even Barbara. It's just me and Serena.

And Janice.

For a brief while, thinking of hot chestnuts and silly things, I had forgotten the Ouija game, but now it's back with its horrible, scary message for Janice and me. One will kill the other.

'I was worried about you,' says Serena, smiling at me. It's a beautiful smile, but I see it growing ever so slightly wary as it moves to Janice.

Janice shrinks.

'Are you going home?' asks Serena. 'Can I come with you?'

My heart patters. Serena wants to come home with me. With me! My brain begins to race, thinking what toys I can bring out, what games we can play, if she comes to my house. It's not a posh house, like hers. Mummy's probably got knickers on the clothes horse by the living room fire and if Daddy's home, he might be in his vest. Will she mind?

'We're going to the allotments,' says Janice.

I had forgotten. What can I do? Which one do I choose?

But Serena must understand, because she doesn't mind. 'Can I come too?'

'Oh yes!' I'm overwhelmed by the relief and the honour. Of course Serena can come.

Janice scuffs the kerb with her broken sandal and looks down, no longer happy. But I can't say no to Serena, can I? I'd never want to say no to her.

'Did you have a nice Christmas?' asks Serena, as we walk on.

'Oh yes!' It's hard not to give a positive answer to Serena. But it isn't true, and I shouldn't lie to her. 'No, not really.'

'Did you play any games?'

No, we didn't play any games. I was too busy making things miserable for everyone else. The last game I played was with the Ouija board, before Christmas. I can only shake my head. The grip of remembered fear has got my tongue.

Janice doesn't speak.

'My cousins came, and Barbara, and Annette next door, and we played Murder in the Dark,' says Serena. 'I didn't like it very much. It was scary, not knowing who the murderer was.'

We are turning into Sawyer's Lane. It's narrow here, at this end, between two tall wire fences, so we can't all walk together. There's only room for two, side by side. I walk with Serena. It's because she's talking to me, so I can't hang back.

I can hear Janice coming behind us. I can hear her breathing. She's got a cold and she breathes through her mouth. It's creepy when you can hear someone breathing, but you can't see them. I keep looking over my shoulder at her, and she's looking at me, but neither of us is smiling any more.

The lane opens out as we reach the trees. Janice comes forward to walk beside me. I am between the two of them.

'Barbara says there's a haunted cottage in this wood,' says Serena, taking my hand, with a little rush of nervousness. 'Is it true? Have you ever seen ghosts here? It is quite scary, isn't it?'

I'd never thought of ghosts before, but she's right. There used to be a building just on the edge of the wood. One corner of crumbling brick still stands. I think it was too small to be a proper house, but it would do for a witch. All the children who play round here call it the witch's cottage. You can see big lumps of stone and brick and concrete, lining the edge of the path and you can see they were once bits of it, but it was knocked down so the witch can't live there any more. Maybe her ghost is angry that her house was knocked down. I hadn't thought of that. An angry ghost is worse than an ordinary ghost. She could be lurking around, among the trees, watching us.

The wood is suddenly really scary. Sometimes I think it's full of fairies and squirrels and things like that, but today it's full of monsters. The trees are naked, tall dark pillars looming up around us. Brambles wave and reach out like claws and the dead undergrowth rattles and crackles. Things move, just out of sight. The winter sky is darkening fast, almost night, and the tiny flakes of snow are getting bigger, falling faster, so everything shifts. The shadows under the trees are gloomy and threatening.

'This is where murderers might be,' says Serena.

She says it and then I feel the tremble in her fingers, the little flinch of fear, as if she said it first as a joke and then realised it might be true.

Janice reaches out for my other hand and I snatch it away. I can't help myself. I keep remembering that spirit message.

There's all the world of meaning in me snatching my hand away. Janice sniffs, her body jerking like with hiccups, but it's not a hiccup, it's a sob. Then she runs forward. She's clumsy, because her shoes are broken, but she runs to put a space between us, so that she can pretend not to care.

We walk after her, down the glooming track. Hanging back.

'Do you remember the spirit message?' asks Serena.

'Yes!'

'It's horrible, isn't it? Not knowing.'

I can barely breathe.

'Mr Dexter is in prison,' whispers Serena. 'He's done a murder. Daddy told me. And one of his sons, only the police couldn't catch him. They murdered a girl. So I expect they'll have told Janice how to do it.'

I shudder and Serena squeezes my arm to comfort me.

How do you do a murder? How would Janice do it? Maybe one of her brothers has got a gun and she might creep up when I'm not looking and shoot me. That's what happens on telly. People get shot. I don't know how else to kill.

Ahead of us, Janice has stopped running. She's reached the bridge and she turns to wait for us, swinging on one of the rail posts until we're nearly there. The best way to make friends again is always to pretend there wasn't a quarrel.

I don't know how much she's pretending.

'Come on,' she says, and she does what we've always done. What we do. What all children who live at this end of the estate do, because it's the law among children. She starts to walk across the iron pipe, holding the rail of the bridge for support. Only adults would think of crossing the brook on the bridge.

Serena doesn't live this end of the estate. She doesn't understand about walking on the pipe. She steps into the bridge.

I hesitate, my hand slipping from hers. Which way do I go? Then I do as tradition dictates. I step onto the pipe.

I hear an intake of breath from Serena, walking to my

left, just above me, her hand brushing mine on the same rail. She leans over and whispers 'Don't go near her, Karen, please. I'm scared.'

And I'm scared too, because suddenly I feel I've done the wrong thing. I have taken the wrong path. But I can't go back. The pipe beneath my feet is wet and slippery. The coldness of it is eating through my shoes and ahead of me is Janice.

She's halfway across, going slowly, looking down as she slithers, her broken shoe dragging on the big riveted joint in the pipe. Snow falls between us, like smoke.

'I'm scared,' repeats Serena, no longer whispering. 'Oh, Karen.' There's panic in her voice.

It nooses Janice too, that panic. She stops, clinging to the bridge rail, and looks back, over her shoulder, as I edge towards her. I can see the fear in her eyes, her chest beginning to convulse.

'It said one of you will kill the other one.' Serena is almost crying, her voice shaking with panic. 'Don't let her kill you, Karen!'

Janice tries to turn, so she can face me, so that I can't creep up on her. Or is she turning to kill me? I begin to whimper. Janice is stumbling and fumbling in her fear, her shoe catching, and suddenly she's slipping, feet slithering from the pipe, her numb fingers scrabbling to grip the rail but her own half-starved weight defeats her and she's gone, down into the freezing brook.

She lands sprawling on stone and garbage, the icy water flowing around her, splattering her as she moans and tries to shuffle up, onto her knees. The grey wet snow, as it falls, makes the water look black. Like it's really deep and she's floating on it. She's hurting, I can see. Tears and snot are pouring down her face and she must have caught on something because there's blood, trickling down her cheek. She opens her mouth and she should be crying, wailing with the shock and pain, but terror stoppers the screams as she looks up at me.

She is looking up at me, blood trickling down her face, wordlessly pleading for help or for mercy.

I am frozen on the pipe. I can't breathe, I can't move. I see Serena's hands on the railings, gripping so hard the knuckles are like white bones poking through.

Then she lets go. She's stepping back, running from the bridge, and I am left staring down at Janice. She is beginning to gulp big breaths, beginning to recover from the shock, the pain and the fear, although the tears still flow freely.

It's silly, being afraid. Her being afraid of me and me of her, because we're friends. It's silly. I'm beginning to unfreeze too. I take a sideways step, gingerly, along the icy pipe. If Janice has already slipped from it, I might too, so I'm carefully clinging to the bridge rails.

Another step. Janice is beginning to pick herself up now, pushing herself onto her hands and knees. If I can get off the pipe, I can pull her up the steep, muddy bank of the brook.

But then Serena is back. I thought she'd run off but she's come back to the bridge. 'Karen!'

She's holding something. I don't understand. It takes me an age, staring at it between her woollen gloves, to work out it's a lump of old concrete. One of the bits along the path.

It's smooth on one side, jagged on the others, with bits of stone sticking out, and a bit of rusty wire. I just stare, trying to make sense of it and of the look of complete panic in Serena's eyes.

'Kill her, Karen, or she'll kill you!'

I gape, not understanding. Serena is standing there, holding out this lump, and she's crying. She's terrified. We all are. I am, on the pipe. Janice is, down in the stream. Three girls, in a dark wood, crying and terrified.

Janice has stopped scrabbling in the water, too frozen with fear to move any more. Serena has heaved the block onto the rails, pushing it at me, too heavy for her to keep holding it out.

'I don't want her to kill you!' she sobs.

My heart thumps.

And then I shake my head. I look down at Janice, my friend, and I can see that little gleam of hope in her eyes. She manages a sniff, and then begins to brace herself on one arm in order to push herself up.

'Take it!' pleads Serena, almost screaming. 'Drop it!'

But I won't. What I'll do is go down and help Janice.

Serena leans over the railings, she holds the block right out.

And she lets go.

She's holding it, and then she's not holding it.

There's a…

It's not a scream. Just a gurgle, and a crunch and…

My head is swimming. I am going to fall into the water, beside Janice. But hands are gripping me, pulling me back. I hear Serena sobbing. 'I'm scared. You scared me.'

I'm hitting her off me as my vision begins to clear. I look down and then I look away, sick and faint. There's blood in the water. And stuff. I crouch on the pipe, my arms locked round the bottom rail of the bridge, and I look up at Serena.

Tears are flowing down her face. The terror is still there, but it's changing. It's like… I don't know what it's like. She's staring down at the water and the fear in her eyes becomes sort of guilty, but there's not just fear, there's this other thing. She keeps looking. Curious.

Then she looks back at me, where I'm crouching and clinging, and her lip quivers.

'You made me do it.'

I manage another shake of my head. Maybe I'm just trying to turn away from her gaze.

'The spirit said one of you would do it. It said so, didn't it? Everyone knows. She was going to kill you, Karen. I couldn't let her do that. I tried to help you, but you wouldn't do it, so I had to.'

I am split. Ripped in two. One half of me is thinking about Janice, who is a mangled mess in the water and she's my friend and I want to cry and I want her back. And the other half is thinking that Serena is disappointed in me. I've let her down, and made her do something terrible. The most terrible thing in the world.

Serena wipes her eyes and then she smiles, full of pity and reassurance.

'I had to do it, you see. Or she'd have killed you.'

I remember the fear as Janice turned on the pipe. Serena saved me.

Then I look down again, at the horror in the stream, and

I can only sob and choke.

Out of the corner of my eye, I catch Serena stamping her foot. She doesn't sound sympathetic any more. 'Everyone will think it was you. Because of the spirit message. They'll know it's come true and you killed her.'

'I didn't!'

'Yes, but you did, sort of. You should have. It's just that I had to do it for you. To save you.'

She's gone, off the bridge again, leaving me, walking away. Leaving me with the thing in the water. I don't know if it's better or worse that she's leaving me. I can't deal with this alone, but—

She's not leaving. She's just climbing down the bank, to the stream, looking at Janice, as if she's something really interesting, like a tadpole. She pulls up a bit of broken branch and pokes at the mess.

I'm sick, the vomit burning my mouth. I'm trembling all over.

'Come down to the water,' says Serena. 'You'll have to pull her out of sight.'

I don't move.

She looks up at me, hand on hip and she's not upset any more, she's just stern. 'If they find her, they'll know you killed her and they'll arrest you. Then they'll hang you.'

No! I can't take this. My insides are clenching and I can feel wee running down my legs. I can't... I can't...

'If you hide her, they won't find her,' says Serena, poking hard at the concrete block, so that it rolls over. My eyes fix on its jagged upturned side. It's covered with blood and hair and goo. It's horrible, but I don't want to take my eyes off it, because if I do, I'll see the thing it was on, before Serena pushed it over. I'll see Janice's head.

'You have to come down,' orders Serena.

I can't think. I crawl back along the pipe to solid ground and slither down the ice-cold mud of the bank. Serena is right. She's in charge. Everyone will know it was me. Everyone who crosses the bridge and looks down into the water will see…it. Janice. And they'll know what I've done.

But when I'm down, in the water, ice up over my ankles like knives stabbing into my flesh, I can't look at Janice. I can't bring myself to touch her. The black water flowing round me is full of…

I start to scream. I can't stop myself. My insides are shredding into a million pieces and each one wants to escape as a scream. Until a slap whips across my face, and I gulp on the last scream, choking on it. Serena is shaking me. She's in the stream with me. Water over her shoes and her white socks.

'Stop it! Stop it! Be quiet! Or someone will come and they'll arrest you!'

I stand there, panting like a dog, staring at the snowflakes as they settle on her coat and then vanish. I want to vanish too.

She's calmed down. 'You've got to pull her out of sight, Karen. Where no one will see. Otherwise, they'll catch you and hang you for murder.'

It's not fair. None of it's fair. I don't want to hang. I look down at Janice's feet. The broken shoe has come off. I grab her ankles and try to tug her under the bridge. Her crumpled body straightens, but her hair is still tangled up with the concrete block that crushed her head. She won't shift.

'Pull her free,' orders Serena.

In reply, I just let go and shake my head.

Serena stares at me for a moment and I go limp under her gaze, but I can't do it. So she bends down and yanks Janice's hair free from the concrete. Some of it comes off in her hand. It's full of…

I am crouching again, so low the water is washing my skirt and knickers as I'm sick. I can't look at Janice's head, but Serena can. She is standing, peering down at it closely, as if it's really interesting. Then she turns to me again. 'I'll have to do it for you. Again. I don't think that's fair, do you?'

I shake my head.

'It's not very nice for me.' Resolutely, she grasps Janice's ankles and pulls. But she only takes one step backwards under the bridge, before she straightens, holding up Janice's thin white legs, scratched and bruised from the fall. 'That would be better.' She's looking along the brook, to where it disappears into the dark tunnel. 'Come on. I think you should try and help me. It's not fair to make me do it all on my own. I'm only doing it for you.'

So I take one of Janice's feet, the one that has no shoe, and I help Serena turn the body and drag it down the stream. I look at the big hole in Janice's dirty sock and I cry for my friend, but there's nothing I can do.

The mouth of the tunnel is half clogged with slimy debris. 'Push it out of the way,' orders Serena.

I obey like a whipped slave. I open a way into the black

mouth. Somewhere deep inside, something scurries. That's it. I can't do any more. I can't look. I sit down, in the water and bury my head in my arms with a sob.

'You're not very helpful,' says Serena, sadly, but I don't care.

When I raise my head at last, she's managed to drag Janice inside the tunnel and she's pushing a foot in, out of sight. She pauses, looking down at her handiwork.

'I think they will find her, though. They'll probably come looking for her— I know!' Her eyes brighten. 'You can tell them she's left home, run away. Daddy says children from families like that are always running away and it's good riddance and a waste of time and money looking for them. If you tell them she's run away, maybe they won't—' She stops, thinking, and she laughs with excitement. 'Oh, I know! I know! Tell them you saw her get into a car with a stranger.'

I gape at her. Mr Cutler, that morning, in assembly, had gone on and on about not getting into cars with strangers, and Angela was whispering, 'Black Jack Coke will get you!' until Miss Protheroe reached along and slapped her hand. I don't understand. What have cars and strangers got to do with me killing Janice?

'Then if they find her, they'll think the stranger killed her. That's what they do, Daddy says. They mess with little girls and kill them. That's what he's done.'

'Black Jack Coke,' I whisper, staring into the tunnel. This culvert, if anywhere, is where Black Jack would live. He could be in there now. Maybe he's just out of sight, looking at Janice, rubbing his hands. Perhaps he'll mess with her.

What does messing with her mean? Perhaps he'll eat her. Perhaps he's about to spring out and eat us too.

I wish he would. I wish something would eat me, so I don't have to be here any more.

'Yes, like Black Jack.' Serena is considering. 'We should make it look as if he's messed with her.'

I can't take this. Not anymore. Make it go away, please. I bury my face again, and when I look up, Serena is struggling back out of the tunnel, holding Janice's knickers. They're sodden, dirty, stinking.

'Poo!' Serena's holding them with her fingertips, her nose wrinkled in disgust. 'Horrible. Yuk!' She throws them and they catch on a bramble behind a hawthorn bush. A little white ghost in the gloom, because it's really dark now. The snow's stopped and everything's just black, except for the dangling knickers.

'Come on.' Serena takes my hand, hauling me to my feet and dragging me up the bank. 'Now you have to get dry.' Like a mother cat and I'm a kitten, she fusses over me, wringing out my wet skirt. She has a handkerchief and rubs my legs dry. She's washed herself clean and now she wipes the blood off my hands, and the tears off my face and she smooths down my hair. Only my shoes and socks are still sodden, ice cold. I can't feel my feet any more. Finally, she turns to see to her own clothes, which are not nearly as wet as mine, although she did most of the work.

For me, she said. She did everything for me.

'Now.' She's very calm, very matter of fact, taking my arm as we walk on down Sawyer's Lane, out of the woods, past the high fence of the timber yard, towards Foxton

Road. 'Remember what you have to say. Tell everyone you saw Janice get into a car with a stranger. Um. I think it was a dark car. And the driver was black. Like Black Jack Coke. No, don't say that. They'll think you're making that up. Say you couldn't see the driver. I know, say you shouted to her not to, because you knew we're not supposed to get into cars, but she wouldn't listen. And then the car drove off with her, and you haven't seen her since.'

She's squeezing my arm as we walk, hugging me, pinching me. 'Are you listening to me? Do you know what you have to say?'

I nod.

'Because if you don't, they'll hang you for murder and I won't be able to help you any more. They'll hang you till you're dead.'

We walk along Foxton Road to the turning into Linden Crescent and she stops to face me once more. 'You will do it, won't you, Karen? You will tell them? Promise me.'

I promise.

'All right. Bye!' And she's on her way, skipping up Foxton Road as if nothing had happened.

If I squeeze my eyes shut very hard, perhaps nothing will have happened. But when I shut my eyes, all I can see is Janice looking up at me and then—

A lump of sharp concrete, in the water, with blood and hair and stuff streaming from it.

A hole in a sock.

A black tunnel.

I want to be in that tunnel. I want to disappear into it and never come out.

I run, down Linden Crescent, to my house. I run round and in through the back door. Mummy is in the sitting room, talking to Hilary. I can hear Children's Hour on the television. *Vision On*.

I want vision off. And hearing, and touch and consciousness.

I run upstairs and into my bedroom. I pull off all my clothes and scrumple them into a ball and push them under my bed, right to the back, behind the bag of toys and the box of books. I climb into bed and I pull the bedcovers over my head and I curl up as small as I can be. If I can just shut it out, it will all go away.

It's dark, under the covers. Dark as the tunnel where Janice is lying.

Are there rats in that tunnel? Or Black Jack? She'll be lonely and cold and afraid. I shouldn't, I shouldn't, I shouldn't…

'Karen, is that you?' My mother is coming up the stairs. I squeeze myself even smaller, gripping the blankets tighter.

She's tugging them back. 'Karen? What's the matter? Are you feeling ill? Tell me what it is.'

But I don't tell her. I can't tell. The words are there, shouting at me in Serena's voice, telling me what to say, but I can't do it. I shan't ever speak again.

Something moved overhead. Flick of a fluffy grey tail. A squirrel.

I was standing by a horse chestnut tree, looking down at the culvert that carried the brook under Foxton Road and the railway embankment. The banks were smooth and green, and the water ran clear, a solitary cigarette packet the only debris catching on the concrete lip of the low tunnel, but even now it was sinister, that black mouth leading into nothingness.

On a dark, cold, January evening, that tunnel had eaten my soul.

My feet were wet. Had I been in the brook? Had I stood staring into the culvert as the memories had come flooding out of me? I looked back at the bridge, and the iron pipe. I must have been doing enough re-enacting to cause alarm. The old man who'd been reading his newspaper was standing on the bridge, looking at me. I looked at my hands. Had I been heaving concrete? They were wet but not bloody. Long-bitten, but not scratched.

And no blocks of concrete around. No jagged lumps embedded with blood and hair and brain.

I raised a hand to shield my eyes as I looked back at the bridge, and the old man took it for a wave and hurried off, newspaper under his arm. Best not to have anything to do with mad women, he'd be saying to himself. That's what they always say. I've had people hurrying away from me, in anxious embarrassment, for thirty-five years.

But just for once, without medication or therapy, I was not feeling mad. I was feeling purged. Thirty-five years of confusion, denial and screaming dread drained out, leaving a vacuum that gave me a moment of perfect sanity. A brief moment. Already, the vacuum was beginning to fill with blubbering grief.

And cold, hard anger.

I walked back to the bench where I'd sat.

This bench, donated by Cpl Kenneth Dexter, is dedicated to the memory of his beloved sister Janice, 1955 – 1966.

In my bag was a nail file. Unused until now. It was a well-meaning gift from Charlie, who despaired of my nails. With good reason. They were always so bitten, the file was useless. But I had a use for it now.

The grey, weathered wood of the bench was soft enough for the file to bite in easily enough as I carved.

S O R R Y.

Vandalism. Defacement of council property. Okay, so arrest me.

The lawn around me had been mown, but not so recently that daisies hadn't sprung up again, spangling the green. Nothing keeps a daisy down. The petrol mowers and rollers used by the silent groundsman at Marsh Green school never kept the daisies down on the playing fields, where we were allowed to play on hot summer lunch breaks. Janice and I were experts on daisies.

I gathered them now, more and more into my cupped hands, then I sat on Janice's bench and made a daisy chain. Solemnly, carefully splitting the stems and threading them through. The stems were too short and my nails were too savaged to use half of them, but I managed to finish up with a small ringlet. I carried it onto the bridge and dropped it in the brook, watching the water dance it away, down towards the culvert.

I was crying. Wouldn't anyone?

I'd cried when Janice died. I'd cried and cried, as much for me as for her. It was all I could do – cry. I couldn't speak. That was what Inspector Whinn didn't understand, when he questioned me. And questioned me and questioned me. He had to, I suppose, because I was a vital witness. The only witness.

*

'Now, young lady, let's have no more of this snivelling. A girl is missing. Janice Dexter, and I understand you know her. You claim to be her friend. Isn't that so?'

'They're not really close friends,' says my mother, but her voice is small, as if she realises, even as she speaks, how silly it is to pretend to have nothing to do with the Dexters when something this serious has happened.

Inspector Whinn raises a hand to silence her, his eyes very stern on me, as I crouch in my chair. I don't want to be in the chair. I want to be under it. I want everything to go away.

'Come along now. You're not a very good friend, are you, if you won't tell me what happened to Janice. She's missing and we believe you saw something. Is that right? Karen, look at me. Is that right? What did you see?'

He's a heavy man. He has Serena's dark hair and her dark

240

eyes, but he's not gentle and beautiful like her. He smokes, and his face goes dark red when he's annoyed, and there's a little tick in his cheek. I know Serena's mother, who is very elegant and wears earrings even in the house, but I've only seen Serena's father once before. He's always at work, because he's very important. He's angry, which would be scary, but I'm already so scared it can't get any worse.

'My daughter tells me you saw something. Is that right, Karen? Stop pretending the cat's got your tongue. I want you to tell me in your own words. Did you see Janice Dexter get into a car?'

I know what I'm supposed to say. I can hear Serena reciting the story that I'm to tell, and my chest is bursting with a longing to say it, to do as she has commanded. But I can't. It won't come out, because it's not true. It's splitting my head in two and the words are like dust in my throat. I can't say anything. I just rock, the tears rolling down.

Inspector Whinn pushes his chair back violently, and goes to the door. He's speaking to someone. Then he comes back and stands over me, like a bear, smoking, watching me with disappointment, like Serena looked at me. I let her down.

The door opens and a policewoman comes in with Serena, holding her hand.

'Let's try again,' says Inspector Whinn, crumpling up a piece of paper. 'Karen Rothwell, tell me what you told my daughter. Did you see Janice Dexter get into a car?'

Still I can only sob.

Serena kneels beside me and takes my hand. 'Tell them, Karen. Tell them what you told me. About Janice. She got into a car, didn't she? Wasn't that what you said? Tell them, please?' She's smiling encouragement.

Her nails are biting into my hand.

I say nothing. A lump of bloody concrete is stuck in my throat.

*

That must have been when Janice was merely missing. How long did it take before her body was discovered? Days, I think. Time enough for sleet and rain and rising waters to wash away all outward sign of what had happened by the bridge. I don't know how she came to be found, but I have a feeling, a dim memory of something my parents said, that it was some man, walking his dog, who discovered her. Maybe, until then, the police weren't really looking. They had to go through the motions, of course, but Dexter children weren't high on their priorities. An inspector would never have been involved, if his daughter hadn't told him that I had told her about the car.

It was all down to her being the daughter of a policeman. If she hadn't been – if I'd been the one to tell the police, as she had commanded, would anything have been done, I wonder? Would the mysterious disappearance of a grubby and unwanted Dexter brat have aroused any more interest than a straying dog? Going off with strangers, just like her mother, probably did it all the time. What would you expect from the Dexters? Wasn't that how Mrs Dexter earned her living, off with strangers in cars? If there's one less of them in our neighbourhood, so much the better.

But Serena was the daughter of an inspector, and she'd come to him with a story of possible abduction, so of course they took it seriously and questioned me. Janice might not count,

242

but Serena did.

Then the body was found. It didn't matter quite so much that it was a Dexter after that, because it was a murder, too serious to shrug off, and the police had to come out in force. And though I still wouldn't talk, Denise did, always so helpful, always so eager to carry tales, pointing the finger at Nigel Knight. Then, Angela, always ready for a jolly game, such as Hunt the Nigel.

Then they came back to me.

*

'Now listen, Karen Rothwell! You hear me? I'm not putting up with any more of this snivelling and dumb silence. Tell me! Spit it out and stop pretending you're a baby! What did you see?'

Inspector Whinn's face is really dark now, the tick in his cheek much worse. I can feel his spittle on my cheek, he's so close.

'She hasn't been well,' pleads my mother. 'I don't know what it is. A terrible cold. She's not right. Pneumonia, I wouldn't be surprised. You can't just keep shouting at her like this. She's not well.'

She's defending me, but only half-heartedly. At home, she's been doing the shouting, shaking me, telling me they can take me away and good riddance if I'm going to be like this. But I don't speak. I can't.

I will not say the lie.

Inspector Whinn is breathing heavily, trying to get control. He must realise that shouting at me isn't going to work. He pulls up a chair and sits down beside me, folding his fingers together, then unfolding them, then folding them again. He's trying to speak calmly. 'You spoke to my daughter, didn't you? Yes? You told Serena that you saw Janice Dexter get into a car. Is that right, Karen?' He draws a very noisy breath. 'It was a dark car, that's what you said. Was it a dark car? Karen, look at me.'

He taps me on the cheek, to make me turn. It's more than a tap. It's almost a slap, but I don't care. I won't raise my eyes. I bite my thumb, really hard, so it hurts, but it won't block out the other pain.

'Was it a maroon Morris Traveller? You know what that is?' Inspector Whinn snorts, starts again. 'Was it a car with wooden strips? Is that what you saw? Your friend, Denise Griggs, says it was. My daughter says Denise sometimes makes things up, so I have to check. What really happened, Karen? Tell me. Shall I fetch my daughter again? Would you like Serena to help you?'

My head jerks up. I can't help it. My eyes meet his.

I don't know what he sees in my eyes, but I know what I see in his. Shock. I am ten but I recognise shock. It fills me up to the brim, so I know when I see it in someone else's eyes. I see the blood drain from his face. One minute he's dark red and the next he's a sort of grey and his face looks like it's melting.

He sits back. I can see his hands on his knees, clenching into really tight fists. White knuckles. I remember Serena's white knuckles on the rail of the bridge, and I begin to shake. His fists go all hazy.

Inspector Whinn coughs. I see the lump in his throat go up and down as he swallows. 'Very well, it's obvious we'll get nothing useful from this child. Take her home, Mrs

Rothwell. We'll just have to manage without her evidence.'

What was the truth he saw in my eyes? He couldn't have guessed the whole truth, in every sickening detail, but he must have seen enough to suspect that he wouldn't want to know more. He was an intelligent man. A busy man, though. Fathers were busy in those days. Sometimes their children only got to see them when fathers sank down in front of the TV after work and told them to keep the noise down. Fathers didn't take their children to the dentist, or go to parents' evening. That was the mother's role. Maybe, as a police inspector, working whatever strange hours the criminal world set, Inspector Whinn saw even less of his child than most. Such a man might well not know his daughter at all – but I think I must have understood, in that instant when I looked into his eyes, that he did know her. He knew more than he wanted to know. I was a child who couldn't cope with the impossibility of Serena's contradictions, her outward angel and inner devil, but he might be a man who lived with the secret knowledge of exactly what his daughter was.

Thirty-five years ago, my child's brain had simply not been able to compute. But I had computed it now.

I left the pretty little stretch of brook, in the pretty, manicured wedge of urban woodland. I walked back down the pretty lane to Foxton Road, and crossed it to the ranks of new housing and small closes that clustered between it and the railway. A gate marked a passage between two houses. It was a metal-framed gate now, instead of the wooden one I remembered, and it swung easily on its hinges, instead of dragging across the grass

245

track that led me through to all that was left of the allotments. A couple of dozen strips, mostly under glass and plastic. The rest, including the old weedy strips at the far end, probably abandoned to nature once the urgency of wartime food production had faded, had disappeared under a new, cramped rabbit-hutch estate. Long gone were the mossy, unpruned fruit trees concealing Nigel Knight's secret hideaway. Gone were the corrugated sheds of the pig farm that had blocked his escape when the police and their dogs came to hound him out. Nothing left of the story but the railway line where his terror had taken him.

Denise had accused him, and Angela had set the police dogs on to him. Who prompted them to do it, I wonder?

I stood in the middle of the allotments, staring at the railway line, the anger in me growing stronger by the minute. Wasn't Janice's death enough for her?

A man emerged from his greenhouse and carefully padlocked the door, eying me warily. I might be feeling sane, but two days in a van and a few agonising hours of running my brain through a sieve didn't leave me looking sane. I don't blame him for locking up. He wasn't to know I didn't want to steal his tomatoes.

I returned to the van, walking gingerly on the eggshells of the past, afraid that the clarity and my understanding of all that had happened might begin to disintegrate at any moment. I was alert for that sense of disintegration, because I knew it would be lurking there somewhere, not far below the surface. It would get me sooner or later, but it mustn't be sooner if I could help it.

I drove back the way I'd come, along the foot of the downs.

Over the humpback canal bridge. The place where she'd suggested I kill myself. Because, of course, that's what she'd been doing. I should have realised, because she'd done it before.

She's done it that last time I'd seen her in 1966. When my parents were packing up to leave Lyford, and wringing their hands over me, and Hilary was refusing to speak to me because I was responsible for ruining her life and taking her away from her friends. I didn't understand that that was what I was doing. I didn't realise that my parents were facing the wrath of their neighbours and an end to all their comfort, for the crime of having a daughter who'd so maliciously and wilfully foiled the police hunt for a child killer.

I'd been aware of that wrath at work elsewhere. I'd seen stones and worse thrown at the Dexters' house over the years. From the back of a police Jaguar, as I was being taken away for questioning, I'd heard the mob turning on Mr Knight. Now, deprived of a lynching, the bestial snarling settled on my parents. Not on me, because I wasn't visible. I'd been hauled out a few times to be interviewed by the police or to see doctors, but other than that, I stayed in my room, in my bed, hiding from everyone and everything. No one seriously expected me to go back to school. Everything would be all right, my parents thought – we could all start afresh, horrors forgotten, if we just moved to another town, another factory, another school.

It was the day before we left that Serena came to call.

*

'Karen. Come on now, pull those covers down. Sit up, please. Look who's come to see you. Serena. Your friend. Isn't that kind of her?'

I try to pull them back, but the blankets are dragged

from me, by hands that are really itching to slap me, though they're stroking my head instead, pretending to be loving.

Serena is standing by my mother, smiling sweetly, and I am sick with fear.

'I'll leave you to talk,' says my mother, softly, as if I'm a sick child.

I scream and back up tight against the headboard.

She snaps. 'Now stop it! Don't be such a silly girl. Please, Karen, just be nice for once! Serena's come specially to see you, so behave yourself.'

'It's all right, Mrs Rothwell,' says Serena. 'I'll look after her. Won't I, Karen?'

'If only you'd just made friends with nice girls like Serena,' says my mother, sounding as if she's near to tears too, as she hurries from the room.

Serena looks at me. She's smiling. I want to turn away, to face the wall, but if I do, what might she do? She is my friend, she looks after me and I am petrified of her.

Serena pulls up a chair to sit beside me. 'You should have done as I told you, Karen. Everyone is ever so cross with you. Daddy says he'd like to wring your neck because you won't tell him what you saw. I told you what to say. It would all have been all right if you'd done what I told you.' She sighs sadly, reaching out to smooth my hair, even though I flinch away. 'Now everyone knows you killed Janice.'

'I didn't!'

'Oh Karen. You know you did, really. It was because the spirit ordered it, so of course you had to do it. I just helped, because I didn't want Janice to hurt you, but you know you did it, really.'

She's smiling, stroking my cheek with her hand. With her nails. Gently up. Then down and the nails begin to dig in. I am paralysed as they dig into my cheek. She is watching as if she's really curious to know how deep she can dig before she draws blood.

'It must be horrible for you, having everyone know you killed her.' Her nails scrape up again.. 'Your mummy and daddy think it too. I heard them whisper. They don't like to say so in front of you, because perhaps they're a bit afraid of you, but they were whispering that they know you did it. They're worried you might kill Hilary too. Would you, Karen? I suppose now you've killed Janice it would be much easier to kill someone else. That's what would scare me, if I'd done it. If I thought I might kill my own sister. I can't imagine how horrible it is, having killed your friend. If I killed my friend, I don't know what I'd do.' She's drawn her hand away at last. She's looking at her nails. 'I think I'd just jump in front of a car or something. Or out of a window maybe. Yes, I think that's what I'd do. I don't know that I could go on living if I'd killed a friend. Because any day the police might catch me and hang me.'

She's picked up my bear and she's hugging him. Then she holds him at arm's length. It's like she's talking to him instead of me. 'They tie you up when they hang you, so you can't run or anything, and you can scream and scream but they don't care. They tie a rope round your neck, like this.' She's got the belt from my dressing gown and she's wrapped it round my bear's neck. 'Then they open a trapdoor and you drop and the rope goes tight round your throat and you die! And they watch and clap their hands.'

My bear is swinging, choking, and she watches, smiling. I lunge for him, to rescue him, but she snatches him away.

'I wouldn't like them to hang me. I think I'd rather anything than that. I'd rather jump. Wouldn't you, Karen? That's what I'd do, if I were you.'

I scream, again and again, till I can't breathe or see.

I can hear my mother, racing up the stairs. Serena is out there, at the top, waiting for her.

'I'm sorry, Mrs Rothwell, I can't make her stop. I only wanted to cheer her up.'

'I know you did, Serena. You're a very nice, thoughtful girl and she doesn't deserve such nice friends.'

My mother's coming in, alone, and my screams quieten.

'What's the matter with you?' she demands, staring down at me. 'Why me? What have I done to deserve this?' She picks up my bear from the floor and throws him on the bed. 'Why can't you be more like Serena?'

*

I drove on, up the steep road to the top of the downs, over into the woodland, to Thorpeshall. A lorry was half blocking the entrance to Braxton Lane. I expect I could have squeezed past it safely enough, but I could picture myself scraping it – I still hadn't confidently grasped the dimensions of Malcolm's van. I didn't want to risk being diverted, at this moment of moments, by some irate driver demanding my insurance details. So I parked on the green, opposite the Black Swan, and walked the quarter mile down Braxton Lane, to the bend where Serena's bungalow nestled.

It was mid-afternoon. Gary the painter had gone, no van on the gravel drive, no ladder against the wall. The woodwork was all complete, smart and glistening. No neighbour in the adjoining gardens either, to note down my arrival for the Watch committee.

Someone was definitely at home. I caught the flicker of a TV screen in Serena's living room. If I knocked, I'd be summoning her from her daytime viewing…

I actually, momentarily, hesitated at the thought of inconveniencing her. It wasn't so much concern for her as the impulse for flight, which had been deep-rooted in me for three decades. I hesitated, then all the anger resurfaced and I brushed the urge to flee aside.

I knocked on the door, then rang the bell, then knocked again. Enough. I stood waiting.

The murmur of the TV grew louder as an inner door opened. A wail of sirens – some police drama. Then the front door opened and Serena was standing there, glass in one hand, the other holding the door. Motionless in mid-gesture, as if we were playing Grandmother's Footsteps. She looked flushed, almost excited as she opened the door, but when her eyes fixed on me, they became utterly expressionless. Stunned.

'Why?' I asked.

—22—

The gravel crunched underfoot. It rang in my ears. I looked down at my feet, staggering through it, but I couldn't focus. All I could see and smell and feel was the blood. I was splattered in it, from head to knees. It blackened my blouse. It smeared my hands. It clung in congealing globules to my hair.

I swayed like a drunken woman, but I was out of her garden, into the lane, and the further the horror was behind me, the more the urge to scream subsided. I could begin to breathe again. How far did I need to go? At any moment, one of the neighbours would look out and see a Halloween horror lurching down the road. They'd call the police, and that would be that. I'd be arrested. It was fine. It was all right. It was time I was called to answer, for Janice, if nothing else.

Perhaps I could just sit here on the verge, and wait for the police to come. But no, the abattoir scene was too close, churning my stomach. I looked at my hand. What was I holding? A towel, of course. A blood-streaked towel. I wiped my face with it, feeling the blood smear, then I stumbled on, waiting for the shouts, the screams, the busybodies who'd be rushing out to tackle me at any moment.

No one came.

No one tackled me. No one looked out and gasped, as

I staggered down Braxton Lane. The beady eyes of the Neighbourhood Watch must have been taking a siesta, because no one peered out of their cottages around Thorpeshall green, or glanced out of the Black Swan. They were in there, some of them. Again and again, I caught the flicker of TV screens, but no one appeared, no one challenged me, no car drove past.

So I got in the van, dropped the bloody towel out of sight in the back, switched on the engine and drove away.

I drove home.

I drove to escape the blood, not the retribution. I had no clear idea of what I was going to do. My sanity, which had lasted this long, was hanging by a thread, pleading to go into shutdown. I'd think about what to do. Later. For now, I just wanted to get away from the blood.

If… So many ifs. If someone had seen me in the village, I'd never have got as far as the van. If I hadn't filled up with petrol the night before, I'd never have made it home without having to stop at a garage. If it hadn't been pitch dark when I arrived, that couple walking their dog in the street would have noticed that my clothes and face were not just dirty brown. But nobody saw, nobody realised.

Back in my garden flat, I stripped off all my clothes, placed them carefully in a plastic carrier bag so that the police could collect them, then I showered. I was in the shower for God knows how long. An hour, maybe. The problem of the electricity bill was for another day. All I wanted now was to be clean, to get it off my skin, from between my fingers, out of my hair. To have the sickening smell out of my nose.

Then I took my medication and I went to bed.

I woke late, with madness sitting by my pillow, waiting to be invited in. Waiting to carry me off to some fantasy world that would block out all the horror and anxiety of this one. I knew it was only a matter of time and I panicked at the thought of losing what I'd only just recovered. The truth.

I went rummaging for paper and pencil, and I started drawing. The bridge, the pipe, the culvert, the trees. The concrete block. I had to get it down on paper before it fled from me. Drawing was the only thing I had excelled at in school, back in those early years of innocence when school had been something you went to every day and did lessons and played with friends. Miss Carmel praised my dogs and cars and buttercups. It was the only teacher's praise I could remember. And my heart had burned with unendurable pleasure, when Serena had marvelled at my horse, with legs that bent in the right directions. I was the one who could draw anything. So I drew now.

Nothing sweet and marvellous about these drawings. No buttercups. No prancing ponies. They were black and intense.

They kept me occupied until a knock on the door brought me back to my present surroundings. I realised I still hadn't got dressed. No time. I grabbed a dressing gown and wrapped it round me, ready to greet the police with some small decency. I'd been waiting for them.

I opened the door and it wasn't the police. It was Malcolm.

'Thank God,' he said.

Of course it was Malcolm. I'd left the van in full view on Thorpeshall green, and though it was smudged with road grime and the paintwork was scratched and faded, the words Gem's Books were still clearly visible. The police would have traced Malcolm easily and he'd have brought them to me.

There were shadows of people behind him, down the passage, in the bright light of the road. They'd be coming down now. Except that they didn't. They just walked past. They didn't even glance down the passage. Not police, just two passers-by, who flitted out of my vision without even registering my existence. Then there was just Malcolm, looking worried and grave and shaking his head, but in relief, not accusation.

'I saw the van, so I knew you must be back. Thank God. I didn't know what to do. I've been worrying myself sick, wondering whether to contact Charlotte or go to the police.'

'Didn't you report the van stolen, when I took it?' I stood back to let him in. When had I taken it? A year ago. No, it was only on Sunday. And this was Wednesday. 'I thought you'd go to the police. I stole your money too. I used your card. Sorry. I needed petrol.'

He didn't hug me, exactly. He rubbed my arms. 'It's all right. I'm just relieved you're safe and sound. I had an inkling you might be having another meltdown. I should never have let you go. Thank God, you're okay.'

'Yes. So far. Sorry I didn't come into work.' Midweek, I thought. 'Why aren't you at work? Who's minding the shop?'

'Never mind that. It's quiet. I shut up for the day, thought I'd come and check here again. So what happened to you, Karen? Where did you vanish to?' His gaze had fallen on my drawings. He was frowning down on them, trying to figure out their significance, which, of course, he couldn't.

I picked them up. 'I wanted to make sure I didn't forget again. What happened in 1966. How my friend, Janice, died.'

'You've been back to Lyford? I thought it might be that.'

'Lyford and Hay and Brecon. Sorry about the petrol.'

'Never mind that. Did it do the trick? Did you find what you were looking for?'

'Oh yes.' I sat down. 'I found it.' I looked up and found him studying me anxiously. Looking for the usual signs, I suppose. I wasn't sure if he could see them or not.

'Good,' he said, still thoughtful. 'Have you eaten today? You haven't, have you? Have you eaten at all since you left?'

'Oh you'd be surprised. I had a huge breakfast. Yesterday. Yes, I haven't eaten since then. I suppose I should. Do you want some breakfast? Not sure what I've got. The bread will be stale by now.'

'All right.' He looked pleased that I was compliant and that there was something he could do. 'A bit late for breakfast, but I'll nip out and get us something for lunch. And you get dressed, yes?'

'Yes, all right.' While he was gone, I dug out clean clothes. Fresh everything. It was one o'clock. I had no idea it was that late. I switched the radio on. By now, Serena's death would probably be on the news. A mention, perhaps of the police search for a blood-soaked killer.

There was no mention of Serena. There was no mention of anything except the one item of news, which drowned out all else.

It was Wednesday, September 12th, 2001.

I listened. Then I switched on the television. The same news. Yesterday's news, but they couldn't let go. I'd had a compulsion to draw the scene of Janice's murder, in order to keep it real. The TV companies and news agencies, it seemed, had the same compulsion to play and replay and replay and replay the impossible and yet unarguable collapse of the World Trade Centre towers.

Malcolm returned with sandwiches, and found me staring at the screen.

'This happened yesterday?'

'Yes. Yesterday afternoon. You didn't know?'

'No.' Yesterday afternoon, I'd been confronting Serena. She'd been watching the TV when I'd arrived. Smoke and screams and panic. I'd assumed it was a thriller movie. She'd turned it off as soon as I'd followed her into the room.

'I didn't know.' Once more, on the screen, in a seething storm of all-enveloping dust and despair, a tower sank into ruin before our eyes. And then another.

Serena sinking into a pool of blood. No choking dust surrounding her. Just blood, endless blood.

'Terrorists,' said Malcolm. 'Almost impossible to believe.'

'No. Terror is very believable.'

'Yes?' He looked at me anxiously, then switched the television off. 'Don't look at that. It's too horrible. Tell me, Karen. What happened to Janice?'

'Serena Whinn happened. She was my terror. Was. Now she's dead. Gone. In an ocean of blood.' I looked at my hands. They were clean, but I could still feel gore on them.

Malcolm was silent. There wasn't anything, really, he could say.

'I thought the police would have come for me by now.'

'Do you think you killed her, Karen?' There was no disgust in his eyes. He was asking what I might be imagining, not what I had done.

'The police will tell you. I should have called them from her house, but I just had to get away. I was covered with it. The blood. I've put my clothes in a bag, so they can take them away for forensic examination, or whatever they do. I ought to call them now, oughtn't I? Can you do it? Tell them where I am. I'll wait.'

He started to speak, stopped, sighed, then started again. 'Look, Karen, I don't think you need to call anyone just yet. I think you need to eat, and rest and see how you're feeling after another good night's sleep.'

'Do you think? But I had your van. They'll probably come to you first. You'll tell me when they come, won't you?'

'Yes. I will. I promise.' He gazed round my room, searching the chaos for something, anything to offer a change of subject. To wean me off this nightmare delusion I was obviously having. 'Would you like me to sort some of your books, Karen?'

Sort my books. Yes, they needed sorting. I began to laugh.

I waited for the police to come. I waited for insanity to return. Neither seemed in a hurry. Malcolm brought me some soup for supper. He was back the next day, and the next, just to check up on me. He could see that I wasn't having a turn, after all, despite this fantasy of bloody death I seemed to be nursing. I couldn't bring myself to press on him the reality of Serena's end. I was saving it for the police.

On the third day, though, he found his own clue to the truth. The bloody towel in the back of his van. He brought it in, shocked. 'You were hurt, Karen.'

'No. That's Serena's blood. I told you I was soaked. All my clothes are in a plastic bag in the bathroom.'

He had to look for confirmation and he emerged with the

bag. I'd taped it shut. He pulled the tape off, opened it and looked in, then flung his head back, choking, and put a hand over his nose. The reek, when it was opened, was sickening. He shut it again, hastily, and looked at me.

'Yes. All right. Karen.' He swallowed hard. 'Did you… What happened?'

'She's dead. I watched her die. Blood was spurting everywhere. It was a matter of minutes, seconds it seemed, and she was gone. I should have called the police right then. I don't know why they haven't come. I wish they'd come.'

Malcolm had his hand over his mouth. He was thinking hard.

'She killed Janice,' I said. 'I remembered. I remembered everything. So I had to go back and face her. Make her answer for what she'd done. She was evil.'

'Yes. Yes, I see.' He couldn't really, but he was trying to, thinking what to do next.

He didn't have to think long, because that was when it came, at last. The knock on the door.

Malcolm started, looked nervously at me, and moved to hold me back. To protect me, maybe. 'Let me deal with it.'

'It's all right,' I said. 'I'm all right. I'm ready.'

I opened the door.

—23—

It wasn't the police, after all. It was four middle-aged women.

Barbara, Angela, Denise and Ruth.

They stood there, huddled, four women who didn't really want to know each other but who stuck together for protection.

I stepped back, an automatic gesture of surprise, but they took it as an invitation to enter. Barbara strode forward with a curt nod. Angela sloped in, not quite focusing on me. Denise trotted by with an anxious attempt at a smile. Ruth, oozing reluctance, pushed in without looking at me.

My flat wasn't big, barely big enough for my books, but now it seemed like a broom cupboard. Six people. It had never held so many before. They'd never have managed to squeeze in if Malcolm hadn't spent a couple of evenings tidying the piles and boxes of books into more compact order. The sofa was empty and a chair had come to light that I'd forgotten all about. Funny, that I was employed to tidy Malcolm's chaotic shop and he'd employed himself tidying my chaotic flat.

He'd returned the bag of bloody clothes to the bathroom, but the smell still lingered. Noses wrinkled. Quietly, he opened the windows, which helped a little. We got a whiff of the bins outside instead.

There was an uncomfortable silence. I wasn't sure what I was supposed to say. I'd been psyching myself up for a different situation.

Barbara took charge. It was only reasonable; she occupied most of the room. She was blunt, no nonsense.

'Serena is dead.'

Denise gave a gasping sob. The others said nothing. They just stood there, watching me.

'Yes, I know.'

'Ah! As I thought.' Barbara spoke triumphantly, as if she'd tricked me into a confession.

They looked at each other. Not at me.

'I'm going to stay,' said Malcolm. 'In case you need me.' He was warning them, I suppose, that they wouldn't have a free hand with me.

'Yes, please stay.' I managed a smile. There was something so utterly sane about Malcolm. He was my lifeline, whatever precipice I was about to hurtle over.

'All right. I'll, um, put the kettle on, shall I?' The standard method of lowering tension.

Barbara stared after him, suspiciously, then she turned back to me. 'If you know she's dead, I obviously don't need to tell you anything.'

'But tell me anyway. Why has no one come? Wasn't she found till now?'

'She was found the day before yesterday. Stabbed. She bled to death. A painter was at her house on the day before. The 11th. They're saying that's when she died. The painter's not a suspect, by the way. A neighbour saw Serena waving him off. The police questioned him though. He told them she'd had a visitor that morning, someone she claimed was an old friend.

Her phone records showed that she'd spoken with me the night before, so the police contacted me. I was able to prove that the visitor wasn't me.'

'No. It was me.'

'Of course it was you. Denise had warned me you were on your way to see Serena.'

'So you were able to tell the police about me. How did you know where to find me?'

'I had someone at the office trace you, after you came up to Carlisle. You still owe for a consultation.'

'Oh for Christ's sake,' said Angela, flinging herself down onto the chair.

'Sorry, yes, sit down, somewhere.' I waved at the sofa.

Denise and Ruth looked at each other as if it were a game of musical chairs, and there was only one seat left. Then they seated themselves a foot apart. Barbara remained standing and magisterial.

'I had to tell the others. We knew you'd been to see Serena and now she was dead. It seemed highly probable that you were involved. But the police told me the painter saw her visitor leave, and that created some uncertainty in our minds.'

'Of course,' said Denise.

Barbara hushed her. 'But since you already know she's dead, there can't be any more doubt, can there?'

'It would look like that,' I agreed.

'It's as I thought. But we agreed we should give you the opportunity to explain yourself, before we went to the police.'

'Yes,' drawled Angela. 'We thought, for once, we'd get it right before we blabbed.'

Barbara sniffed. Denise gave a whimper. Ruth continued

to stare straight ahead of her, refusing to open her mouth. I wondered how they'd persuaded her to come. Barbara's brute force, perhaps. I could just see her frogmarching little Ruthie along Farnham Drive, she'd done it before.

'Are you going to tell us what happened?'

'First I should tell you what happened in 1966.' I squeezed back to let Malcolm in with a tray of mugs. Did I have six mugs? Apparently. He handed them round silently. It wasn't the moment for polite enquiries about milk and sugar.

'I went to see Serena, to learn the truth about Janice. I knew I was to blame, but I couldn't remember why. I just wanted Serena to spell it out. And she did. She told me how I'd killed Janice, in a fight, and then invented the story of her getting into a car to cover it up.'

There was an intake of breath. Of shock only from Malcolm. From the others it was a gasp of satisfaction.

'It's better to confess and face up to it, Karen.' said Denise, earnestly. 'Believe me. Only that way can you find true redemption.'

'Oh shut up,' said Angela.

'Why did you always suspect I'd killed Janice?' I asked. 'You did, didn't you?'

They weren't expecting the question. They exchanged querying glances, waiting for someone else to speak.

'It was obvious. The car story simply didn't add up. We believed it at first, of course. But later…' Barbara, naturally.

'Later, when Serena sowed doubt in your mind about it, perhaps?'

'Well of course, she could see as well as any of us that it was simply absurd. It made far more sense that you killed her.'

'So much sense that I believed it, too, when Serena told me so. I did drive away from her home, like the painter said. But I didn't do what I was supposed to do. I was supposed to go and drown myself in a canal. Instead, I went back to Sawyer's Lane, in Marsh Green, and when I was there, I remembered how Janice really died.'

I told them. I spelled it out in as much detail as I could bring myself to describe. I could feel my body trembling, but inside I managed to keep calm. Denise was quite right. Confession did bring a sort of redemption. I was telling them the truth, and they might be incapable of believing a word of it, but there it was, whether they believed it or not.

I stopped.

There was silence. Total silence.

'No…' Someone whispered it, but I don't know who. Of course they wouldn't believe it.

Barbara began to sway, dropping her mug. Angela was out of her chair and guided Barbara to it. Barbara sank down heavily. Angela settled on the floor, staring at the carpet, then softly, with hiccups, began to laugh.

'Stop it!' said Denise. 'Stop it!' She burst into tears.

At last, Ruth looked at me. 'Serena said I really ought to tell the police about my father's photographs. Because he was always taking photographs of children and he might have taken pictures of Janice and caught the murderer on film. She actually made me feel proud that I'd provide the vital clue. So I told them. They wanted to see his latest film, and he didn't want to hand it over. But he had to, and when they saw what was on it, they came to search the house and found the whole filthy lot. She got me to inform on my father. My father, the pervert.'

Barbara was shaking her head, more in convulsion than in denial. 'How could Serena have known he'd been hoarding kiddie porn?'

'She knew! I saw a lot of those photographs. Of me, and all my friends. All of you, including Serena. None of us suspected he was doing it, did we? He had us all, getting undressed, or in the bath or on the toilet or in bed, but we all looked completely unaware. Except Serena. He captured her looking straight at the camera. And smiling. I could never understand why.

'Why did I always do as she ordered? She said I had to be friends with you.' Ruth glared at me belligerently. 'All that pretence I had to go through. I didn't even like you.'

'That's all right. I didn't like you, either.'

Ruth scowled and then laughed. 'Bloody performing monkeys, weren't we?'

'Like a puppet on a stri-ing.' Angela's attempt at singing ended in a croak. Or a choke.

'She told me it was Nigel's car,' whispered Denise, clawing her knees. 'She said afterwards she didn't, but she did. Almost. Really she did. She said you'd seen Janice getting into a dark car, and then she started talking about how dark didn't have to mean black. It could be brown or purple, like Nigel Knight's car, and how you'd definitely mentioned something about wood, and what a pity it was that you were the only one who saw it happen, because you were being naughty and refusing to talk to the police, and if only someone else had seen it, they could describe it properly. And I thought – I thought...'

'She knew you loved to tell tales,' said Ruth.

'I didn't!'

The others said nothing, just looked at her.

'God forgive me.'

'She bet me I could outrun the police dogs,' said Angela. 'I was itching to try, too. She said even Nigel could probably outrun them, but we'd never find out, because the police had no clue where to look, and Nigel probably had a secret hiding place somewhere, which they'd never find. So I had to go and tell them, didn't I? Where the poor innocent would be hiding like some cornered hare. I don't know why she had to get me to give him away? They'd have found him easily enough without me. That's what dogs are for. Why did she have to manipulate me?'

'Because she could,' I said. 'I think she was addicted.'

Barbara was staring at me, broodingly.

'She got you to propose the Ouija board at Christmas, didn't she?' I said.

'Yes.'

'She tried to convince me you were the one moving the glass.'

'Good God, it wasn't me!'

'It was the Devil!' said Denise. 'If you mess with satanism—'

'It was Serena, for Christ's sake.' Angela tossed a book across the room. *The Snow Goose.* Malcolm silently retrieved it.

'Of course it was Serena,' I said. 'I knew it couldn't have been Barbara. She had a message too. The cat.'

Barbara clamped a hand to her mouth. We waited. She swallowed hard. 'She got me to kill a cat.'

'Jesus.'

'She knew I loved cats. One of her neighbours had one, a lovely thing. It used to roam along the row of gardens. She told me her other neighbour hated cats and he threatened to catch it and burn it alive if he ever found it on his vegetables. She was terrified he'd do it, so she told me we needed to frighten it off, so it would never dare go anywhere near Mr Michael. Her parents were out. And the neighbours. No one was around. She went in and fetched this gun.'

'Gun!'

'Yes. A revolver. It was big and heavy. She told me, later, her father had it because he was a policeman. I don't know if that's true. Maybe it was a relic of the war. She said it was too heavy for her, and I'd have to do it. I'd have to fire straight at the cat, so the bang would scare it and it would go home and be safe. It was just sitting there, in the sun. I suppose I thought the gun wasn't loaded, or maybe that I couldn't possibly hit it. But I did. I killed it. We hid it in next door's compost heap. I killed the cat!'

Barbara sobbed, and Denise rushed out of her seat to pat her. 'I don't care what you say, it was the Devil. I think Serena was possessed.'

Barbara wriggled free and sniffed. Her jaw set. 'When she reappeared in England, after all those years abroad, she contacted me. Said she'd heard I was a solicitor and she'd love to have an old friend managing her affairs. She came to see me, at my office. She pulled this... this bloody gun out of her bag, said she'd been trying to get rid of it for years, and could I take charge of it? What could I say? I thought she must have forgotten how I'd shot the cat. She never mentioned it.'

'Like she never mentioned my father's filthy photographs,' spat Ruth. 'But she turned up on my doorstep one day and said how wonderful to meet up again and wasn't it a lovely time at school, and here was a photo to remind me of all of us.

It was us, all of us, at the swimming pool, getting changed. Angie and me were still wriggling into our suits. I don't know who took it. Maybe it was one of my father's. She handed it to me, like it was a prize. Said how we must all keep in touch, in future.'

Denise, who had been pulling faces of abject misery, crumpled on the floor with a loud wail. 'She came for me, said she'd take me out for a drive. Because we were old friends and she wanted us to be friends again. She came in a Morris Traveller. Maroon!'

'Came to sympathise,' said Angela. 'With me being lame. After being such a good athlete. How tragic. I'd been so good, I could even out-run police dogs. Did I remember how I'd raced against them? I was just beginning to forget. After that, I couldn't forget, ever again. Never will, now.'

There was a moment's silence, then 'Dear God,' said Malcolm.

'Why?' asked Ruth. 'Why did she do it?'

'Why did we let her?' added Angela. 'She only had to say "dance," and we'd dance. All except Karen. What's your magic? How did you escape?'

'Did I? Twice she had me set on committing suicide. The first time, I nearly succeeded.'

'And the price of resistance was madness?'

'So it seems.'

'Oh.' Ruth managed a laugh. 'And those of us who didn't resist remained sane?'

Barbara dabbed her eyes. 'We were children. How were we supposed to know our best friend was a psychopath?'

Another prolonged silence. Then Denise came to me,

gripping my hands, so hard she threatened to cut off the blood supply. 'Forgive me, Karen, for having ever suspected you. I should have known you couldn't kill Janice. You weren't guilty like me. I killed Nigel Knight with my lies. That's the truth! The whole truth.'

'Not the whole,' I said. 'I'd like to know the rest. What happened to the Dexters?'

Another exchange of glances. 'The council moved them,' said Ruth.

Angela barked a laugh. 'They caused trouble. Imagine. The nerve of these people. A couple of the boys were arrested for riot or something. So, sweep them away to another estate. Out of sight, out of mind.'

'And Mr Knight?'

'Mr Knight died. Heart failure. Brought about by an overdose of something, but Dr Winterton kindly ignored that. Wasn't so much the death of Nigel as the way his good friends and loving neighbours turned on him so readily. We were a lovely bunch, weren't we?'

'And we moved,' said Ruth. 'To the other end of town. Didn't make any difference. We could have moved to another country and it would have followed us. Know what it's like, being the daughter of a man everyone calls a pervert?'

'Know what it's like being…' They were all saying it. Except me. I didn't need to say it.

Barbara coughed, bracing herself to address me again. 'So. You remembered the truth, and you went back to confront Serena?'

'No one saw me arrive or leave. I didn't know what was happening in New York. I didn't realise that anyone who was home would be glued to the TV. Watching another edifice come down.'

'And you killed her.' Angela struggled to her feet and came at me, to stare into my eyes. 'Good. I'm glad.'

'Don't worry,' blurted Denise. 'No one blames you. She deserved to die, that's the truth.'

'I don't know.' Barbara looked uncertain, possibly for the first time in her life. She was a lawyer, after all. She didn't inhabit the world of wild justice. 'I understand that, in the heat of the moment—'

'No!' Ruth leaped up. 'Don't you start saying the police should be told about this. I'm glad she's dead. We're all glad. I wish I'd done it myself. I wish I'd driven the knife in. You're not going to the police, you hear!'

Barbara gaped. She was the one who made decisions and told the others what to do. But three women were facing her down. She opened her mouth, then shut it again.

'We'll say nothing,' said Ruth.

Barbara gave the smallest nod, then coughed. 'After all, we don't know what happened.' She glanced at me. 'You haven't told us, have you?'

'No...' I hadn't told anyone what had happened in Thorpeshall.

— 24 —

For long seconds, as I stood facing Serena on her doorstep, she didn't stir.

'Why?' I repeated.

At last, with an effort, she composed herself. 'Why what, my dear?' She stepped back, holding the door open. 'Goodness me, Karen, you've taken me quite by surprise. Turning up on my doorstep twice in one day, when I haven't seen you for more than thirty years. But come in. Come in.'

She led me back into the living room, stooping to switch off the TV. Fire and mayhem vanished from the screen. Some violent thriller, I thought, finding her choice significant. The Serena that I'd always thought I'd known would have been watching a romance, a classic, or Shakespeare perhaps. But instead she chose violence.

'Sit down then.' She led me solicitously to the sofa, where I'd sat before. Putting me back where I'd been. She leaned over me, raising her glass and setting the slice of lemon bobbing. 'Can I offer you a drink? I suppose I shouldn't, if you're driving. And I expect you're on medication which mustn't be mixed with alcohol. Are you? Can I get you something else? An orange squash perhaps?'

Her concern sounded so genuine, I began to wonder, just

began to wonder, if I had been inventing memories after all.

It must surely have been the prism of medication I'd been looking through, a few hours earlier, when I'd landed on her doorstep and convinced myself she'd barely changed from the lovely girl I'd known at school. I looked at her afresh. She wasn't the same at all. She looked middle-aged and dried out, but denying it as most mortal women do. Of course she looked a thousand times better that I did, but age was one thing she hadn't quite managed to manipulate. She looked tired.

'Tell me why,' I repeated. 'Why did you do it?'

'Do what, darling? I don't think I did anything, did I? I was going to offer you help, but you rushed off before I had a chance.'

There was nothing in her voice to suggest she was wilfully misunderstanding me. She sounded gentle and sincere. I must have been fantasising.

I looked into her eyes and I believe I was on the verge of apologising.

Then I saw my bear, swinging by the neck, Serena watching, head on one side, smiling...the same smile.

'You know what you did. You did everything. Everything and yet nothing, because you get other people to do it, whatever it is. That was what you wanted from me. You tried to make me kill Janice.'

'My dear.' Her face was distorted with sympathetic distress and then, in front of my eyes, it all melted away. She stepped away, drew a deep breath, and then laughed. It was an unpleasant laugh, full of weary contempt. 'You know what? Shall we abandon this charade? To be absolutely honest, I'm tired of it. All of it, the whole bloody game. It's no fun any more and I really don't know that I can be bothered to keep playing.'

She took a quick swig of her gin, shut her eyes briefly, and then considered me, head on one side, just as she had studied my bear. Just as she had studied Janice, dead in the stream.

'You see, games are only fun if you win. And keep winning. I've always liked winning this one, this push and pull puppet game. I've always been so good at it. I could be the Olympic champion. But then I come up against you. Always you. Karen Rothwell, messing things up, keeping me from the podium. You're a weird one. What is it with you? Why is it that you're the one person who won't ever do as you're told? I think you have to be the most obstinate person I've ever had anything to do with. Why can't you just play the game?'

'Because it's not a game.'

'Oh rubbish. The whole of bloody life's a game – and I really don't like losing. Why on earth did I ever let you into my life? You were a nobody. Who were you to mess things up? You let me down, and here you are, thirty years later, doing it again. What's so special about you, Karen Rothwell? Is it some mysterious twist of your brain? Something an autopsy might reveal?'

'If I'd killed myself, like you wanted, you might have had a chance to find out. But I didn't.'

'No you didn't, did you? And God knows why you didn't. What's so wonderful about your life that you insist on clinging on? Has it really been worth the effort? Most of it spent in a straightjacket, from what I hear.'

She was attempting to rile me. I wasn't sure of her purpose, but she must have had one. I knew that Serena never did or said anything without it having a hidden purpose. She was trying to prompt me to something – but what did it matter? I wasn't listening to her complaints. I just wanted an explanation. 'Why did you do it?'

She walked to the French windows, and looked out across the empty lawns, sipping her gin. 'Why?' She mused on the question, then turned back, with a triumphant smile. 'Because I could. Because I can.'

'That's all you can say?'

'What more do you want? It's the only reason I do anything. Because I can. What makes you do anything? Being a madwoman, I'd have thought it might be voices in your head, but that wouldn't be the case with you, would it, Karen, because you won't do what voices tell you.'

'I'm not the only madwoman in this room.'

'Ah. You think I'm mad. A psychopath, maybe? Or sociopath. I'm never quite sure of the distinction, but I'm sure you can explain it to me. You must be an expert in psychiatrist jargon. What labels do they use for you?'

'Lots. Anything to explain why I behave the way I behave and do the things I do. Things I sometimes don't know I'm doing. But it seems you always know what you're doing, Serena.'

'Mm. So what is it, exactly, that you think I do?'

'You twist people round, till they're tied in knots. You manipulate them. You get them to do vile things they'll regret for the rest of their lives. And you sit back, all innocent, and laugh.'

'Oh, please. You make me sound like a monster. I may have had unfortunate moments, but mostly what I do isn't horrible at all. If I can persuade and prompt others, it's usually for their benefit, not mine. I provide motivational courses, you know. Get people to face their darkest fears and overcome their sense of inadequacy. Well, after all, if you have a gift, why not milk it? One has to make money somehow.'

'You seriously call it a gift?'

'Oh yes.' She sat herself down on a sofa, one arm ranged along the back, ankles crossed, quite relaxed. 'Like perfect pitch. I discovered it when I was about – what was I? Four, I think. I persuaded my cousin Jimmy that he could fly. I had a magic powder. Talc. He believed me. Flew from the bannisters. Broke his arm. I remember wondering why on earth he believed me, and then realising that it had been easy to make him believe it, because he wanted to fly. Offer people what they want and they become totally gullible. It's simple.

'Getting people to do something they didn't want to do – that's much more of a challenge, but I cracked that too, eventually. What I found, you see, is that it pays dividends to be a sweet little angel. I watched kids all around me having tantrums, sulking, screaming if they didn't get their own way, and occasionally it worked, but not very often. Parents were made of sterner stuff in those days. Anyway, it seemed a lot of effort for such an uncertain result. Where's the profit in screaming your head off if you just finish up with a smack for your troubles? It was so much easier to smile and say pretty please, and then, if they said no, just look sad but resigned. Sweet and loveable. Ninety-nine times out of a hundred, they'd cave in in seconds. One little tear spilt in sorrowful acceptance buys far more than a gallon spilt in raging anger.'

'"Two ginger nuts for your infant piety."'

'Quite so.' She laughed. 'A fan of Jane Eyre, I see. You would be. Taking on all the Reverend Brocklehursts in this world, with your obstinate little fists flailing. Yes, I've always preferred to be the pious little angel and get double the rewards. It's so incredibly easy to wrap adults round your finger if you understand the game. And other kids too. That was the real eye-opener.' She gazed into her glass. 'The Dawson boy. He was the one who showed me how easy it was to get people to do things, even when they didn't want to. Ian Dawson, at infants' school. Do you remember?'

I remembered the name, but not the boy. I shook my head.

'No, well, he wasn't there long. Lived on Foxton Road, just along from Rowlands Avenue. Our parents though we should play together. Nice children from the right sort of homes. He was so tiresome. Like an obedient puppy, following me around. I was tossing a sun hat and it got stuck up in an apple tree. I really liked that hat and Ian was at hand, so I begged him to get it back for me. He wasn't what you'd call an athletic boy, but he tried to climb the tree for me. And it turned out he really didn't like heights. I mean, really didn't. He was so scared he started crying. Stuck there on a branch and sobbing in fright, saying he daren't go any further. So I just smiled sadly, and said it was all right, I understood, even though I really, really loved that hat. So he crawled on. What a prat. He was crying, but he kept crawling. I stood there, looking sad, waiting to see just how far along he'd go.'

She shrugged. 'The branch broke and he landed on his head. He never went back to school. Some sort of brain damage, I think.' She stirred the drink with her lemon slice, then drew it out and licked it. 'I suppose you think that was wicked.'

'And you don't?'

'I couldn't have been more than six. Can a child of six be wicked? We aren't born with precise concepts of right and wrong. We learn that there are things we can get away with and things we can't, that's all. We push boundaries as we explore the possibilities. I didn't know that he'd go on climbing, just because I looked sad. I didn't intend him to fall. But it happened, and I learned. Extend your wings, and if people think they're angel wings, you can keep flapping forever.'

'I really did think you were an angel.'

'Don't feel bad. Everyone did. All the teachers adored me. It was almost embarrassing at times – but ultimately worth it. I was such a good child. I never understood this need most children have – rebellion for its own sake. Much more comfortable to be worshipped. To have a harem of willing slaves, knowing that just a smile, a look, an oblique word will twitch their strings and have them hopping around like bunnies.'

'Why did you choose me?'

'Oh God, why indeed? Karen Rothwell. I couldn't have chosen worse, could I? And in any other circumstances, I wouldn't have chosen you. You were always a spectacularly insignificant nonentity. Apart from an ability to draw horses with knees, I don't think you ever exhibited any trait that could possibly be of interest to anyone.'

'So why did you pick me?'

She looked surprised that she had to explain. No, not surprised. Weary. Bored. 'Because you were Janice Dexter's friend, of course. Her only friend, as far as I could see. Other kids had more sense than to go anywhere near her. But there you were, sticking by her, so I decided to prise you away.'

'But why? Why pick on Janice? What had she ever done to you?'

'She attacked me.'

'What? Janice? That's a lie. She'd never hurt anyone. She hadn't a violent bone in her body.'

'I mean, she confronted me. She didn't hit me or anything. God forbid, or I'd have had to disinfect. That revolting brother of hers, Kenneth – he'd knocked me down. It hurt. No one had ever hurt me before. It was unspeakable. He was caned for it, I'm glad to say. Quite right too. You have to have discipline in schools, or thugs like him could go around punching and kicking anyone they liked.'

'He didn't punch or kick you. It was an accident. I remember it. He wasn't looking where he was going and he just ran into you.'

'That's what Janice said. Standing there in front of me, like she'd suddenly crawled out of the slime and grown a backbone. She challenged me. Saying it was my fault her brother was caned, because I should have told Mr. Cutler it was an accident and I was mean and she hated me.' Serena was whining, contemptuously. 'Poor little Kenneth. I ask you, was there ever a day when he didn't deserve to be caned? He was a foul beast. They all were, the Dexters. The filth at the bottom of the Neanderthal swill bucket. The world would be better off cleansed of the lot of them. I expect Kenneth finished up in prison with the rest.'

Cpl. Kenneth Dexter. 'No he didn't.'

'No? Well, if you ask me, it's a pity they did away with hanging.' Serena dismissed my contradiction. 'It would have been the kindest way to dispose of all of them. Except that none of them were adventurous enough to do anything worth capital punishment. They just needed culling. And I helped.'

'Janice objected to her brother being unjustly punished, she said a few words because she was upset, and for that you decided she had to die?'

Serena stared at me, lost in her own thoughts. Then she laughed. 'Oh, good God, no. Or then again, perhaps, yes. Depends on whether you really want to think of me as a psychopath, with an insatiable urge to kill people. Which, on this particular day, as it happens, is rather ironic. The insatiable urge to kill. Very much alive and well in this world today. There are truly deranged and obsessional killers out there, Karen. Perhaps they're over our heads right now, as we talk, waiting to consume us in hellfire.'

'I don't know what you're talking about.'

'No, you don't, do you. Mass murder, that's what. You can't equate me with such people. I don't go round lusting for blood. So no, I didn't exactly intend that Janice should die. Not at first. I just wanted to see if I could take away her only friend.'

I stared at her, speechless. Angel and devil like two sides of the same coin. What I found it harder to come to terms with was her sheer pettiness. It wasn't monstrous, it was pathetic.

She sighed heavily, frowning at me. 'I suppose you were simply so cussed that you had to choose the one girl no one else wanted to be friends with. I should have figured that out, watching you together. You were bound to be a perpetual disappointment to me.'

'I'm glad of that, at least.'

'I was deceived, you see, because you came running so

eagerly when I crooked my little finger. I thought you'd snap into line, like everyone else, but you just would not turn your back on her. You were supposed to become best buddies with Ruth, instead. How difficult was that? Two nobodies – you'd have made a perfect match. But no, you had to keep running off with Janice bloody Dexter. So I came up with the Ouija Board for our little Christmas get-together.'

'Of course. It was you.'

'I nearly had you thinking it was Barbara, didn't I?'

I ignored her crowing. 'You as good as told me to kill Janice.'

She laughed. 'Hell, I didn't plan on you going through with it. Either of you. I just wanted you to be so scared of her, you'd never go near her again.'

'Just because you wanted Janice to have no friends.'

'Put like that, it does seem rather small-minded, doesn't it? I plead guilty. I was eleven. Children are often small-minded at that age. I wasn't always petty, though. Admit it, usually I was quite nice. If you'd just walked away from Janice, as I was asking, I'd have been nice again. I might even have forgiven her. See what happens when you don't do what you're told?'

'You're evil.'

'Rubbish. I was merely a little girl with a child's amoral curiosity. I wanted to see what would happen. And, I suppose, in my own way, I had obstinacy to match yours. The more you resisted me, the more I just had to bring you to heel. Even when that spirit message had you wetting yourself with fear, still you went back to Janice. Hopeless. I had to do something, or I'd have lost the game.

'Even on that last day, when I saw you both, I wasn't thinking actual murder. I was just going to whisper in your ear, that's all. I could come up with any number of disgusting stories about the Dexters. But then…' She shrugged. 'Ah then, you headed for Sawyer's Lane. I ask you, a dark lane in a gloomy wood. Wouldn't anyone think of murder? It had me scared witless, and I was supposed to be the one doing the scaring.'

'No.'

'No?'

'I don't think you have the faintest idea what being scared is really like.'

'Oh I do, believe me. You should try being in a Cessna with a drunken husband who thinks looping the loop in a dust storm is all part of the fun.'

The husband, presumably, who then died in a plane crash, insisting on flying in poor conditions. The husband before the one who committed suicide because he was falsely led to believe he had cancer. I wondered. How could I not? 'How many people have you killed, Serena?'

'I've never killed anyone. I've never hurt anyone. Surely you understand how entirely innocent I am. What other people choose to do, that's their business, but my hands are clean. I don't kill.'

'What about Janice?'

'What about her? Janice Dexter was murdered by person or persons unknown. The poor police never did get to the bottom of it. All right, we know the truth, don't we? You killed her, Karen. Smashed her head in. But I think it's perfectly reasonable to call it self-defence, because the chances were, she would have done the same to you, if you hadn't got in first. Don't blame yourself too much. You really were petrified.'

She was so smooth, so casual in what she said, that for a

moment I wondered if she could be right. I had seen and unseen so many things, over the years. Over the last few months even more. Was she right?

I could feel, in my flesh, the pitted iron of the sewer, the ice cold water, the roughness of the concrete block. I could smell the exhalation of chill, stale air from the tunnel. I could see the pathetic hole in Janice's unshod sock. I could hear...

She was wrong. All that I'd remembered, standing on the bridge in Sawyer's Lane, was the truth.

'No, Serena. I was petrified, all right. So petrified, it screwed up the rest of my life, but I didn't kill Janice. I didn't drop the block. You did it. You are the one who killed her.'

She was very still, very white, her eyes wide. Was she waiting to see if I would waiver in my certainty, or was she facing up to a truth she'd been denying even to herself? I stared her out.

'You're fantasising, Karen. You do, you know. I understand that at one time you thought you were Jane Eyre. And Flora MacDonald, apparently.'

'And Éowyn. Yes. I did. I imagine you're telling me that because you want to divert me. I'm supposed to start worrying about how you got to see my records, but I don't care. Yes, I've done a lot of fantasising, but I'm not fantasising now. You killed Janice Dexter.'

'You want to think that. Understandable, I suppose. A scary business, murder – enough to tip anyone over the edge, especially when you're convinced you'll be hanged, if you're caught.'

'Did you enjoy threatening me with that? Did you believe it, yourself? Or did you know they didn't hang children, even when they were still hanging adults?'

'I certainly got some satisfaction from it. It was punishment for your recalcitrance. Of course they'd stopped capital punishment by then. Only just, but you didn't know that. Current affairs and ten-year-olds don't really mix. I knew about it, because it was a sore subject with my father. He disapproved of abolition. He thought the death penalty was essential to the administration of justice. I tend to agree… Don't you?'

'Do you have any idea what justice is?'

'Of course. Just rewards and just punishments. That's what it was all about, in '66. If people misbehaved, they had to be put right.'

'With you as their self-appointed executioner.'

'Never executioner. Not even judge. Counsel for the prosecution, maybe. Some people needed to be prosecuted.'

'Like poor Nigel Knight? What did he do to offend?'

'He tried to paw my hair once. Ghastly. They should have put him in an asylum or something. Anyway, blame Denise for that. She was the one who set the police onto him.'

'With your prompting.'

'I didn't *do* anything. I never do.'

'But you did. You can try and make me think black is white all you like, but I know that you killed Janice. You dropped that block on her. You dragged her into the culvert.'

As I spelled it out, I saw the twitch in her neck, the suddenly speeding pulse, although otherwise she didn't stir a muscle.

'You murdered her, because I refused to do it.'

She sighed, with a hint of irritation. 'I always suspected this memory loss business wouldn't be quite as permanent as the others seemed to think. You wiped it out, like a good girl, but you've come running back with it, like a rotten bone. That's your trouble, Karen. Totally unreliable. I can't trust you to do anything. You wouldn't even kill yourself. Twice I laid it out for you, and each time you failed.'

'You nearly succeeded the first time.'

'Yes. Bad luck.'

'For you.'

'For both of us, judging by the end result. What did you gain by surviving the fall? Just misery for yourself and all around you. You should have died. After all, whoever dropped the block, you were the one who was crippled with guilt about it. And so you should be. I did it for you.'

'No you didn't, Serena.'

'Oh but yes. I protected you. You were both so scared, in that lane, one of you was going to finish up committing murder, and I didn't want it to be her. You should be flattered. I wanted you to be the survivor. And then I came up with a perfectly convincing story, so that you would never be suspected, remember?'

'By making it look as if she'd been sexually assaulted.'

'Weren't we all so innocent in those days? I'd do a much better job if I were an eleven-year-old today. Mind you, dragging her filthy knickers off was bad enough. I'm not sure I could have faced getting any more intimate with her. Ugh. I had to scrub my hands raw, when I got home.'

'Did it hurt? I hope so. I hope your skin's been rubbed raw ever since.'

She smiled, mockingly. 'A little hand lotion works wonders. I was over it in no time.'

'It was Mr Cutler's lecture in assembly that made you think of it, wasn't it?'

'It was 1966. They'd only just caught the Moors Murderers. The trial wasn't for another few months, so I'm not sure if the full shock horror had hit the press yet, but my father certainly knew all about it. All the nasty details – and he repeated enough in front of me to tell me it was about children being picked up in cars and having unspeakable things done to them. If he'd been more specific, maybe I'd have made it more convincing. Anyway, as it turned out, Janice's foul pudenda hanging loose was enough to do the job. Everyone was primed to suspect the worst.'

She drained the last of her gin and shrugged. 'At least I didn't record her screams. Or even yours. It was you doing most of the screaming, as I recall. Yes, see? I'm not a psychopath like Brady. Not that stupid. Far from it. I don't think anyone has ever suspected me of anything. Except you.'

'You're wrong. Your father suspected you. I saw it in his eyes.'

She took a deep breath, tapping her fingers on the arm of the sofa. 'I hate to say it, but you're probably right. But he hated to say it too, so he didn't. Not then.' She laughed. 'He made such a mess of the investigation, didn't he? Didn't do anything by the book. Bullied you into a complete breakdown. I think that might have been intentional. If you were too doolally to say anything, you couldn't hint at anything I might have done. He could never be quite sure. That's why he didn't object to being shunted off to some distant colony, I suppose. I wouldn't be a threat to the suburbs, in Hong Kong.'

'Just a threat to Hong Kong. How many people did you kill out there?'

'I don't kill,' she repeated, primly. Then smiled. 'Never you mind. Whatever happened out there, it pushed my father

285

beyond his limits. He blurted out all his suspicions about the Janice Dexter case. Not that it did him much good. He had a fatal heart attack moments later.'

'Another of your triumphs.'

'Nothing triumphant about it. It was bloody inconvenient. We had to find somewhere else to live.'

She stood up. 'I'm getting myself another of these. Sure you won't have one?'

'Quite sure.' I followed her to the kitchen door, half suspecting her of intending to escape across the garden. 'I wouldn't trust you not to poison it.'

She laughed, scooping fresh ice from the freezer. 'How many times do I have to tell you? I don't kill people. Other people do it, or kill themselves. The whole world is so obliging. Except you. Karen Rothwell. Why did you always have to be so damned awkward?' She gestured to the table, littered with salad ingredients and a board with half a lemon and a sharp knife. 'Cut me a slice, would you?'

I reached automatically for the knife, then stopped myself. 'Cut it yourself.'

I caught a flicker of fury at my little show of defiance. She stared at me a moment, then picked up the knife and started slicing the lemon. 'Won't do a single thing to oblige me, will you. Wouldn't turn your back on the Dexter brat. Wouldn't finish her off. Wouldn't tell the police what I told you to say. Wouldn't kill yourself – twice! You really have no idea how much you annoy me.'

'I don't care how much I annoy you. Complain to the police. I'm sure they'll sympathise.'

'Oh, good Lord, you don't really mean to go to the police,

do you? With a cockamamie story about a murder in 1966? You do realise they'll laugh you out of court. Or lock you up in a hospital, more likely. Which is where you ought to be. Because you are totally mad. They'll only have to look at your medications or speak to your psychiatrist. And to me, of course. I don't have your trouble with little white lies. I can be totally convincing.'

'I'm sure you will be. You'll have them at your feet as soon as look at you and I don't suppose for one minute that they will believe a word I say. But still, I'm going to the police. For Janice's sake. Let the heavens fall.'

She was watching me as she sliced, with that contemptuous, confident smile, and her words rang so true that I was completely unprepared for the lunge she made at me with the blade.

Maybe some schizophrenic instinct took over, because, prepared or not, I lurched to the side, toppled, grabbed the kitchen table, scattering its contents, knocking over a chair, and I dragged myself out of her reach. A can crashed, a bottle smashed, tomatoes rolled on the floor.

She came at me again, round the table and I felt all the old terror wash back into me. She was going to kill me. Why hadn't I realised she would? She was mad.

And then… Then she wasn't there.

I didn't understand how Serena could just vanish. Had I blanked out? Was I hallucinating? I'd been feeling horribly, icily sane since I'd left Sawyer's Lane, but I knew my confusion and delusion, my panic and denials were gathered around me like armed guards, waiting to grab me, the moment I glanced their way. Perhaps I was blocking her out, because I didn't want to see her.

No. It couldn't be that. I'd heard a thud, I'd heard a gasp, and now I saw red.

Bizarre. Like some strange abstract art. Glistening red spraying the kitchen walls beyond the table. Why? It didn't make sense.

Then I heard her groan, and a gory hand grasped the table top. Tried to grasp and then it slipped back. I stepped round the table to make sense of it, my heart beginning to thunder, my vision beginning to blur.

She was there on the floor, behind the fallen chair. There was a broken olive oil bottle too, but I couldn't connect the two. An olive oil bottle. Serena. Lying. Trying to sit up, the knife slipping free from her groin, blood spurting and spraying from the wound. So much of it. An unstoppable flood, and her face growing paler and paler as I watched.

She tried again to scrabble for a grip on the table and haul herself up. Serena Whinn. Janice's murderer. Part of me wanted to stand and watch her die, crowing for vengeance.

Another, more human, part of me couldn't do it. You can't just let someone die. Not even a murderer.

'It's all right. I'm here. I'll get help. I'll call an ambulance.' I doubted there was even time for that. I knelt down, leaning over the chair to support her. I felt and smelled her blood drench me. It wouldn't stop. I looked round, grabbed a tea towel and tried to press, but it was utterly pointless. The flow was too great. There was nowhere to tie a tourniquet. The towel was sodden before I'd even brought it near the wound.

Serena grasped my hand in both of hers. I understood. At

least, for one short moment, I thought I understood. She was asking for help. For forgiveness, maybe. At least for a human touch, at the end.

Then I realised how wrong I'd got it, yet again. I could see what she was doing. She was trying to force my fingers onto the handle of the knife. I snatched my hand away.

She struggled to speak, through bared teeth. 'Why…won't… you…ever…' Fading. Fading. She never finished the words. Her eyes were no longer seeing me. She sank down into a sea of blood and oil.

I rocked back, wanting to be sick. I raised my hand to my mouth, but it was so wet and sticky, with warm gouts of blood, that it made me retch even more. I had to get away. No point in calling an ambulance now. She was dead. Blood was no longer spurting, just oozing, but the kitchen was awash with gore. The fallen chair had created a dam, but blood was beginning to seep under it. It would be circling my feet soon.

I stepped back. I should call 999, of course I should. The police.

I would. But not here. I had to get away, out of this abattoir. It was the blood. I couldn't take it. My head was spinning.

I stepped away, stumbling to the kitchen door, and seized the handle, but my slippery hand couldn't grip. I grabbed another towel, hanging beside the door, swallowing hard as I wiped the handle clean, and gripped it, through the towelling. The door opened and I threw myself out, gulping down clean air, forcing it into me. Get me out of here. Get me away.

— 25 —

'No, I won't tell you what happened. You can work it out for yourselves, I imagine.' Yes they had no trouble working out how and why I had killed Serena Whinn. 'I'm sure the police are looking for me, so why not just tell them where I am?'

Ruth, Angela and Denise glanced at Barbara, willing to leave her in command, this time. Passing the buck. I could see her hand still trembling as she plucked at her coat. She swallowed.

'Actually, the police don't suspect murder. The painter chap told them she'd been drinking when he left. They found a broken bottle of oil in the kitchen and signs that she simply slipped in it while slicing a lemon. They have to ask questions, of course, but the coroner's verdict will almost certainly be accidental death.'

'After all,' said Ruth, bitterly. 'The whole world loved her. Who could possibly have any motive to murder the saintly Serena Whinn?' She waited some seconds for a reply that never came.

'We shall say nothing,' announced Barbara.

'I'm not asking you to keep it quiet,' I said.

She brushed it aside. 'If the law is satisfied, why complicate the matter? We'll say nothing.'

The others nodded.

Then Ruth shrugged. 'Look, no offence, not that I can't stand your company or anything, but if that's it, can I just go home?'

'Oh yes.' Angela hauled herself to her feet. 'Good idea. Let's all go home and get on with our wonderful, bloody lives.'

There was a hesitation, some shuffling, some wondering what to do next, but finally Barbara nodded her consent, and they trooped out. One by one, they shook my hand. Denise tried to kiss me.

I closed the door behind them and was alone with Malcolm.

'Karen—' he began.

'I know.' I smiled. 'You're honest. You're not going to tell me that it was all right to kill her because she deserved it. You're going to tell me to go to the police.'

He winced and sighed. 'Karen, it was wrong. Murder is always wrong.'

'Yes. But I didn't kill her.'

'But then…' He ran his fingers through his thinning hair. 'I don't understand.'

'I went to confront her. I wanted her to confess, and she did. I don't know why, after all these years. I think she'd just got tired of it. She admitted it all. She didn't care that I knew. But when I told her I was going to the police, she went for me, with a knife.'

'My God! So it was self-defence.' Poor Malcolm looked so relieved.

'Not even that. In fact, it was just what the police think. An accident. I knocked over a bottle of oil. She slipped in it. She fell and accidentally stabbed herself. It must have been an artery, here.' I indicated my groin. 'There was so much blood.

And it was so quick. So quick. There was nothing I could do. She died, there on the kitchen floor, and I just had to get away.'

'Of course. Of course. Oh Karen.' He hugged me. 'How could I have suspected you? But why didn't you tell the others? They're convinced you killed her.'

'They've spent thirty-five years believing I killed Janice. I can't expect them to cope with too much enlightenment in one day.'

'But if they do go to the police, after all…'

'If they do, I'll tell them exactly what happened, and maybe I'll be believed, and maybe I won't. You believe me, which is enough.'

'No, it isn't.' He frowned, beginning to worry. 'Have the police really accepted it was an accident? What if they're still asking questions? If they find any suggestion that somebody else was there…'

I moved to the window, staring out across the yard, remembering the scene in Serena's kitchen – the scene I had been trying to forget.

'She offered me a drink, but I said no. There was no second glass. She really had been drinking. She really was slicing a lemon. The blood…' I shut my eyes with a shudder. 'I was the other side of the room. The blood sprayed, right across the wall before I got to her. No void, showing I was there. There was a fallen chair, holding the blood back. I didn't tread in it. I didn't leave footprints.'

'Fingerprints, though, surely.'

'Not on the knife. She tried to make me touch it, but I wouldn't. The door handle – I got blood on it, but then I wiped it off. With the towel. So that I could get a grip. I took

292

the towel with me. I wasn't trying to hide. I just wanted to get away from the blood. If they are looking for a murderer, I'm sure they will find traces of me. But they're not looking, because it really was an accident. Only Barbara and the others would have any reason to suspect otherwise.'

'So. Thank God. But my poor, poor Karen, nursing such horror all these years. No wonder...'

I sat down, suddenly weary. 'No wonder I'm mad as a hatter, you mean.'

'I mean, no wonder you've spent your life trying to escape from it.' Malcolm started gathering up mugs, the tea barely touched. Then he slammed them down again, shaking his head. 'All these months, Karen, you've been killing yourself trying to track down this angel, and she turns out to be a complete monster. I'm only just realising how easily she could have killed you?'

'I wonder.' I curled up on the sofa with a cushion. 'It's a nightmare, yes, but I go over it, and I wonder. What game was she playing, even at the end?'

'The murder game, that's clear enough!'

'Maybe. And maybe not. She'd had forty-six years of getting people to do whatever she wanted, and in the end, where did it leave her? Locked in a role she'd have to keep playing forever. Whoever the real Serena Whinn was, somewhere deep down, she could never come out. Even with me, when she knew I'd seen right through the lovely compassionate angel act, she simply put on another role. The heartless, contemptuous bitch act. I think she was trying to goad a violent reaction out of me. She'd got hold of my medical records, somehow. She knew I had it in me.'

'Because you once gave Dr Pearce a wallop? Rubbish. You think she wanted you to attack her? Then she could finish you off and claim it was self-defence.'

'Maybe that was all there was to it. Or maybe… I can't help thinking that she'd just had enough.'

'And she wanted you to kill her?'

'While making sure I'd be blamed, of course. I had to be punished for not murdering Janice when she told me to. I don't know. I'll never know what demons were driving her.'

'Look, Karen, I think there's a bit of you so bewitched by that woman that you're still trying desperately to think well of her. You want to blame yourself in some way, instead of her. Stop it. See her straight, for what she was. A psychopath.'

I considered the cushion. I began to unpick its threads. 'I know she lied and twisted things. Probably did it from habit as much as anything. But she was right about children, wasn't she? We aren't all born with a sense of good and evil. Or perhaps your Christian teachings say that we are. I think we start with a blank canvas and learn as we go along. It's what childhood's supposed to be for. Serena just picked up the wrong lessons. She discovered the key to persuading anyone to do anything, and she used it, just like all children use what they learn.'

Malcolm scratched his head, shaking it. 'She tried to manipulate you into killing your best friend. That wasn't a childish learning curve. That was evil.'

'Did she really plan it, though? If she set out from the start to make me kill Janice, that would really be evil, but I don't know. She wasn't nice. She was petty and self-centred, but I think she was just being spiteful – with a smile. She was going to steal Janice's only friend and it got out of hand. She was only ten or eleven.

'So were you. So was poor Janice.'

'We were all just children. Too young to calculate the consequence of everything we did. What really happened with Barbara and the cat? Barbara was besotted with cats, and Serena was probably just jealous of the neighbourhood moggy, so she thought she'd persuade her cat-loving friend to chase it away. I don't suppose she planned on Barbara actually killing the poor thing.'

'And it was just a good joke, I suppose, to scare you to death with a fake message from the spirit world.'

'Except that she did too good a job, and scared herself into the bargain. When she came with us down Sawyer's Lane, it got too much. I think she killed Janice because, by that point, she was as terrified as we were.'

Malcolm tutted his exasperation. 'Oh, that's all right then.'

'No. No, it wasn't all right. But it was a child's terror that made her drop that block. Not premeditated murder. What came after – that was vile. That was really was just plain evil manipulation. She knew she'd done something unforgiveable and all her sweet saintliness wouldn't save her. There'd be retribution and she couldn't be doing with that. It wasn't part of her vision. So she wanted to make sure someone else would get the blame.'

'You.'

'Me, or Nigel Knight, or some unknown stranger in a car. Or Black Jack Coke. Just so long as it wasn't Serena Whinn. I suppose she thought she'd got away with it. She hadn't, though. It had her forever, after that. She'd crossed the line. If she really was a psychopath, it began that day. Any innocence in her was smashed beyond repair.'

'I don't give a toss that she smashed up her own life. It's all the other lives she damaged on the way. A girl murdered, a young man dead, her friends still screwed up by guilt and neuroses, decades later, and you—'

'The obstinate cow who wouldn't do as she was told.'

'The only one who ever resisted her, by the sounds of it.'

'Do I get a medal?'

'You should. But what did you get instead? Years of medication and psychiatric treatment.'

'I did get to be Éowyn, warrior princess of the Rohirrim. And Jane Eyre and Flora MacDonald and Joan of Arc.'

Malcolm burst out laughing. 'You never stopped fighting the monster. But don't joke. It's way beyond a joke.'

'Yes. It is.' I put the cushion down, what was left of it, and sat up. 'So what do you think I should do now? I am still ready to go to the police, if you think I should.'

He took my hand and squeezed it. 'No. Sorry I even suggested it. As you say, it was an accident. If you speak up now, it will become a suspicious death. You'll be facing a police interrogation for God knows how long. Karen, my love, you've faced down your monster and you've come through, but you're still—'

'Nuts.'

'Fragile. You're not up to coping with what they'd throw at you. Don't do it. Serena's dead. Let it go.'

'And Janice?'

'Janice is dead too. Let her rest in peace. You know who the real murderer was. So do I. So do your four friends. She's not going to get any more justice than that. Not in this life.'

'She was never going to get that, was she? I should tell someone, though. Maybe not yet. In a while. For now, to be honest, all I want to do is sleep for a fortnight.'

'A very good idea.' Malcolm fetched a blanket and tucked me in, like a child.

So here we are, twelve years after Serena's death, gathering at the Lyford Crematorium, to watch Angela's coffin rumble slowly through the curtains into oblivion.

The service was short and muddled, which seems wonderfully appropriate for Angela. Mostly humanist, because her brother, Colin, had taken charge of his sister at the end. After Serena's death, she'd accepted belated counselling for post-traumatic stress. I don't know if it really worked, but she had started to pull herself together. Her career picked up again, briefly, and she even started to cut down on the alcohol. But it was too late to undo years of determined abuse. A liver can only manage so much self-repair and it got her in the end. When it was obvious there was no saving her, and she grew tired of the struggle, Colin persuaded her to accept a place in a hospice near him in Lyford.

'To rescue her from Denise,' suggests Ruth, as we gather outside to slip cheques into in a bowl held by a funereal attendant. 'No one deserves Denny at their deathbed.'

Ruth has two of her children with her, quietly, politely in the background. She makes the occasional irritated remark about still being stuck with them, but it's obvious to everyone else that they're there for her, to jolly her up if she starts to rant and hug her if she starts to weep, cheerily tolerant of their mother's sour mutterings. A strange family.

Ruth raises a hand to greet Barbara, who is coming towards us, in full black, every inch the solicitor still, though she's semi-retired and working for a cat charity.

'We haven't changed much, have we?' says Ruth. 'Except you, Karen. You look okay. And you're still together then.' She nods at Malcolm, who's emerging from the office – even a crematorium has an office. He's clutching a piece of paper.

'Looks like it.'

'So far. People never stick together, these days.'

'You and Russell have. Forty years, isn't it?'

'Yes, well.' She shrugged off this small achievement. 'Inertia, that's all. Managed to sell the bookshop, in the end, then.'

'Yes, but not as a bookshop. They're out of fashion. It's all internet these days. You know how it is. The shop sells cupcakes now.'

'Right, now, I think we should all make our way…' Denise comes up. She's a nun, at last, but there's nothing of divine peace about her. She is bustling, desperate to organise us. I'm not sure what she wants us to do. Whatever it is, she stops short at the sight of the cellophane-wrapped bouquet I'm carrying. 'Oh. Karen. Flowers. Now there were specific instructions – no flowers, by request. Just contributions to the hospice.'

'We've left a cheque,' I say. 'Don't worry. These aren't for Angela.' I push the flowers aside to reveal a biscuit tin beneath.

Denise frowns, a sort of deliberate puzzlement. Her breathing begins to quicken.

I open the tin and show her the papers inside. Her hands fly to her mouth as she swallows hard. 'Oh! Oh!'

'We agreed.'

'Yes. Yes we did.' She clutches her own capacious satchel to her, hugging it like a teddy bear.

'Angela's?'

'Yes, I've got hers.'

'And mine,' say Barbara and Ruth together, in the same subdued tones.

'So, do we...?' Denise looks round vaguely.

I catch Malcolm's eye. He's standing on the periphery of our little crowd. He nods.

'You found it?' I ask.

He holds up the sheet of paper. 'It's three blocks across, over by those purple beeches.'

'Good. Then let's go and do this thing.'

The others take deep breaths, preparing themselves, but no one says a word and we walk in procession through faint autumn drizzle, past row upon row of gravestones and markers weathered by age. Further along the vast acres of the cemetery stand the ranks of newer slabs and crosses and rose bowls, among which lies the grave of Serena June Canterbury.

Here in Lyford municipal cemetery. There had been an assumption, when the coroner released her body, that she would be buried at the quaint little church in Thorpeshall, but when advice was sought, it seemed she had no relatives left to arrange it. No husband, no lover, no close friend. Plenty of humble admirers and general well-wishers, who thought her charitable work was wonderful, but no friends. So Barbara, as her executor, took charge and had her quietly interred here. Ruth told me the grave still receives occasional floral tributes from her charity beneficiaries. She's not having mine, though.

The grave I seek is more neglected. Quite forgotten. No other mourner around in this quarter. No flowers in sight, fresh or withered, among these plots.

Janice Eileen Dexter, beloved daughter and sister, 1955-66. Rest in perfect peace.

And in memory of her brother, Sgt Kenneth Ian Dexter, DCM, 1954-96.

'Good God,' says Barbara, blunt as ever. 'They let him in the army.'

'Why not?' I say. 'He was always strong on defending those he loved.'

'Yes, well. Even so.'

'He got the medal in the Falklands, dragging a wounded comrade to safety. And he was killed, protecting some aid workers, when his vehicle crashed, under sniper fire in Bosnia. I tried to trace them all, you know. The Dexters. I thought they should know the truth.' I felt the stillness relax into relief as I added, 'But no luck.'

No luck with a single Dexter. The father never rejoined his family after his last spell inside. Whereabouts unknown, like four of his children. Mrs Dexter fell drunk under a bus, two years after Janice's death, and the younger children had been taken into care. Two of them died of drugs, one died in a knife fight, one in prison, with Aids. And one died in Bosnia. I was six years too late to reveal the truth to Marsh Green's bad boy, who'd stripped the emperor's new clothes off Mr Jefferson and got the cane for bumping into Serena Whinn and won the DCM.

But the truth is going to be recorded, about the long-forgotten girl who lies in this grave.

Nothing grows here except some weed, up against the stone, which escaped the last strimming, and a mat of couch grass and moss that has crept across the green stone chippings on the grave. I stoop to pull it clear. The chippings beneath had once been loose, but time has compacted them. Still, they will have to do.

I straighten and open my biscuit box again, offering it to each of them in turn.

With her little mouse squeak, Denise gropes in her satchel and pulls out a small ring-bound pad and a child's exercise book. She holds them out, obviously expecting me to confirm their contents, so I flick their pages.

The exercise book is full, from start to finish, of Denise's childish writing, many words heavily underlined. *Guilty, wicked, lies, vile, horrible.*

The notepad is half-full of Angela's untidy scrawl, which grows more and more illegible, till, at the end, it's merely a series of jabs and scratches. I did make out a few phrases. *Pathetic little cow. Poor bloody innocent idiot.* It had all been her idea, this recording of our confessions. Denise wanted her to speak to a priest at the end, but she'd said no, she'd write it down. So we'd all agreed to do the same. To state the truth and acknowledge our parts in it, for a posterity that might, one day, demand to know, even if the present no longer cares.

Barbara hands her case notes over, neatly typed on legal-looking paper. I catch phrases like *notwithstanding* and *in respect of*. Dry and legal, but the truth.

Ruth's is a small notebook, filled with neat tiny writing, one word, whenever it appears, even smaller than its neighbours. *Father.*

I add them all to the papers already in the '
The one you've read. Then I shut the lid and
a hole in the chippings on Janice's grave. I have
with a trowel, not knowing what to expect, but th
need. Denise is on her knees beside me, scrabbling int
hardened gravel like a demented dog, bruising her bitten nai
and fingers, until she's excavated a hollow deep enough to take
the tin, with a thin scattering of stone to cover it.

I get up off my knees and lay my bouquet against the
grey headstone. Nothing exotic or elegant for Janice. Just
Michaelmas daisies for the daisy girl.

That's it. We've done what we all agreed to do. One more
look at the brittle beech leaves overhead, then we turn back to
the well-trodden paths and drift our separate ways.

Finished.

'Home?' suggests Malcolm, softly in my ear, as my tears
begin to well.

Behind us, the chill breeze rustles round the grave, and the
daisies wave at the empty sky.

ABOUT HONNO

Honno Welsh Women's Press was set up in 1986 by a group of women who felt strongly that women in Wales needed wider opportunities to see their writing in print and to become involved in the publishing process. Our aim is to develop the writing talents of women in Wales, give them new and exciting opportunities to see their work published and often to give them their first 'break' as a writer. Honno is registered as a community co-operative. Any profit that Honno makes is invested in the publishing programme. Women from Wales and around the world have expressed their support for Honno. Each supporter has a vote at the Annual General Meeting. For more information and to buy our publications, please write to Honno at the address below, or visit our website: **www.honno.co.uk**

Honno, 14 Creative Units, Aberystwyth Arts Centre
Aberystwyth, Ceredigion SY23 3GL

Honno Friends
We are very grateful for the support of the Honno Friends:
Jane Aaron, Annette Ecuyere, Audrey Jones, Gwyneth Tyson Roberts, Beryl Roberts, Jenny Sabine.

For more information on how you can become a Honno Friend, see: http://www.honno.co.uk/friends.php